Hereafter

Books by Jody Hedlund

Young Adult: The Lost Princesses Series
Always: Prequel Novella
Evermore
Foremost
Hereafter

Young Adult: Noble Knights Series
The Vow: Prequel Novella
An Uncertain Choice
A Daring Sacrifice
For Love & Honor
A Loyal Heart
A Worthy Rebel

The Bride Ships Series
A Reluctant Bride

The Orphan Train Series
An Awakened Heart: A Novella
With You Always
Together Forever
Searching for You

The Beacons of Hope Series
Out of the Storm: A Novella
Love Unexpected
Hearts Made Whole
Undaunted Hope
Forever Safe
Never Forget

The Hearts of Faith Collection
The Preacher's Bride
The Doctor's Lady
Rebellious Heart

The Michigan Brides Collection
Unending Devotion
A Noble Groom
Captured by Love

Historical
Luther and Katharina
Newton & Polly

Hereafter

JODY HEDLUND

NORTHERN LIGHTS PRESS

NORLAND
HIGHLANDS
HIGHLAND CONVENT
ST. CUTHBERT'S
IRON HILLS
STEFFORD
MIDDLETON
EVERLY
EASTERN PLAINS
WEST MOORLAND
MERCIA
EAST SEA
CANNOCK
CISTERN BOGS
LANGLEY
CRESS RIVER
DELSWORTH
CENTRAL HEATHLANDS
SMITHTIDE
WELLMONT RUINS
N
INGLEWOOD FOREST
WARWICK
GREAT ISLE

Chapter 1

Emmeline

I brushed my hand over the crushed grass and examined the nearly invisible footprint beneath. Only a pace away, a broken twig and a patch of flattened bellflowers confirmed my suspicion. A stranger had made it past the ravine and was quite possibly still lingering.

My chest tightened, squeezing the air from my lungs and forcing me to stand. I scanned the thick woodland and brush, picturing soldiers in black chain mail converging upon me.

The late afternoon sun tried to penetrate the leafy ceiling, but only a handful of dappled rays filtered through. With the recent summer rain, vibrant moss stretched lazily up tall oaks, hazel, and birch, while pale lichen drooped from branches. A badger peeked out from among the nettles and elder, and a purple emperor butterfly hovered over a nearby pile of deer dung.

As far as I could see, everything was as it ought to

be. I sniffed the air, catching only the usual smoky remnant of burning charcoal. I heard nothing but the quick trilling chirps of a pair of hawfinches, the intermittent buzz of cicadas, and the breeze rustling the treetops.

At the nudge of a wet nose against my hand, I released a breath and scratched Bede's pointed snout. "Whoever was here isn't any longer." Otherwise, my ever-vigilant red fox wouldn't be so relaxed. I could always count on the little creature's sharp instincts to alert me to danger when my own senses failed to pick it up.

Still, I needed to follow the intruder's trail for a short distance and attempt to discover who had come so far into the forest, and why, especially since so few crossed the ravine. My father would expect me to study the details and figure it out. He'd spent years preparing me for such things—teaching me every skill he knew about tracking, hiding, hunting, weaponry, and more.

With a stealth and lightness he'd beseeched me to perfect, I followed the trail several additional steps before halting. Shivers crawled over my skin at the prospect of someone lying in wait for me ahead in the brush. "Maybe we should go home."

Bede watched me, his head cocked, his tongue lolling with a slight pant.

"Mother will be expecting me to be back on time today."

The fox's pointed ears flickered, but otherwise his attention didn't waver.

"And Father will be home soon. I don't want to miss his arrival." He'd been gone for over a week, taking our recent batch of charcoal to one of the West Moorland villages to sell for provisions.

He'd promised to return by today, and I'd been waiting with mounting anticipation, knowing he'd bring me a gift as he did every summer on the day we remembered my birth. He and Mother always skimped and sacrificed for many a fortnight in order to make the purchase. And I loved them all the more for it.

At the crack of a branch to my left, I dodged behind the nearest tree. It happened to be a young beech. Though I was thin and petite, the tree's diameter wouldn't hide me for long, even if my dark hair, breeches, and shirt blended into the surroundings.

As nimbly as a squirrel, I scrambled up the branches and disappeared into the foliage. From my high perch, I surveyed the forest below.

Bede rose onto his hind legs, braced his front paws on the trunk, and peered up at me. He wagged his tail and let out a short yip.

"No, Bede," I whispered, glancing around, waiting for someone to jump out.

The fox pawed at the tree as though attempting to climb. His ears perked expectantly, and he let out a soft whine.

"Quiet, Bede! Go hide."

Just then a raccoon poked its nose through the brush. The fox spared the masked culprit a glance before dropping down and lifting his face to stare at me, his mouth curling up almost as if he were laughing.

He had every right to ridicule me. I was letting my anxiety get the best of me. If a true threat had approached, Bede would have warned me long in advance. Even so, my heart pounded out an ominous rhythm, and my body tensed in anticipation of an arrow or knife embedding my chest.

In my nightmares, I always died one way or the other, usually unexpectedly, while I was hiding.

After a minute of waiting in which Bede simply stood, staring at me, I reached out trembling hands to begin my descent. I needed to return home. I'd be safe there. And when Father came back from the market, he'd have a logical explanation for a stranger's footprints in this part of the forest, in the depths of the woodland where we rarely had visitors.

I hopped to the ground, took a final look around, and then started off. As I leaped over windfall and ducked under low branches, my pouch thumped against my hip. I pressed it firmly, the outline of the small leather-bound book inside reassuring me of its safety. I'd already read the historical chronicle countless times, but I never tired of starting anew and had spent the afternoon high in my favorite oak tree doing just that.

My fingers also brushed against the familiar form of the key I always carried, along with a smaller lump at the bottom of the pouch—the ruby signifying my true identity. An identity my parents never let me forget.

"You are Princess Emmeline," my mother had reminded me often, "of the house of Mercia, the daughter of King Francis and Queen Dierdal."

"I don't want to be Princess Emmeline," I'd responded as often. "I just want to be Emmy, the charcoal burner's daughter."

Of course, only Father called me Emmy. Mother insisted on using my given name, Emmeline, because it was more ladylike. While she hadn't wanted Father to teach me how to be a soldier like him, she'd understood his reasons for doing so: that he wanted me to be prepared for the future, with the ability to fight the enemy and keep myself safe. To balance Father's training, Mother had worked even harder to shape me into a proper lady worthy of the title of *princess*.

Bede raced along next to me, easily keeping pace, his paws barely touching the ground. While his tracks wouldn't matter so much, I made sure not to leave a trail, stepping on stones, large branches, and outcroppings where even the most skilled of trackers would have difficulty tracing my path.

When I reached the coppiced woodland adjacent to the earthen kilns, I allowed myself to slow down. The stumps left from trees Father had once felled had regenerated with new shoots. Some from as far back as ten years ago had grown into multiple stems that were ready to cut again. Others were still young and needed protecting from browsing deer.

The forest was thinner here, lighter and airier, allowing the sunlight to penetrate so the trees could grow again and continue to provide the wood Father needed for making charcoal. At midsummer, bluebells, violets, archangels, and wood anemone formed a colorful carpet all around the copse that I was loathe to trample.

I skirted the new growth and entered the clearing where Father had constructed several domed kilns made of alder and covered with damp turf. Today the kilns were cold and smokeless, waiting for the next production, which Father would start soon after his return. His was an endless job, one he did year-round during the heat of summer as well as the frigid days of winter.

Yet, even with all his hard work, we struggled to survive from one year to the next. The rugs Mother wove on her loom fetched a fair profit when Father sold them at the market. But rather than letting Father buy her anything, Mother always insisted on saving the earnings to use on something for me.

Across the clearing and beyond the herb beds and large vegetable garden, the cottage sat tucked against the edge of the forest, partially concealed by blackthorn and covered with ivy. A thin wisp of smoke rose from the chimney, a sign that Mother had been busy cooking all afternoon in preparation for a special meal to celebrate my eighteenth birthday.

At the sight of Father's mule grazing in the shade of the maple closest to the cottage, my pulse spurted with renewed anticipation. He was home earlier than I'd expected, and I prayed that meant he'd had easy and profitable trading.

"Race you!" I called to Bede.

The red fox bounded with a snort. When I picked up my pace, he scampered to remain at my side.

As I sprinted the last of the way, my worries dissipated, and I couldn't keep from smiling at the thought of the special evening ahead. We'd feast on the delicious meal Mother had prepared with my favorites of roasted duck and baked vegetables fresh from the garden. Afterward, we'd enjoy a slice of honey cake—the only sweet delicacy we ever ate, and only on my birthday. Finally, after we'd washed dishes, Mother and Father would present me with a gift— always a book that Father managed to find on one of his trips to the market.

What book would they have for me this year? A collection of poetry? Perhaps a text of ancient history? Or maybe even a compilation of maps and descriptions of faraway places?

Whatever it was, I'd adore it, as I always did. And I'd read it until it was near to falling apart, just as I had all the books in the hidden cupboard.

Bede yipped as he ran beside me, his eyes sparkling with excitement, his head bobbing with his effort to outrun me. I lengthened my stride and reached the cottage first.

At the door, I stopped short and pulled myself up straight. Lifting my shoulders and chin, I tucked loose strands of hair back under the cap I wore. Father required me to wear boys' clothing whenever I went beyond the clearing. Although Mother never liked to see me in the plain garments, she acquiesced so long as I cast them aside and returned to my skirts at home.

From behind, Bede jumped up onto me, tail wagging and tongue lolling again.

"No, I won this time." I turned and playfully nudged him down.

He tossed his head as though arguing with me.

"I can't help it if I'm faster than you." I rubbed a hand between his ears and was bending to plant a kiss there when the door wrenched open with such force I stumbled back.

"Emmy. There you are." Father filled the doorway, all muscle and brawn. With broad shoulders, a strong square jaw, and rich brown eyes, I guessed he was as handsome now as he'd been eighteen years ago when he'd first met Mother. That had happened during the dangerous days as an elite guard fighting against King Ethelwulf's invasion of Mercia.

"Father!" I vaulted into him as I always did upon his return. His strong arms surrounded me and lifted me up in a tender but all-encompassing hug. I breathed in the woodsmoke that permeated every part of him, a scent he couldn't scrub off even when he washed away the black grime he accumulated while tending the kilns.

"I was about to set off in search of you." He gently lowered me to my feet, studying me with his typical keenness, which told me he hadn't missed a single detail. He'd likely already figured out where I'd gone, what I'd been doing, and how long I'd been away.

"You're home earlier than usual." I eyed him in return. In simple garments that were patched and mended beyond their usefulness, I saw nothing out of the ordinary except he favored his stronger leg, the sign he'd overtaxed himself in his haste.

Every time I pleaded hard enough, he'd tell me the story of how he'd injured his leg while saving Mother, me, and my two sisters, Adelaide Constance and Maribel, from a wolf attack when I'd been but a few days old. He'd single-handedly thwarted the pack sent by King Ethelwulf to track us down. One of the wolves had taken a bite out of his calf, and he'd almost died from the severity of the wound.

Mother claimed she'd saved Father by giving him true love's kiss. And of course, whenever she brought it up, Father asked her to demonstrate the kiss she'd given him, which she gladly did every time.

Father stood back and waved me into the cottage with his cane. The scent of roasted duck enveloped me and made my stomach rumble. Only when he moved to close the door did I notice the extra energy in his step—an energy that shouldn't have been there, an energy he never had after days of trekking many leagues to town and back.

I expected Mother to be bustling around the table setting out our wooden trenchers and cups or busily carving the duck. Instead, she was kneeling in front of our clothing chest and folding items into neat stacks on the floor, a bag open at her side.

A vise seized my lungs and squeezed. Was she packing for a trip?

As though sensing my question, she halted and sat back on her heels. Only seventeen years older than me, she could have passed for my sister, not my mother. If she'd been beautiful when she was younger, she was only more so now with her long, lustrous dark hair, her pale and perfect skin, and her trim and yet womanly body. Father said I resembled Mother, which was why Sister Katherine had chosen them to raise me and not one of my siblings.

Her striking green eyes met mine, and I saw in them a mingling of fear and excitement I'd never seen before.

"Emmeline," she started, her voice containing a note of apology.

I turned my attention to my father. "Is something amiss?"

He didn't meet my gaze this time and instead limped to the corner where he'd dumped his sacks. "Much has changed in the outside world since my last trip during the winter."

My muscles tensed, and I braced myself for

whatever news he'd share, sensing it wouldn't be to my liking. "What changes?" I forced the question even though I didn't want to know.

"Your twin sister has come out of hiding and is living with Queen Adelaide Constance in Norland."

I took a rapid step back and almost tripped over Bede, who'd followed me inside and now sat on the rush mat in front of the door. I sank down beside him.

Father was watching my reaction carefully. "Maribel married young Lord Chambers of Chapelhill."

"Should I know that name?"

"No, you wouldn't, and that's not important. What matters is both Maribel and Adelaide are now married."

Last year on Father's visit to town, he'd come back with news that my older sister Adelaide—as she preferred to be called—had finally begun her quest to reclaim Mercia's throne from King Ethelwulf. Upon reaching the age of twenty, she was old enough to rule of her own right.

As such, she'd sailed to Norland and had married the Earl of Langley, who'd left Mercia years before and had been in Norland forming an army of rebels. Since the earl was like a son to Norland's King Draybane, Adelaide's marriage had solidified an alliance with Norland as well as gained much-needed troops and financial backing.

Ever since discovering the news, Father had been thrilled. A spark had flared in his eyes and only burned brighter with each passing month.

I, on the other hand, hadn't wanted to talk about the news with Father, much to his disappointment. I'd done my best to forget all about it.

Now, I had no wish to speak of Adelaide again. And I certainly had even less desire to hear of Maribel's marriage. "I don't know why either of their marriages should matter. They don't affect me."

"Their marriages do affect you, Emmy. Very much."

"Why?" My question came out more defiant than I intended. Father knew I had no aspiration to involve myself in Mercia's affairs, that I was perfectly content with my life the way it was and didn't want it to change.

He shifted several stones in the interior wall to reveal the hidden cupboard filled with books. He'd discovered the compartment shortly after moving to the cottage and had taken to storing his weapons there. "Everyone I talked to said King Ethelwulf had wanted his son, the crown prince, to marry Adelaide or Maribel, and by doing so, squelch the uprising."

"Then my sisters are free to continue plotting their uprising. But as you know, I have no inclination to be a part of it." Bede pushed his nose against my hand, and I tangled my fingers in his hair to keep them from trembling.

"Now that the king cannot have Adelaide or Maribel for Prince Ethelrex, he may set his attention upon you."

"We are safe here in the forest."

Father didn't respond except to lift his double-edged sword from his arsenal. At the sight of the imposing blade, a chill skittered over my skin and caused me to shudder. He rarely took out his weapons, but every time he did, I had the same reaction. Although he'd made certain I knew how to use them proficiently, I hated touching them. Even more, I hated the thought of bringing harm to anyone.

"Emmeline." Mother stood and brushed down her simple skirt fashioned from the same coarse linen as my clothing. Again, her features radiated apology. "My sweeting, I know you want things to continue as they always have, but we have taught you that this life is not your true destiny." She waved her hand to the humble cottage.

"It can continue." My voice wobbled with a plea. "We're a family, and we're happy here, are we not?" Mother had always claimed she was happy even though she'd never had other children. After experiencing several miscarriages, she'd told me she was all the more grateful for the opportunity to raise me.

Mother's eyes shone with sudden tears. "We have cherished each moment of every day we have had with you. But 'twould be selfish of us to hang on to you when your sisters and the cause need you."

"They need my key and our map. Not me." I patted the leather pouch at my hip. "We shall find a way to deliver them, and then they'll be able to locate the treasure without me."

"They need more than the key and map," Father cut in, "and you know it."

I was well aware they needed more. When I'd been but a girl, Father and I had found in the key's shaft a tiny piece of parchment containing the words, "W.M. Land." We'd put our minds together and figured out the six letters stood for West Moorland, which spread out to the northwest of Inglewood Forest.

I'd recognized the intricate engraving of the wild

boar on the bit of the key as symbolizing strength and courage. I hadn't needed to study much further to discover West Moorland had long ago been known for its wild boar hunting ground.

Though Father knew the trip would take weeks, he'd traveled to West Moorland to the old hunting ground. After searching for days, he'd finally located the foundation of a hunting lodge that had once belonged to the royal family. He'd dug through mounds of rubble before uncovering a column base in the shape of a boar's head. There, he'd discovered a keyhole hidden at the back of its open mouth amidst sharply pointed teeth. He'd returned home with a third of the map to the Labyrinth of Death.

Although Father had heard of the fabled labyrinth during his years of elite guard training, like most others he'd doubted its existence. But after finding a portion of the map, we'd both realized the labyrinth was no fable and was likely the resting place of the much-sought-after treasure.

After that, we'd scoured the old books and scrolls in the cottage's hidden cupboard. Though the pages were yellowed with age, the stone walls had preserved the parchments from mice and other wild animals.

We'd always assumed the manuscripts were simply old history texts. But after finding the map, we'd finally understood just how valuable the books were and why they'd been stored in the isolated cottage. Most of them had references to a labyrinth in one form or another and contained countless clues regarding not only the layout of the maze but also the traps within.

It had taken us several years, but together Father and I had studied the books, cataloged details, deciphered codes, and solved riddles, until at last we'd sketched what we believed to be the rest of the labyrinth, adding in the letters of the various passageways, along with the center room, which we agreed contained the treasure.

I was fairly certain our re-created map was accurate, although I wouldn't know unless I compared the drawing with the other two original pieces.

The truth was, I had no desire to see the real sections of the map—likely in the hands of my sisters by now. I had no desire to visit the labyrinth. And I had no desire to find a hidden treasure. All I wanted was to stay in Inglewood Forest where I was safe with the two people I loved more than life. And I didn't want to leave my best friend—Bede.

I scratched behind the fox's ears and earned a lick. "The ancient prophecy indicates that a wise young ruler—not *rulers*—will rise up."

In the process of strapping on the belt he used to carry his weapons, Father paused. "Sister Katherine told us it would take the three of you working together to find the treasure."

Sister Katherine was one of the nuns at St. Cuthbert's who had shielded Father and Mother when they'd arrived in the Iron Hills with me and my sisters. She'd helped to orchestrate our hiding places so that King Ethelwulf hadn't been able to discover our whereabouts. She and another nun were the only two who knew where Mother and Father had taken me. After all these years of seclusion and safety, we were certain they'd never given away the location. We could continue to live together in the forest forever enjoying life as we always had.

And that's what I planned to do.

As if sensing my resolve, Father shared a glance with Mother. She nodded at him, and he squared his shoulders, took a breath, and then met my gaze levelly. "We're leaving for Norland at nightfall."

I stiffened. "No."

Bede rose to his feet, his fur bristling and his eyes darting between Father and me. Although Bede would never attack Father, he'd do anything to defend me at the slightest hint of aggression. I placed my hand upon his head to soothe him even though I was anything but reassured.

"I don't want to go." I tried to speak calmly, but my voice wavered anyway. "You know that." Father had already tried once to convince me to go to Norland after he'd learned Adelaide was there. I'd refused to leave. He had to know I hadn't changed my mind since last year.

"We must go. I heard rumors that the king's men are searching Inglewood Forest for you. It's only a matter of time before they track you here."

"The forest covers hundreds of square miles. They won't find us." Even as I spoke, I knew I wasn't being rational, that I was letting my emotions cloud my judgment.

Father's expression turned grave. "I saw tracks on my way back into our part of the forest. A soldier's tracks."

I should have known Father would notice the tracks too. "We can't assume the worst. The tracks could be from a woodcutter coming to assess the land, or a hunter who's wandered too far, or even another charcoal burner."

Father shook his head and pursed his lips. "People are looking for you. And since we don't know who may be friend or foe, we must go."

People had always been looking for me, especially in my nightmares, but this couldn't happen here, not in our safe place.

"No one realizes you and Mother have a child." Every time we'd had a rare visitor over the years—usually just another charcoal burner—Father had distracted the guest until Mother could hide me.

"Emmy, please try to understand—"

"Why can't you try to understand how *I* feel?" My voice had risen with my growing anxiety—an emotion I didn't want to experience but one that nevertheless swelled in my chest. I scrambled to my feet.

"We only want what is best for you." Mother held out her hands and walked toward me.

"This *is* the best. I have all I want."

"Whether you acknowledge it or not, God made you for more." Father's voice turned firm and his eyes steely. "Now, resign yourself to leaving. Help your mother pack. We'll partake together of your birthday meal, and then we'll be on our way."

Tears stung the back of my eyes. Why was Father being so stubborn? Was he thinking again of how poor we were and that I deserved more than this kind of life—something he oft lamented? As much as I'd tried to accept everything they'd taught me about duty and being a princess, I didn't want or need anything beyond what I already had.

"I know you don't like my decision now," he said, "but I pray one day you'll see the wisdom in it."

Mother drew near, her arms open wide to console

me, her expression tender and compassionate. "Emmeline, sweeting."

If I allowed her to hug me, I wouldn't be able to stay strong. I'd crumble and cry and do as she asked. Instead, I needed time to think, to come up with a new plan, to gather my wits together. And I couldn't do any of that here. I had to get away.

I fumbled with the latch and swung the door open. Before Mother could enfold me in her arms, I backed out of the cottage, nearly falling in my haste. Hurriedly, I righted myself, spun, and began to run.

Chapter 2

REX

At another anguished scream from our prisoner, I gritted my teeth. On the edge of our camp and surrounded by my toughest warriors, the captive dangled by his arms from a rope looped over a sturdy branch of an oak. His feet were only inches from the ground, but not close enough to give him any relief from the rope pulling his arms from their sockets or rubbing his wrists raw.

Stripped to his drawers, he writhed, his back and chest displaying the welts from the glowing red iron Magnus was using to torture him. So far, our prisoner had endured the pain without giving away anything. Sooner or later he had to divulge the information we wanted . . . or die.

"Tell us what you know about Princess Emmeline," Magnus said again as he had already numerous times.

The man lifted his chin defiantly, the same response he'd given us since we'd strung him up an hour ago. We'd been lucky to find him. In fact, I'd almost lost his trail on several occasions. But when he'd circled around and headed toward his small rebel search party, I'd cut him off. He'd put up a decent chase, but he'd been no match for my speed or skill.

Magnus pressed the hot iron to the prisoner's lower back at the tender spot in the middle. The man immediately arched up in another scream worse than any of the others. I hated the sound. More than that, I hated the torture we were inflicting. But I knew of no other way to get the information we so desperately needed.

We'd been searching for the lost princess for many a fortnight, nigh onto months. None of our leads had amounted to anything. None of the people we'd questioned knew of a young woman who was coming of age. None could supply us with any helpful clues.

Now our time was running out. The soldiers bringing fresh provisions yesterday had informed us that ships carrying Queen Adelaide Constance, her rebel army, and Norland's forces were sailing south toward Delsworth.

Not only would we soon be under attack from outside the kingdom, but it was also possible that malcontent citizens from inside the country would rise up to fight with Queen Adelaide Constance. Thus, the king and his advisors believed my marriage to Princess Emmeline would help appease the masses. The king even held out hope it would prevent Queen Adelaide Constance from attacking altogether.

I swallowed an angry oath. I was failing not only myself but also my vow to the king to find the princess. After spending years working hard to become the best elite guard in the kingdom, I couldn't fail now. Not when the king trusted me to find this last princess after others had fallen short of capturing her sisters.

As the king's firstborn son and heir to the throne, I'd waited many long years in Warwick for him to call me back to Delsworth so I could show him how capable and dedicated I was and that I was worthy to succeed him someday.

This was my chance. And now I had to finish the job. Even if it meant torturing one of the rebel scouts.

At least I could take comfort from the knowledge I wasn't the only one having difficulty finding Princess Emmeline. The queen's rebel search party was apparently experiencing trouble too, for we continued to have sightings of their harpy eagle which meant they hadn't yet called off their quest.

If the queen's people were still looking for Emmeline, then most likely the princess hadn't escaped yet to Norland. She remained lost somewhere deep in the heart of the thick forest in a place that was practically impossible to find.

Magnus glanced at me, his eyes gleaming. My younger brother was taking too much pleasure from his task of attempting to extricate information from our prisoner. Time to relinquish the job to someone else, no matter how much Magnus pouted.

"Let Dante take over," I ordered.

Magnus didn't remove the iron from the rebel's back. "Why?"

I crossed my thick arms over my chest and braced my feet apart, hoping to send the message to my brother that I wouldn't be moved in my decision.

He held the iron a moment longer before lowering it. Even though an angry shadow flitted across his handsome features, Magnus dared not defy me. He handed the hot stick to my head commander.

Dante took the iron and then gave a slight bow of respect to Magnus before standing back and looking to me for guidance.

During the exchange, I'd kept half my attention upon the prisoner and realized he'd expelled a breath, likely one of relief. The slight action on his part was the indication I'd been waiting for, the sign he was breaking and on the brink of giving us the information we needed.

"Put the iron away," I said, without taking my half-attention from the prisoner.

Magnus cursed under his breath, his glare condemning me for being too soft, too lenient. And once again, I wished the king hadn't commanded me to bring him along. I hadn't spent much time with my brother growing up since he'd remained in Delsworth during my years of training in Warwick. Nevertheless, upon my arrival in the royal residence, it hadn't taken long to realize Magnus was prideful and bloodthirsty—a combination that made him dangerous not only to himself but to all of us.

At the release of tension in the prisoner's abdomen, I knew I had him right where I wanted. He'd inadvertently shown me his weakness, that the torture was becoming unbearable. It wouldn't take much more to get him to talk.

I nodded at Dante. "Take your dullest knife and start severing his toes, one at a time."

"I like it," Magnus said, offering one of his rare compliments even as he crossed his arms and waited much too eagerly.

The prisoner's body stiffened.

Dante moved to do the task with unquestioning obedience, his face stoic, his eyes determined. Wisely, he positioned himself to one side of the prisoner to avoid any kicking. Then, before our captive could wrestle away, Dante grabbed the man's calf, bent the knee, and wrenched the foot back, the knife already pressed against the large toe.

As the dull blade cut into the man's flesh, I didn't breathe.

"The princess is living with a former elite guard who is now a charcoal burner," the prisoner called out, his voice desperate, his features taut with pain.

I raised my hand.

Dante halted his sawing and lifted the knife away.

"A guard who used to go by the name Lance," the captive rushed to speak. "And a noblewoman by the name Felicia. That's all I know. I vow it."

A former elite guard. And a noblewoman. Surely with that description, other charcoal burners would be able to point the way. After all, an elite guard and noblewoman could hardly live in the woods all these years without gaining some attention.

And yet, if such details had been enough, why hadn't the queen's search party located the princess? Why were they still looking?

"I need more information," I said with a nod to Dante.

He lowered his knife to the prisoner's toe and began to cut again.

For several seconds the man attempted to endure the blade biting through his flesh, but then he released a guttural cry and yelled, "Wait!"

Dante glanced at me. I raised my hand again, and he stopped.

The prisoner lifted his tormented eyes to meet mine. I kept my face void of any emotion. If this man knew how much I detested torturing him, he'd refuse to say anything more and cling to the hope I'd release him— which I likely would.

"I came upon a new trail this afternoon," he said in a ragged voice. "A few footprints that were slender and small enough to belong to a young woman."

Finally. This was information we could use. "Where?"

"If you release me, I'll take you to the footprints."

I motioned Dante to resume the torture.

"Three-quarters of a league to the southwest," the prisoner shouted quickly, "and then perhaps half a league west."

I studied his face. From the earnestness and fear in his expression, I knew he was telling the truth. "Give us other landmarks."

Already my mind was carving out a path in the direction he'd given us. I added more detail as the prisoner described stones, trees, and setting particulars he'd memorized in order to take the rebel search party back to that area.

With the information fresh in my mind, I was anxious to go before darkness settled. I pivoted and stalked toward my tent.

"Cut the prisoner down and bind him hand and foot," I called over my shoulder. "If he's lying, I shall not only cut off his toes upon my return but shall sever his fingers as well."

"That's rather severe, isn't it, Your Highness?" Father Patrick fell into step next to me, his short legs scurrying to keep up with my long stride.

"Sometimes severity is necessary." Father Patrick knew me well enough to realize I'd never carry through with cutting off our prisoner's toes or fingers, that my threats were only meant to scare and nothing more.

"Sometimes mercy is even more important," Father Patrick remarked.

My faithful priest had never been afraid to speak the truth even when no one else dared. He'd been a loving presence and faithful tutor while I'd been growing up in Warwick, and I'd been grateful he'd accompanied me to Mercia. But there were times like these when he didn't understand the increasing pressure I was under.

His flowing brown habit billowed around his portly frame as he tried to keep pace with me. "You have a good heart, Your Highness. I can always count on you to do what's right in the sight of God and man."

What was right in the sight of God and man? Sometimes I didn't know anymore—especially when the king's deeds—deeds that seemed unnecessarily harsh or even selfish—didn't settle well within me.

Of course, I'd always known the king was a ruthless ruler. Every time I'd visited him or he'd traveled to Warwick, he'd emphasized that a king must do whatever is necessary to retain his power.

I'd just never realized the extent to which he took his power. Now after a year in Mercia, I'd witnessed acts of lawlessness and cruelty I couldn't condone, particularly his calloused attitude toward the many who'd suffered during recent years from failed crops and a shortage of food. He'd done nothing to ease their hardships. Even I, though I wasn't yet king, had taken pity on the people of Warwick and had labored with other nobility to find ways to provide for all.

I could only pray the distress would ease in Mercia now that the drought was over. Already the hardships were lessening, and the land was growing more fruitful. The dissatisfaction would abate, especially when I found the princess and married her. And hopefully, all would be well with the king.

"Yes, you are a very good man, Your Highness . . . which is why you must make sure the prisoner suffers no more abuse, even during your absence." Father Patrick looked pointedly at my brother before raising his brows at me. A ring of trim brown hair surrounded the large bald spot on the top of his head, which was shiny with a layer of perspiration. His cheeks were flushed too. And I sensed his reaction had more to do with witnessing the torture than with the summer temperature.

I stopped and faced my men again. Dante was in the process of cutting down our captive, and the others were gathering their weapons in preparation for our next mission. Only Magnus remained unmoving, watching the proceedings with disinterest.

"No one is allowed to harm the prisoner while I am gone," I barked out. "We may yet have use of him."

I threw back the flap on my tent and retrieved a cloak that would help me blend into my surroundings. If there was one thing I'd learned these past weeks of hunting for the princess, she was well-hidden. And now I understood why. An elite guard of the former king had been assisting her all these years. He was an intelligent man to have gone undetected for so long.

Backing out, I tossed the cloak over my chain mail.

"Your Highness." Father Patrick was waiting patiently outside my tent, his forehead creased in worry. "Always remember we can accomplish more through wise strategy than through brutal force."

Though my nerves strained with the need to be on my way, I clasped the priest's arm gently and dropped my voice to a whisper so no one would hear my confession. "Father, you know I detest displays of torture as much as you do."

He reached up and patted my cheek as he'd done when I'd been a boy. "God go with you."

I squeezed his arm. "Make sure your prayer book is ready upon my return with my bride. I shall wed her ere the night is over."

At least I hoped so.

Taking my swiftest men, we set out at a run. I led the way through the thick brush, following a deer path to make our movement easier. We traveled the long distance quickly, arriving in a new area of the forest we'd never explored.

A steep ravine separated it from the lower woodland, a ravine that lengthened in both directions and seemed impassable. If not for our prisoner's instructions to locate a creek that trickled underneath, I might not have found the low cavern hidden behind hanging ivy. The cave narrowed into a passageway that led gradually uphill and opened on the opposite side of the ravine.

After traveling another half a league west, we easily located the rotted hawthorn our prisoner had indicated. So far I'd only spotted the prisoner's imprint, although he'd been careful not to leave much of a trail.

Now we studied the area meticulously and finally discovered a faint, slender, human footprint that most definitely could belong to a young woman. Even after combing the surrounding woodland, we found only two more, and then the trail vanished, almost as if the person had never been there.

Curiously, fox prints covered the ground. From what I could surmise, the fox and the woman had been there at approximately the same time.

Crouched low, I traced the outline of the fox's paw on first one print and then the next. They were close together, almost relaxed. If the fox had shown aggression toward the person, the paw prints would have been deeper and farther apart.

I stood and silently surveyed the unchanging landscape. Through the leaves overhead I gauged the condition of the evening sky, still hazy as always from the numerous charcoal burners who made the forest their home and were constantly burning wood.

Sniffing, I checked again for the thickening scent of woodsmoke that might signal a charcoal burner nearby. If only I could find an elevation high enough to look down on the forest and map out the various sources of the smoke. As it was, even from the highest of trees, I couldn't spot any distant plumes.

"The footprints face south, Your Highness," Dante said quietly from behind me. "Maybe if we split up, we can pick up the trail."

I bent again and studied the fox prints. The fox was no foe to the woman. What if the creature was a companion?

For the first time in weeks, the thrill of pursuit spurted in my blood. I'd landed upon the first viable trail. And now I needed to move into the mode of hunter closing in on his prey.

I stood, pulled up my hood, and drew the cloak around my chain mail. "We shall follow the fox prints. No sounds. All eyes alert."

Understanding dawned in Dante's eyes, but he said nothing and only lifted his hood, motioning for the others to do the same. We would become invisible wraiths, blending into the woodland, creeping forward undetected. This was no time for carelessness or amateur mistakes.

Soundlessly we moved through the forest following

the fox trail, constantly surveying the terrain and checking every detail we passed. The prints led us to the border of a wooded copse—one we'd never been to before, unmarked on any of the maps I'd memorized.

I motioned for the others to stop, get down, and remain invisible.

My blood pumped harder. The fox had done well and had led us exactly where I'd wanted. The coppiced land with thinner growth and new shoots belonged to a woodcutter or charcoal burner. Though the air wasn't any thicker with smoke, I suspected kilns awaited on the other side of the area. If so, a hut would also be nearby.

"Take half the men," I whispered to Dante. "Stay wide. Circle around to the front of the living quarters."

Dante nodded to three of the men. In an instant, they were gone.

Without a moment's more hesitation, I led the other half of my men the opposite direction, using all the speed and stealth we could muster. If the fox caught wind of us, we'd lose the element of surprise.

As we crept through the woodland, a break in the brush revealed turf-covered kilns. Without a trace of smoke coming from any of them, I suspected the charcoal burner was between burnings. With any luck, he'd be away at the market, leaving his wife and children unattended.

We skirted the clearing, remaining concealed. And finally, after long, tense minutes, I was rewarded with the sight of the backside of a cottage. From what I could tell, the abode was in good repair, tidy, and well-kept.

To the north of the cottage, Dante rose just slightly and signaled to me. I motioned for him and his men to stay hidden. My senses were keenly alert, taking in the silence and stillness of the place. Had the family learned of our coming and already fled? Were we too late?

I scanned the surrounding area for any clues as to what we might face. A lone mule was tied to a maple. A few chickens pecked the grass, and a goat lay in the shade of the home. A large fenced-in garden spread out behind, filled with leafy produce that would soon be ready for picking.

The cottage was quiet. The shutters of the window in the back were open, but I saw no movement inside the mostly dark interior.

I signed for Dante to take his men and attack through the front door while I led my contingent in the back window. I gave us twenty seconds. Any longer and the fox—if he was around—would sense our presence. Once the fox was alerted, his master would be too.

With quiet haste, we kept out of sight as best we could, crouching close to the ground, climbing the fence, and passing through the garden to the open window. My mental count landed at fifteen. Unsheathing my knife, I slid up the wall.

As I silently reached twenty, I hopped through the opening, alighting without a sound. At the same moment, Dante burst through the main doorway.

In an instant, he and his three men engaged in hand-to-hand combat with a large muscular man. The surprise on the man's face told me he hadn't expected the invasion. But the speed and agility with which he was counter-attacking confirmed his identity as Lance, the elite guard who'd been hiding Emmeline.

At a gasp from near the table, I wasted no time in lunging for the other occupant, a beautiful woman with long, dark hair and pale skin. She was young, but not young enough to be the eighteen-year-old princess.

Her eyes were wide with horror as I grabbed and spun her so that my knife grazed her neck. Of course, I didn't press the blade into her skin. But I had to make the most of my advantage to bring Lance into submission and gain his cooperation. I suspected threatening this woman would do just that.

"Drop your weapons," I said firmly. "Or I shall slit her throat."

At the sight of my knife blade as well as the fear in the woman's expression, Lance froze. That instant of taking his attention from Dante and his men was all the time they needed. Within seconds, they'd disarmed him and had his arms twisted and tied behind his back.

"Let my wife go!" He craned his head to plead with me. "Do anything you want to me, just let her go."

I drew his wife closer, tightening my grip. At the movement, I could feel her stiffen in fear, just as I wanted.

"Please!" Lance's voice turned desperate.

I nodded at Dante to shut the door. As far as I could tell, the princess wasn't inside the cottage. We would need to wait for her return. If she didn't realize we were present when she came home, we'd be able to capture her without having to resort to unpleasant tactics.

As my men quietly closed the door, I watched the elite guard, taking in every detail about his appearance, size, and skills. And I sensed I couldn't underestimate this man.

"Lance," I said.

This time he didn't react, had schooled his face so it remained emotionless—void of surprise, anger, even fear.

"I am Prince Ethelrex of the united kingdom of Bryttania, eldest son and heir of King Ethelwulf, the rightful ruler of the house of Warwick and Mercia."

Again Lance's face was unreadable. His wife, on the other hand, trembled beneath my grip. I guessed she was Felicia, the noblewoman who'd been a part of sheltering Emmeline. I shifted her, making a display of letting my knife slip so that it poised above one of her major arteries.

"Let her go," Lance said again, his voice harder.

Dante shoved the hilt of his sword into Lance's back. "Show proper respect to His Royal Highness."

Lance didn't move, not even to lift his chin, which told me this man—unlike our prisoner earlier—would not be swayed. Not by words, not by threats, and not by any form of torture. He was the kind of man I respected.

In this case, however, too much was at stake. I couldn't afford to give him any respect or leniency.

"I have come for the Princess Emmeline," I continued. "If you cooperate in handing her over, I shall spare your wife. If not, I shall cut her apart piece by piece."

Father Patrick's words from earlier resounded in the deep places of my mind, the warning that I needed to use wise strategy rather than brute force. I prayed my threat was a wise strategy and would convince Lance to do my bidding since he obviously cared more about his wife's life and safety than he did his own.

He looked at his wife, and I sensed I had him right where I wanted him.

"Do not even think about cooperating with the enemy," Felicia said, her trembling ceasing. "Do whatever you can to break free and take Emmeline to safety."

"Where is the princess?" I asked, moving Felicia's arm behind her back and forcing her down to her knees.

"You will never get her!" Felicia cried out, pain and fury in her voice. "She will never turn herself over to you. Never!"

Lance closed his eyes and dropped his head, but not before I caught a glimpse of the indecision there. Would he let his wife suffer to save the princess? I hoped I didn't need to find out. One thing I did know is that they were both strong. And my battle with them for the princess had only just begun.

Chapter
3

Emmeline

Bede whined softly at the base of the tree. Again.

From my comfortable spot high in the branches, I sighed. Above me, beyond the canopy of leaves, the sky had shifted to a darker hue of blue, the sign evening was growing late.

And the sign Father, Mother, and I must be on our way . . .

For the past hour, I'd slowly resigned myself to Father's decision. As much as I hated the prospect of leaving my woodland home, in the end, I trusted and loved him enough to do as he wanted. If he truly believed we must go this time, then how could I defy him?

I sat forward and swung my legs over the branch.

Bede peered up at me with sad eyes, almost as if he knew I'd made my choice and that it would mean the end of everything we'd both loved. He darted a glance around, his ears pricking, before whining again.

"Be patient, Bede. I'm coming."

I'd half-expected Father to follow me into the woods. In my haste and in my frustration, I hadn't covered my tracks. But even if I had, he was well aware of my favorite hiding spots. He'd easily find me if he set his mind to it.

But I suspected he'd held back, hoping a little time away would allow me to see the wisdom in his decision and to accept the inevitable. Truthfully, I'd always known that someday my time with Lance and Felicia in Inglewood Forest would come to an end. They'd been frank about my identity as a princess, their role in my life, and what my future held.

In recent years, they'd even tried to convince me to stop calling them Mother and Father. But I'd insisted they were the only parents I'd ever known, that they'd always be my mother and father, that nothing would change our relationship.

Of course, they'd exchanged a glance as they always did when I said something they didn't agree with. But at least they hadn't protested any further.

In all his arguments, Father never failed to remind me that through the hidden books, I'd been given incredible amounts of knowledge regarding the labyrinth. He emphasized that with such knowledge came great responsibility. Deep inside, I knew I couldn't shirk that responsibility.

"I shall go to Norland," I said as I started the climb down. "I'll deliver the key and map, tell my sisters everything I know about the labyrinth, but then I shall return here. Eventually, I'll come back."

I paused on a low branch. What if Mother and Father didn't want to return to the forest? What if they longed for the comforts and luxuries of their old lives?

What if they resented the loneliness and hardships that came with living here?

Whenever I'd asked them if they missed having a normal life, they always responded that they wished for nothing more and that raising me had been the greatest privilege of their lives.

Nevertheless, what if now I could give them the opportunity for more?

I hopped the rest of the distance and landed on my feet. Remorse hit hard at the bottom of my chest. I'd been childish and selfish to insist on staying, thinking only of what I wanted and not of what would be best for them.

Bede turned and trotted in the direction opposite of home. When I didn't follow, he halted and cocked his head at me, as though beckoning me to come along with all haste.

"While I'd love to see whatever it is you have for me, it's time to head home. Otherwise, Father really will come after me."

He was a determined man, always had been. And that strength had been the reason we'd survived, especially during the first few harsh winters. Although I couldn't remember the difficulties of starting out in the cottage since I'd been but a newborn, Father and Mother liked to reminisce about those early years when they'd come to the forest as newlyweds.

If only I had a fraction of my parents' inner fire.

Maybe this trip to Norland was a chance to develop some strength, to face unknown siblings and an unknown future. Whatever the case, I couldn't put off heading back to the cottage any longer. I had to help finish packing. And I wanted to enjoy one last eve together. After all, Mother had worked hard to prepare my special birthday meal, and they'd still want to give me my yearly present.

"This way, Bede," I called as I started forward.

When Bede didn't immediately follow, I paused and looked back at him. "I know you don't want to leave either, but we have to trust Father."

Bede yipped.

"Come now." I began to jog toward the cabin. "I promise I'll give you a taste of honey cake."

I didn't have to wait long for Bede. He was soon racing along beside me. As we neared the clearing, however, he reached over, snagged my tunic, and jostled against me, giving me no choice but to stop.

I yanked my garment to wrest it free and was about to rebuke my fox when the skin at the back of my neck prickled. I ceased my struggle and dropped to the ground on my stomach. Bede flattened too, stared straight ahead, and growled.

Something wasn't right. I didn't know what. But maybe that's why Bede had been acting strangely.

For long seconds, I listened for unusual sounds and scoured the surrounding area for signs of trespassing. Then I crept closer to the edge of the clearing until I could peek through the foliage.

The expanse was silent and deserted. At first appearance, everything was as it ought to be. But when I studied the area again and paid attention to detail, I realized the mule was still tied to the tree where Father had left it. By now, Father would have fed and watered the tired creature, as well as brushed it down, especially since he'd soon load it with the belongings we planned to take with us.

And the chickens were still roaming around. Father should have killed and dressed the fowl to use during our journey. He certainly wouldn't leave them behind.

Next to me, Bede growled again, louder this time, and bared his incisors. His dark eyes were focused on the cabin.

Something had occurred while I'd been gone, but what? Had the visitor whose footprints I'd discovered earlier happened upon the cottage? Was he inside with Father and Mother?

Nothing about our home seemed amiss. Except that perhaps it was too quiet. Did I dare approach? If I could get closer, I'd be able to look for footprints and any signs that might give me more information. On the other hand, what if the visitor was a foe?

I rose to my hands and knees, uncertainty gnawing at my insides. "What should I do, Bede?"

Bede didn't take his eyes from the cabin, as though he sensed danger.

Scenes from my nightmares flashed through my mind, and I was tempted to retreat the way I'd come and return to my hiding spot high in the tree. But at the same time, loyalty to my parents demanded I hasten to their aid if they were in trouble.

Trying to gather my courage and still my trembling, I stood. For several pounding heartbeats, my throat was too constricted to speak. Finally, I managed a short whistle, one I used to communicate with Father when hunting.

Bede didn't move except to twitch his ears.

After long moments of silence, I whistled again, this time hopefully loud enough he would hear me if he was still in the cottage.

"Go, Emmy!" came Father's voice from inside. "Run. Hide!" He was abruptly cut off as though he'd been hit, and Mother's scream was muffled.

The urgency of Father's tone was all the warning I needed to begin racing away.

The door of the cottage banged open. "Come out and show yourself," a commanding voice carried across the yard. "Or you will force me to hurt your parents."

I stopped. Hurt Mother and Father?

"No, Emmy!" Father shouted louder. "We'll be fine. Just go!"

I retraced my steps to the edge of the clearing and peeked through the brush. The door of the cottage was open. Several soldiers stood outside with Father between them. His hands were bound behind him, and his feet tied with ropes so he could hardly walk. His weapons were gone, and he was disheveled, a bruise already discoloring the skin around one eye.

"Get away, Emmy!" Father called. "And don't look back!"

One of the guards backhanded Father in the mouth, but he continued to shout instructions at me to run, hide, leave. Quickly, another of the guards twisted a gag that cut through Father's mouth and silenced him—or at least made his words indistinguishable.

Several more soldiers came out of the cottage holding Mother between them. Her hands were bound, but thankfully her feet were free, and her captors appeared to be treating her with more care.

I counted eight men wearing cloaks of gray and brown. One soldier stood apart from the others and had cast off his outer garment, revealing the black chain mail that haunted my dreams—the chain mail belonging to the elite guards of King Ethelwulf.

Again my chest burned with the need to run and hide. I wouldn't be a coward for doing it. Running was what Father had pleaded with me to do. He wanted me to get far away and stay out of the clutches of the king. I couldn't let him down. Not after the sacrifices he'd made to keep me safe all these years.

The knight wearing the chain mail took several steps from the cottage, his gaze roving over the brush until his sights locked upon me. An ordinary man wouldn't have been able to spot me so quickly amidst the foliage, especially since I, like his companions, wore garments that blended well with the woodland.

But of course, this was no ordinary group of soldiers. These men had been drilled like Father to do the near impossible. Faced with so fierce a foe, I ought to be on my way now. I'd need every inch of a head start I could gain. Even then, I'd be sorely outnumbered.

My advantage was that I knew the woods better than anyone except Father. My hiding places would prove challenging to even the best of trackers. With all the skills Father had made sure I learned, I'd have a very good chance of outmaneuvering these soldiers and making my way to safety.

And yet, how could I leave Father and Mother behind to suffer at their hands?

The guard at the forefront seemed to size me up, though I was mostly hidden. I took him in, too, noting his fair hair braided in the three warrior strands over his scalp and tied together at the base of his neck. His face was rugged, perhaps even handsome, behind the layer of unshaven scruff. His shoulders were broad and his arms thick with muscles that bulged against his chain mail. From the confident way he held himself, I had no doubt he was the commander of this group if not of the king's entire guard.

When his gaze locked with mine, I drew in a sharp breath. Though he was too distant for me to distinguish the color of his eyes, I had no trouble seeing their fierce intensity. I dropped into a crouch, hiding in the thickness of the brush—but not before witnessing him motion to several of the men to surround me. In my mind, I could picture the paths they would take in the woods, drawing closer until I was trapped. If I wanted to get away, I had to do so now.

"I can see you have no wish for any more trouble to befall your parents," he called out. "If you hand yourself over to me, I shall let them go, unharmed."

He was stalling me, giving his men time to circle around me.

"Do not give in, Emmeline." Mother's voice rose distinctly into the evening, unwavering and strong. "You know what you need to do."

I cringed, waiting for a backhand to her mouth. When the captain didn't silence her the way he had my father, I whispered a prayer of gratefulness. Perhaps the commander was a decent man toward women. Or perhaps he was allowing my mother to speak and so further halt my escape.

At a nudge from Bede's nose, I made my decision. I sprang away and leaped over windfall, intent on making my getaway before the soldiers closed in.

"String them both up!" the captain shouted so I

would hear, obviously seeing my attempt at escape. "And heat an iron."

I faltered and stumbled to a halt. A glance over my shoulder told me the captain wasn't issuing an idle threat. The soldiers were shoving my parents toward the large maple where Father had tied the mule. The captain tossed a rope over a high branch so that it hung on either side.

"No," I whispered, my blood turning cold.

Bede bumped against me, urging me to run. But as my father reached the tree, one of the guards forced his bound hands upward above his head while another began to secure him to the dangling rope.

Although I'd never witnessed torture or anything remotely cruel, I'd read enough in my history texts to know the damage that could be wrought on the human body. I also knew I wouldn't be able to turn my back upon my parents and allow them to go through that anguish. Not for my sake and not for any reason.

I couldn't see the soldiers advancing, but I sensed their presence to both my right and left. I spun and stared into the heart of Inglewood Forest, knowing that's where I needed to go.

Yet, at a cry from my mother, I couldn't make my feet run as she'd instructed. Instead, hot tears stung my eyes. My parents might have been able to leave a loved one behind to face torture, but I couldn't do it. I wasn't as strong as they were. I never had been.

My shoulders slumped. For a moment, the weight of my failure pressed heavily upon me. I hadn't become the courageous woman they'd worked hard to develop.

At the slight crack of a step to my left, I dodged

away and broke through the brush into the clearing. One of the guards was already pulling the rope attached to my father, dragging him up so that his feet no longer touched the ground. His arms stretched tightly above him, the twine digging into his wrists. Though he kept all emotion from his face, the tightening of his torso told me of the pain he was already experiencing.

A soldier had strung another rope and was beginning to tie my mother's hands above her head. At the sight of me racing across the grassy yard, her eyes widened, revealing panic. "Emmeline! Please! Go!"

I picked up my pace, my attention homing in on the rope holding my father. I'd already unsheathed the small knife Father had insisted I always carry with me. While I'd long past vowed I wouldn't use it for harm, I'd found it was useful from time to time for cutting roots or shaving bark or even some whittling.

Now I was glad more than ever Father had made me wear it. I aimed at the rope and threw it. In one swift slice, it severed the twine, and Father dropped to the ground. He was on his feet in an instant, his eyes upon my knife, which had embedded into the trunk.

Before he could figure out a way to retrieve the weapon, however, the daunting captain of the guard grabbed a fistful of his hair, jerked his head back, and laid a sharp blade against his neck. It pierced Father's skin, quickly drawing blood.

"No!" I halted and held out a hand, not realizing it was trembling until too late. "Don't hurt him!"

The commander didn't budge. Only his gaze flicked behind me. His men had followed me out of the woods and now stood a short distance around me, and he'd communicated something to them. Had he told them to draw closer and grab me?

The captain turned his attention back to me, and for an endless moment, he took me in from my boy's cap down to my boots. His eyes were a vivid blue, the same as the clear evening sky overhead. But they were unreadable, like my father's. If he was curious, surprised, or even appalled to find me attired as a boy, I couldn't tell.

I suppose it didn't matter to him what I looked like. His assignment was merely to bring me to the king in Delsworth. If Father was correct, the king would marry me off to his son, the crown prince, with the hope that such a union would undermine the rebellion.

Perhaps if I cooperated for the time being, I'd not only save my parents, but I'd find a way to free myself from the clutches of these soldiers, hopefully before we were out of Inglewood Forest.

The commander watched my expression carefully.

"Release them," I said. "If you bring them no more harm, I shall accompany you without further resistance."

Father said something behind his gag. Of course, I couldn't make out his words, but the message within his eyes was loud enough. He didn't want me to give in.

"Please try to understand," I said to him. "I had to come back. I wouldn't be able to live with myself, knowing I allowed you to suffer."

Father tried to speak again, his eyes pleading with me. Could I somehow make him realize this was the best way to save us all for now? That soon enough I'd find a way back to him?

"Bede." My faithful companion was right by my side, his low snarl warning the soldiers to keep their distance. I tangled my fingers in his fur. "You and Mother will keep Bede."

At my unthinkable offer, Mother's gaze snapped to mine. I'd raised the fox since finding him as a wee motherless pup. We'd never been apart. Ever. Bede went with me everywhere. If I willingly left my dearest and most beloved friend, surely they could comprehend my unspoken message—that I'd never leave him behind if I didn't plan on returning.

Father gave me the barest of nods, which told me he finally understood and that he trusted me to find a way to escape.

"Release them," I said again to the commander. "You vowed you would let them go unharmed if I handed myself over to you."

"And are you handing yourself over, Princess?" he replied in a strangely disquieting tone. "Or are you planning to run once I free them?"

I lifted my chin, hoping he couldn't see how close he'd come to the truth. "Of course I'm handing myself over. I could have easily escaped your men if I'd so chosen."

He watched me a moment longer, and I forced myself not to squirm under his scrutiny. He was rather bold for a captain of the guard.

"Prove your cooperation." He shifted the blade lower on my father's neck, nicking the skin and drawing more blood. "Go change into clothing suitable for a princess and pack any items you wish to take with you. For every misstep you make, I shall press my knife deeper."

His voice was cold and held no room for bargaining. Everything about this man, from his arrogant bearing to his hard demeanor, testified of his leadership and his ability to command unquestioning obedience.

Though he frightened me, and I feared he'd slit my father's throat regardless of what I did or didn't do, I had to remember I was a princess, of royal blood. My status was far superior to his. He wouldn't dare harm me. Not as long as the king needed me. Not even if I tried to flee a hundred times.

The trick was figuring out a way to keep this guard from hurting my parents.

Chapter
4

WHEN EMMELINE EMERGED FROM THE COTTAGE A SHORT WHILE later, I appraised her again. In spite of an ugly skirt that appeared as though it had been laundered in a cesspit, she was still stunning.

Without the boy's cap, I could see that her hair was as dark as a raven, the color matching her long eyelashes. While her hair was still bundled in a messy knot, a few strands had come loose and fluttered about her face. I suspected her tresses were long and thick and wavy and would add to her beauty—if it were possible for her to be more beautiful.

The simple truth was that I'd never met a young woman even half as lovely as Emmeline, and I'd certainly met many noblewomen over the past year. From the moment I'd spotted her through the brush, I'd known her delicate, exquisite features belonged to the princess. It was almost laughable that she'd believed a boy's cap and breeches could fool anyone.

I'd been impressed by her speed when she'd come out

of the woods to save Lance. I'd even been slightly impressed by her ability to throw her knife with such accuracy. But I hadn't been surprised. Lance had trained her to protect herself just as any good elite guard would have done who'd been guarding the princess.

Her keen eyes assessed first Lance and then Felicia. Though I hadn't wanted to gag Felicia, I'd had to do so to prevent her from further communicating with the princess and attempting to make plans. Then my men had bound them each to different trees. They'd used many ropes and tied complicated knots that would be difficult to undo. But I suspected Lance would be able to free himself within a day. A day was a far enough lead that we'd be well on our way back to Delsworth with the princess, and he'd never be able to catch up.

The rich dark brown of Emmeline's eyes was expressive—probably more so than she realized, giving away her feelings quite easily. And as she paused to set down her full sack and take in the state of her guardians' well-being, her relief was palpable. She'd clearly been worried I'd slit open Lance's throat during her absence. No doubt she considered me a brute.

I suppose I couldn't blame her. After all, I'd used Lance and Felicia to bring her into compliance. Once we were away from Inglewood Forest, and especially once we were back at the royal residence, I'd work at changing her opinion of me and find a way to win her affection. Eventually, she'd even be grateful to me for sparing Lance and Felicia when many others in my position would have killed them on the spot.

Yes, I'd have a challenge in wooing her. But I always relished challenges, and this would be one I'd especially enjoy. For now, however, I had to keep up a show of strength and power, even if she temporarily despised me for it.

Dante reached for the princess's sack only to have the fox snap at him. She bent and gently touched the creature's head, and he immediately calmed.

"Let Dante search your bag," I ordered.

She lifted her chin. "I have no other weapons besides the knife, which it appears you now have."

I'd sheathed it with mine, not sure if I'd eventually return it to her or not. Would we ever come to the point of being able to trust each other? I prayed so but knew it would take time and effort.

Dante took hold of the sack again, and this time the fox allowed it. When he flipped it over and began dumping the contents, she yanked the sack away from him, her eyes flashing and her body bristling. "How dare you?"

Books littered the ground, most of them worn and falling apart. Pages of parchment came loose from several and fluttered in the breeze. She dropped to her knees and gathered the pages, tossing a glare at Dante. "Have you no care? These are worth more than gold."

"We cannot take the books." I approached her. "Only clothing and personal necessities."

"My books are my necessities."

I halted next to her and snatched up a drawing that resembled a maze—a very large and intricate maze.

Upon seeing what I'd picked up, she sprang up and lunged for the paper, leaving me with no doubt that this was a map of great importance.

I held it high out of reach.

"That's mine."

"It's mine now." I started to fold it, hoping it was

indeed a map to the Labyrinth of Death, which was a maze in the Highlands that had been discovered over the winter.

She glared at me now too, and her anger only made her more stunning. The brown of her eyes turned almost ebony, and the pulse in her neck beat harder, drawing my attention to the graceful and elegant lines.

Under different circumstances, I might have allowed her beauty and anger to sway me to let her keep a few of her books. But with the closing of the evening soon upon us, I couldn't afford to waste time sparring. Instead, I bent and swiftly slit the leather strap of the pouch in her pocket and snatched it up before she knew what I was doing.

She grabbed it quicker than I'd expected. "Give that to me at once!"

I wrenched it free of her fingers and then held it out of her reach as I'd done with the map. From the corner of my eye, I could see Lance shaking his head and attempting to say something to Emmeline, confirming my suspicion that whatever was in the pouch was important.

"I demand you return it to me this instant." She clawed at my arm, and her fox crouched low, snarling at me.

In addition to a small book, I traced the hard contour of a key through the leather. A brief glance inside showed me the large gold key that matched the one the king already had. Before the princess could wrestle the pouch away, I stuffed it, along with the map, down my tunic behind my chain mail then dropped my hands to my side, daring—no, inviting—her to retrieve the items.

But as I suspected would happen, the princess immediately ceased her efforts and merely stared at the bulging spot on my chest, her eyes rounding. She was innocent and unaccustomed to men, to be sure.

"We must go." I eyed her now empty sack lying on the ground. There was no sense in wasting time sending her back into the cottage to repack. I suspected any other garments she had would be in the same condition, if not worse than what she was wearing. She'd need a completely new wardrobe when we arrived in Delsworth, something worthy of a future queen.

Once again, she knelt and began to pick up the books, dusting them off and carefully stacking them.

"Say your good-byes," I ordered.

She ignored me, tucking pages back into one particularly old book.

I planted my feet wider, crossed my arms, and narrowed my eyes—a look that never failed to make men quiver.

"I will pack my books first," she said.

"You are not bringing them."

"Yes. I must."

"No."

She glanced up at me, her eyes dark again and flashing, her chin jutting stubbornly. "Yes."

With a growl, I reached for her, scooped her up, and tossed her over my shoulder.

"Put me down!" She wiggled within my grip, attempting to slither down.

I tightened my hold and stalked toward the woodland while she pounded on my back with her fists and tried to kick her feet against my ribs, this time attempting to use the strength in her torso to free herself. She exerted more force than I'd expected, but she was no match for me, and I continued forward without faltering in my stride.

I wanted to make it back to our camp before nightfall. Since my men could pack up and be mounted in little time, I hoped we'd be out of Inglewood Forest—at least the better part of it—by sun's first light. Now that I had the princess, we'd be safest out of the forest, away from the land she knew, for I suspected that if she broke free, she'd do her best to make sure we didn't find her again.

Besides, it wouldn't be long before the queen's rebel search party discovered we had the princess. When they did, they'd try everything possible to catch up and take her away.

At a sharp bite of teeth in my calf, I pinned Emmeline with one hand and with the other unsheathed my sword and swung it back.

"No!" she screamed. "Please don't!"

I paused, giving her the chance to save her fox's life.

"Bede, go back!" she shouted at the fox. "Go back to Mother and Father, and stay with them."

The red fox continued to bound through the tall grass behind us. The creature was as loyal as a dog, if not more so. I hoped for Emmeline's sake he would obey her. I didn't want to injure—or kill—her pet. But I couldn't have him following and slowing us down.

"Go home, Bede!" she called again, and this time her voice cracked. "Go! Now!"

The fox finally stopped. I could picture his eyes upon Emmeline, probably confused and worried. A thin needle of guilt pricked me. I was taking the princess away from everyone and everything she'd loved and doing so against her will.

As I headed into the forest, for just a second I was tempted to put her down and let her say a proper good-bye to her pet and family. But at the sight of my men in my periphery, I put the soft-hearted notion out of my mind.

I was securing the princess for my men and others like them who didn't deserve to be dragged into a needless war against Queen Adelaide Constance. I was securing the princess for all the people of Bryttania, to keep the land peaceful and prosperous under their rightful ruler. And most of all, I was securing the princess to show my loyalty and worthiness to the king. He was counting on me, and I couldn't let him down.

"Stay!" she shouted at the fox. When she said nothing more, I knew the fox had listened to her. She'd ceased struggling and had grown limp. At the soft sniffles, the guilt came back with stabbing force. Was Emmeline crying?

A part of me knew I needed to say something. But I sensed anything I offered at this point would only offend her and make her angrier. She needed time to adjust and accept the lot that had befallen her.

"Run ahead," I called to Dante. "And alert the others to be ready to leave."

My commander nodded and then picked up his pace, disappearing into the woodland ahead of us.

Even with my extra burden of carrying the princess, we made it back within the hour. Darkness had fallen and several torches had been lit, illuminating the camp and showing we were nearly ready to go. Dante, along with the rest of the men, except for Magnus, were busy tying our belongings to our horses.

At the sight of me, Magnus pushed up from the log he'd been sitting against and came toward me. Father Patrick followed on his heels. The others paused in their work—likely to get their first glimpse of the princess.

Gingerly, I lowered her, guessing that after having her head down for the past hour, she'd experience a rush of blood that might make her dizzy. However, the second her feet hit the ground, she launched away from me into the woods, and started to run, the darkness of the forest swallowing her up.

Chapter 5

Emmeline

I grabbed handfuls of my skirt to prevent it from tripping me and wished I'd kept my boy's clothing on underneath. Even though the way was dark, I'd been plotting my escape route the entire time my captors had hauled me away.

I picked a deer trail slightly to the west of the one we'd traversed, knowing it would lead to the brook at the ravine too. I needed only to reach the steep rocks, cross to the other side, and I'd be free and could make my way to one of the tallest and thickest of trees where the king's soldiers would never find me.

At the shouts coming from the camp behind me, I pushed myself harder, having only a few seconds' lead. I was counting on the king's guards being tired, especially the commander who'd carried me.

My skirt snagged on a branch, but I kept running, wrenching it loose even as part of it tore away. The pounding of the earth behind me, the crashing of limbs, and the snapping of twigs told me soldiers had begun the chase.

For an instant, I considered climbing a tree and hiding up high. But such a move could prove risky. Even if I snaked my way from tree to tree using the branches, the king's men would hear me and follow my trail, biding their time until I returned to the ground.

At the brush of fingers against my upper arm, I twisted and dodged into a different path. Though the forestland was an inky black and the leaves overhead allowed very little moon or starlight to penetrate, the dense trees and windfall couldn't slow me down—not when Father had made me practice running in the dark many times. I'd always thought he pushed me too hard, had agreed with Mother that he didn't have to teach me everything he knew.

But now that I was fleeing for my life, I finally understood why he'd insisted.

Love for both him and Mother swelled painfully in my throat. I pictured them again tied up, their desperate gazes following my departure. My father's eyes had silently implored me to do whatever I could to break away.

Although I wanted to return to the cottage first and cut them loose, I forced that thought from my mind. I had to make my way to Norland. Though the king's men had done a thorough job in binding my parents, Father would eventually free himself, and then he and Mother would waste no time in heading north too. They wouldn't risk staying and having the king's men recapture and use them again to bait me into doing the king's will.

The labored breathing of the soldier behind me matched mine. From the burning in my lungs, I wouldn't be able to keep up the pace for much longer. Hopefully, I could last until I lost my pursuer.

Another unsuccessful grasp at my back was followed by a blow against my lower legs. As my body jolted forward, I cried out, knowing I'd land hard and probably gouge open my hands and arms in bracing my fall. But before I slammed into the underbrush, fingers made contact with my tunic, slowing my momentum so that the force of my plummet knocked the wind from me and skinned my hands but didn't inflict the damage I'd expected.

I should have used the descent to my advantage, rolling, jumping back up, and slipping away—employing stealth and silence to escape the enemy rather than trying to outrun him. But for a second, I was startled by the gentleness of the hands at my back, the same strong hands that had carried me away from home. Hands that belonged to the commander.

My pause gave him time to secure his grip on my tunic. I wrestled to free myself, twisting and turning and hoping the linen would rip and allow me another opportunity to escape. But he jerked me to my feet and pulled me back so that I tumbled against him. In an instant, his arm wrapped around me, trapping me.

I expected the sting of his knife upon my throat but heard only the harshness of his breathing and felt the rise and fall of his chest.

My mind scrambled to remember any tricks my father had taught me about breaking free from this type of hold. Maybe if I bit him—

"Do not try anything else." His voice was a low growl. "You might be proficient in the woods, but you will only find I am better."

I bent my head, intending to sink my teeth into his wrist so that he'd reflexively loosen his grip. But somehow he anticipated my move and linked his other arm around my neck, forcing my head back.

"I did not wish to do this, Princess," he said. "But you leave me no choice but to tie you up."

Though I resisted and made the tying difficult, within minutes he'd bound my hands behind my back with his belt and had tied my feet together with strips of my skirt.

"If you try to bite me again," he said, straightening, "I shall gag you."

I should have been afraid of this man. His strength and speed, as well as his quickness of mind, surpassed even Father's abilities. But strangely, I didn't fear him—at least not for my own well-being. If he'd wanted to hurt me, he could have done so already. Instead, he'd treated me cautiously, even carefully.

Perhaps he was concerned what the king or prince would say if I accrued any injuries or bruises while under his command. Perhaps the king or prince would discipline him, maybe dismiss him from his post.

In one easy swoop, he picked me up as if I weighed no more than a feather coverlet. I expected him to drape me across his shoulder again—something I dreaded. My ribs were sore, and I wasn't sure I could take anymore jostling. So when he positioned me in both arms, comfortably against his chest, I was surprised.

He whistled through his teeth, which I guessed to be the signal to his men that the search was over. Then he began to carry me back to the camp. From the brief glimpse I'd gained before I'd started running, the soldiers were almost finished packing. They'd be ready to ride out before long, taking me away from everything familiar and safe.

I couldn't let it happen, but how could I prevent it?

"I'll get away from you eventually." I tugged at the binding on my wrists. Although it wasn't painfully tight, he'd made certain I couldn't wiggle out.

"You will never get away from me unless I allow it."

"You think too highly of your abilities."

"I speak only the truth."

"Perhaps you've proven yourself to the king and prince, but you've yet to prove yourself to me."

"The prince?"

"The one they call Prince Ethelrex." I wasn't accustomed to speaking to men. In fact, the only man I'd ever seen or spoken to was Father. And so, I found the interaction quite strange.

"And what do you know of . . . Prince Ethelrex?" The commander's tone had changed, less hard and more curious.

"I know nothing, and I wish it to remain that way."

"Nothing at all?" Surprise laced his voice.

"Only my father's warning that since Adelaide and Maribel are married, the king may try to force me to wed the prince."

The commander didn't respond.

Through the darkness, I wished I could read his face, but I could only distinguish his strong jaw and chin. "You can try to take me to him, but if you succeed, I will never marry him."

"*Never* is a very strong word, Princess."

"No one can make me speak wedding vows."

"The prince can be persuasive when he needs to be."

"He will find I can be stubborn when I need to be."

The commander's stride was long and sure, almost as if he knew the woodland as well as I did. The only sound was his breathing and the crunch of his footsteps until we drew nearer to his camp and heard the other soldiers again.

I had to do something—anything to free myself. If I could distract the commander, take his attention from my hands tied behind my back, I might be able to reach for a knife in his belt and inflict enough injury that I could get away.

"Do you like your master?" I asked.

"My master?"

"The prince." I stretched my fingers and brushed against the hilt of his sword.

"The prince is the strongest and fiercest warrior in the land."

"I'm surprised you can admit someone is better than you." Again, I groped after his weapon, only to have him heft me higher in his arms, far away from any chance of snagging a weapon.

This man was indeed as sharp as he was strong. Perhaps I'd need to wait to make my escape until he placed me under the command of one of his men. Surely he didn't intend to watch me every second until he handed me over to the prince.

"Is my father's warning true?" I asked. "Will the prince attempt to marry me?"

"Yes, it is certain he will marry you."

"Does he not wish to meet me first? What if he cannot bear the sight of me and loathes my very presence?"

"He will marry you regardless of his personal

feelings in the matter."

"I see." Was the commander insinuating the prince had some hesitations? "Does the prince already love another woman?"

The commander snorted as if my question was ludicrous.

"You do not believe in love, Commander?"

Before he could answer, we stepped through the brush into the clearing where his men had returned and resumed their preparations of packing and loading. A young man wearing the finest garments I'd ever seen approached. I guessed he was close to my age—either eighteen or nineteen. Wavy dark hair framed his aristocratic face along with a pointed beard. I'd only seen one drawing of King Ethelwulf from his younger years, and this man looked almost identical.

Was this Prince Ethelrex? Had he come along on this quest to find me? His clothing and bearing certainly set him apart from the others. But he didn't seem to be the strongest and fiercest warrior in the land. The commander had likely been resorting to flattering his ruler, was probably accustomed to puffing the prince up to keep him happy.

As the younger man halted in front of us, I expected the commander to bow or incline his head out of respect. But the prince was too focused on me to notice the slight from his commander. His brows rose higher with each passing second of scrutiny.

Was he surprised by my appearance?

A short, stout priest carrying a torch hurried toward us, illuminating the prince's face even more.

"She is not what I was expecting," the prince said, his eyes taking on a glimmer that made me want to shrink back and hide.

Unfortunately, I had no place to go except further against the commander. But strangely, within his arms I felt safer than I did facing the prince.

"Her clothing is appalling, and she is in need of grooming," the prince continued, taking the torch from the priest and holding it above me. "Even so, she is strikingly beautiful."

He reached out to touch my cheek, and I recoiled, fear pressing hard against my chest.

I was surprised when the commander took a quick step back, pulling me away from the prince. I didn't know why he'd risk defying his master, but I was grateful nonetheless that he seemed willing to protect me.

But for how long?

"It is regretful you are having so much trouble keeping hold of her." The prince eyed my bound feet and then my arms tied at my back. "If she attempts to get away again, I shall have no difficulty in subduing her."

Something in the prince's tone insinuated a danger I couldn't begin to understand. I sensed this was a man I would never like or trust. And I most certainly couldn't marry him. I'd have to redouble my efforts to get away. And soon.

"The princess promises to be on her best behavior from now on," the commander said. "Do you not, Your Highness?"

Your Highness? No one had ever called me that.

Before I could contradict him, he lowered me to the ground. He held my arm and steadied my awkward balance caused by the binding around my feet. Keeping a firm grip on my elbow, he turned to the priest. "Shall we get on with the wedding with all haste?"

"Right now?" My voice came out a squeak.

"Immediately." The commander didn't look at me but rather motioned at his men, who at once abandoned their packs and horses and began to congregate around us.

As though sensing my fear and revulsion, the prince's lips curled in a slight smile, one that made his eyes glint again. The expression told me I was in for a life of pain and discord if I went through with marrying him. Panic bubbled in my stomach, churning acid. I had to get away. Now.

Darting a glance around the woodland and then the camp, I noticed a knife two dozen paces away, discarded among several other tools. If I could get to it and slit the binding from my feet, I'd take to the trees.

As if sensing my mounting panic, the commander's fingers tightened and drew me closer to his side.

"There's no hurry to have the wedding now." I jerked my arm to free myself. "We can wait until we arrive at Delsworth and have a proper wedding there."

The priest opened his prayer book.

"The king will want to be involved and witness—"

"The king was the one to suggest the wedding take place immediately after locating you," the commander said, "which is why Father Patrick is with us."

I gave one last futile yank of my arm, knowing even if I managed to free myself from the captain's hold, I wouldn't be able to get far. Not with so many soldiers surrounding me. "As I said before," I hissed to the commander, "you cannot make me state my vows."

"If you do not," he growled, "I shall send out my

fastest men and command them to return with Lance and Felicia."

"They will be gone by now."

"Not yet. I made sure of it."

He was right. It was much too soon for my father to have freed himself.

The commander's gaze flicked to a man who remained in the shadows at the periphery of the camp. Naked but for his braies, he was tied to a tree with his back exposed, revealing festering blisters and welts. His condition left me no doubt he'd been tortured, and I guessed it was on account of me. Perhaps he was the one whose footprints I'd found earlier in the day.

If the commander could bestow such torment on this man, what might he do to my parents if he caught them again?

I swallowed the rising bile.

"Are we all gathered?" The priest glanced around the half circle behind him before looking at the commander, who gave a curt nod. The priest held up his book, cleared his throat, and began. "In the name of the Father, Son, and Holy Ghost. Amen."

I closed my eyes as if by doing so I could block out the nightmare in which I found myself. But the burning in my stomach kept me all too awake to the fact that I was trapped with no way out.

Chapter 6

REX

I HELD MYSELF RIGIDLY AND CLENCHED MY JAW TO KEEP FROM commanding Father Patrick to cease the wedding ceremony. I had no wish to start my marriage under such adverse circumstances, forcing the princess to comply by threatening to torture her parents. I would have preferred to wait, to show her the life that would soon be hers, to give her all the luxuries she'd never had, and to allow her to become comfortable with me.

But I had no choice. Whether I liked the conditions or not, I'd marry her as the king had commanded. I understood the urgency—that I had to secure our future together straightaway. Too much was at stake, especially with the queen's army on the move.

As before, I tugged Emmeline closer to my side. In the torchlight, her delicate features were taut with anguish, and her eyes pinched shut.

A strange sense of self-loathing invaded me. In all these weeks, I'd never once thought about how the princess would feel being snatched from her home and forced to wed me. I'd only thought about how the union would keep a war from breaking out, how it would prevent bloodshed, and how it could be the solution to the fight over the throne. With Emmeline by my side, no one would be able to oppose the kingship, not with both royal families united.

Once I explained to Emmeline all the benefits of our marriage, she'd see the wisdom in it and learn to accept her fate as much as I had. After all, few royal children could choose their own spouses. Such decisions were left to the kings and their advisors and were often political in nature. Surely, she understood the way of things.

Whatever the case, I needed Father Patrick to perform the ceremony as quickly as possible. Before I changed my mind. Once it was done, no one and nothing could undo the marriage—not even me. Our fate and the fate of the rebellion would be sealed.

"Skip all but the essentials." I interrupted Father Patrick's rambling. "We need to be on our way."

"It is all essential," Father Patrick responded, leveling upon me one of his censuring looks.

"Just the vows. The declaration of being man and wife. Only what is necessary to make the union binding."

Father Patrick frowned. "You know I'm already having difficulty agreeing to this—"

"There will be a formal ceremony later." Yes, Father Patrick had voiced his concerns about a forced union on several occasions. I didn't need him doing so again and undermining my resolve. "Be on with it. We are wasting valuable time."

With a nod, Father Patrick flipped ahead a page in his prayer book. He cleared his throat and began. "Your Royal Highness, wilt thou have this woman to be thy wedded wife, to live together after God's ordinance in the holy estate of matrimony?"

Emmeline's arm against mine shook, and again self-loathing pulsed through me.

"Wilt thou love her," he continued, "comfort her, honor, and keep her, in sickness and in health; and, forsaking all other, keep thee only unto her, so long as ye both shall live?"

She tensed as though praying for miraculous intervention, anything that would save her from this moment. If only I could reassure her I never took vows I didn't intend to uphold, that I truly would do my best to love, comfort, honor, and keep her.

Father Patrick glanced up at me expectantly.

"I will," I said, adding a silent vow to prove I was a worthy husband.

At my clear declaration, she startled and pulled back as much as she could against my firm grip. I could feel her gaze upon me, studying my profile, almost as if she was seeing me for the first time.

After I'd recaptured her in the woods a few moments ago, I'd realized she didn't know I was the prince, that she believed I was merely a commander of the elite guards. I'd assumed once we rejoined the camp, she'd quickly discover my true identity. But obviously, she hadn't.

I slanted her a sideways look.

"You're Prince Ethelrex?" The brown of her eyes was as rich and thick as sable.

"Yes."

She shot a glance at Magnus. Had she assumed my brother was the prince? Had she believed she was marrying him instead of me? I supposed after weeks of living in chain mail and scouring the forest, I wasn't particularly at my finest. In fact, compared to Magnus in his princely attire and freshly groomed appearance, I was rather barbaric.

Father Patrick looked between Emmeline and me, then cleared his throat. "Now that we have clarified who is marrying whom, shall I continue?"

I nodded.

"Your Royal Highness," he said more gently, with a kind look at the princess. "Wilt thou have this man to be thy wedded husband, to live together after God's ordinance in the holy estate of matrimony? Wilt thou obey him, and serve him, love, honor, and keep him, in sickness and in health; and, forsaking all other, keep thee only unto him, so long as ye both shall live?"

She didn't respond. In fact, her pretty lips were clamped tight.

I squeezed her arm, hoping to persuade her. *Everything will be all right*, I silently encouraged. *I promise I shall be a good husband.*

"Your Royal Highness," Father Patrick said softly. "You must say, 'I will.'"

Her face was pale, and the movement of her swallow in her long, graceful neck was pronounced.

I didn't want to have to send Dante and several others back for her parents. But she had to understand that she'd leave me with no choice if she didn't comply. As if remembering the same, she finally spoke. "I will."

Though her words were barely more than a strangled whisper, the tension eased from my shoulders.

"For as much as this man and woman have consented together in holy wedlock, and have witnessed the same before God and this company, and thereto have given and pledged their troth each to the other, I pronounce therefore that they be man and wife together, in the name of God, our bishop, and our King, who is the protector of our people. Amen."

"Amen," I whispered, bowing my head in a moment of reverence to God and silently acknowledging I'd do everything within my power to fulfill my wedding vows. If I worked hard enough to love Emmeline, maybe she'd eventually accept me and our marriage. I could only hope and pray.

In the meantime, our union wasn't secure. Although we were officially married, there would still be many who would attempt to nullify the ceremony and take her away from me. The sooner I could confine her within the royal residence at Delsworth, the better.

"Let us be on our way," I called out, and the men immediately broke away to finish readying for departure.

Before I could sweep Emmeline back up into my arms, Father Patrick moved in and began speaking to her. "Your Royal Highness, I know this is all rather sudden, but rest assured. God has given you a very good man in Prince Ethelrex. I have known him all his life, and although he is sometimes stubborn, I attest that he will make you a kind and noble husband."

"Thank you." She nodded at the priest, taking his words of comfort with a dignity and grace I admired under the circumstances.

I gave Father Patrick a curt nod as well, hoping he understood my gratitude not only for performing the ceremony against his better judgment, but also for his affirmation.

Then, without further ado, I swept the princess up into my arms and started toward my large warhorse. The creature would tire faster carrying two of us, and I'd eventually need to hand Emmeline over to ride with Dante in order to sustain the pace I desired. For now, however, I'd keep her with me and ensure she didn't attempt any other escapes.

"If I release the binding around your hands," I asked, "will you promise not to thwart me?"

Her chin jutted in defiance. "You may have forced me into marrying you, but you cannot force me to stay."

Just as I'd expected. I'd need to keep her bound, even though doing so would make traveling more uncomfortable for her. I signaled to Dante with a slight cock of my head.

He left his horse, crossed to me, and bowed.

"Retie the princess's hands so that they are in front rather than behind her. And then lift her up to me."

As my oldest, most loyal friend, I trusted Dante more than anyone else. His father was Lord Kennard, the wealthiest noblemen in Warwick, and had been the one to train us both along with the other knights who had come with me to Delsworth. I owed much of my skill as well as my strength to Lord Kennard. He'd been a strict man but ultimately kind and trustworthy.

While I mounted my horse and situated myself and my weapons, Dante repositioned Emmeline's bindings even as she resisted his every move. Finally, he lifted her into my waiting arms. I positioned her sideways in the saddle in front of me. Although the fit was snug and left little room for movement, I had her exactly where I wanted her.

She scowled and held herself away from me. "This is highly inappropriate, as I'm practically in your lap. 'Twould be much better if I rode behind you."

The gleam in her eyes told me if I moved her to the rear, she'd have an easier time freeing herself without my awareness.

I reached for the reins, purposefully drawing her closer and surrounding her within the confines of my arms so she was pressed to my chest. She remained stiff and unyielding. Not that I expected anything less. Yet.

With a nudge to my horse's ribs, the beast started forward, the momentum further pressing Emmeline into my chest. Her hair tickled my chin and cheek, and I slanted so I was near her ear. "You are my wife now. As such, there is nothing inappropriate with your sitting upon my lap."

I could feel her entire body pause at my bold words. And I could not stop myself from taking advantage of the situation with more brazenness. "In fact, I give you leave to sit on my lap whenever you so desire."

"I shall never desire it," she retorted hotly.

"I shall ensure that you do."

"I should like to see you try."

"You should know I never back down from a challenge. And also that I never lose."

She drew herself up higher. "There is always a first time for everything. Even losing."

I liked her sass. It was unexpected and different from the docile, ingratiating attitude of most young women I'd met at court. Even so, I wanted the princess to know I was serious about my vows and that our marriage wasn't a game.

"I meant my vow to you." My voice dropped to a harsh whisper. "And I will choose to love and cherish you unto death."

I could sense her ready retort fade away and her shoulders soften—even if just a little. At that moment, I knew I would win her affection or die trying.

Chapter
7

Emmeline

After endless hours of riding, I was sore beyond endurance. Though I'd ridden our mule on occasion, the experiences left me woefully unprepared for the rigors of being upon a horse.

I'd done my best to remain stiff and aloof for most of the night, but it had taken every ounce of strength I possessed. I'd kept myself awake by plotting all the ways I might be able to flee, although I'd not been able to find a method that might actually work.

When the prince had halted briefly at dawn to water our horses, I'd hardly been able to stand when he lowered me to the ground. If not for Dante, I would have collapsed. And now, after riding with Dante all day, I suspected I'd never walk again. The prince could cut my bindings and have no fear of my escape.

From my spot in front of Dante, I had a perfect view of the prince's rigid back, his broad shoulders, and his strong arms. Though we'd ridden as hard during the daytime as we had all night, he remained as alert and vigilant as he had been from the start.

The thinning of the vegetation and the change in flora and fauna told me we were nearing the edge of Inglewood Forest, that soon I'd leave my familiar woodland home behind. From the northeasterly direction we traveled, I'd long since guessed we were headed to the Central Heathlands.

Fear had been building inside me with each passing hour and the widening distance from my parents. Although overcome with weariness, I hadn't allowed myself to sleep even for a minute during the hours of traveling, and now my eyelids lay heavy with both grit and the need for slumber.

Every time my head bobbed, I sat up with a firm reminder to stay awake and alert for an opportunity to make my escape. So far, none had presented itself.

If only I hadn't run off into the forest when Father had told me we were going to Norland. If only we'd left at that moment . . .

My regrets sat heavily within my chest, next to my fear.

Out of everything that frightened me, I still wasn't afraid of the prince, though I knew I ought to be. Even now, the way he rode with purpose and skill and determination commanded respect. His men jumped to obey his every word, not out of fear but out of reverence and adoration, even though everything about him radiated fierceness and danger.

I meant my vow to you. And I will choose to love and cherish you unto death. His whisper had replayed in my mind countless times, as had the priest's comment about the prince. *Rest assured. God has given you a very good man in Prince Ethelrex.*

Rex—as his brother called him—a very good man? While the prince was brutal when he had to be, I'd been surprised by the kindness in him as well. He'd treated me more decently than other men would have in his situation. He'd even spared the tortured prisoner when his brother had insisted on killing him.

"We need him alive as a witness to the wedding ceremony," the prince had said. "When his people find him, he will tell them what he saw so no one will doubt I have married the princess."

His wise words had silenced any further argument, and we'd left the prisoner alive, bound to a tree, just as we had my parents.

Although I wasn't afraid of Rex, I couldn't claim the same regarding his brother. Something about Magnus gave me chills in a way I couldn't explain. I sensed Magnus would have been far less lenient with me and my parents. So while I resented all that had happened, I was relieved I was married to Rex and not to his younger brother.

As if sensing my thoughts and gaze upon him, Rex shifted in his saddle and cast a glance at me over his shoulder. In the daylight, his blue eyes were vibrant, making his scruffy face all the more handsome.

He always seemed to take in more with a swift glance than I was capable of even after careful studying. Such attention to detail was something elite guards learned. But the prince was especially keen.

His face betrayed no emotion, but he held up his hand and gave a short, piercing whistle, bringing our party to a halt.

"Thank the saints," grumbled Magnus from somewhere behind Dante. I caught the eye of Father

Patrick and could see from his hunched shoulders and sagging head that his weariness matched my own. When he offered me a sympathetic smile, I gave him one back. But just as quickly as the smile came, I let it fall away. How could I smile at a time like this?

"We shall water and feed the horses and let them rest for a few minutes," the prince said in his usual tone of authority. "Then we shall ride on again."

My inward groan matched Magnus's outward one. For how much longer would we push on without eating a proper meal or sleeping? I suspected Rex and his men could go for several days, but I hoped that wasn't the case this time.

Dante slid off the mount. Before he could reach up for me, the prince was there, his large hands upon me, lifting me down. Again, as moments ago, he assessed me, the blue of his eyes even brighter up close.

When my feet touched the ground, my knees buckled, and I would have fallen if the prince hadn't caught and steadied me. His long fingers spanned my waist. The pressure was gentle and yet firm at the same time, making me all too aware of his nearness just inches away.

Examining my wrists, his brow furrowed. "Dante, cut the princess's bindings."

"Hands and feet, Your Highness?" the young man asked.

"Why did you not inform me the ropes were chafing her?" The prince's tone was laced with irritation.

Dante bent to look at my wrists and noted the red, raw skin. He shook his head apologetically. "I didn't see it, Your Highness."

The prince's scowl deepened, and he seemed to refrain from lashing out at his second-in-command as he cut away the binding.

"I was trying to loosen the ropes," I admitted, not wishing Dante to suffer on my account. "And thought to hide my efforts from him."

Rex turned his scowl upon me. "You should have slept."

I lifted my chin.

With a growl under his breath, Rex swung me up into his arms and carried me to a fallen log. Gently, he lowered me, but the moment my backside touched the wood, I couldn't contain my cry of pain. My bones ached in every part, but especially where my hindquarters had bumped in the saddle for hours.

He hovered above me, worry clouding his eyes. "What ails you, Emmeline?"

I started to motion toward my backside but then stopped, unable to speak frankly with him about my predicament. Instead, heat climbed into my cheeks.

As if sensing what I couldn't tell him, he quickly straightened. For the first time since meeting him, he was not only at a loss for words, but he fumbled before he lifted me and positioned me in a cushion of tall grass.

"Better," I said, appreciating the stillness and the softness of the earth more so than I ever had before in my life.

He shoved a hard roll and an apple into my hands. "Here, eat these."

My stomach was growling, and I couldn't turn down his offer, although part of me warned against accepting his favors. He left me, posting two guards beside me as I reclined in the grass and nibbled on my food.

Our break this time was longer than the prior ones. I suspected the prince had extended the respite for my sake, and I was grateful. Finally, he approached. As he stooped and picked me up, I couldn't protest or struggle, even though I knew I should.

Dante helped to settle me on the horse in front of the prince. When I found myself sitting on a cushion of blankets, I couldn't contain my surprise at the prince's sensitivity in trying to ease my discomfort. I tilted so I could see his face.

He held himself tall and straight, his head high, his sights probing the woodland. For the first time since meeting him, I seemed to really see him—not as my captor, but as a man. His face was only inches from mine so that I could take in every scar, smudge, and mark. Beneath a thick layer of stubble, his jaw was long and chiseled. His cheekbones were broad and his nose the perfect shape.

As though sensing my scrutiny, his gaze flickered to mine before returning to our surroundings. "Do I meet with your approval?"

I turned my attention to the woodland, too, and pretended to study it, although all my mind could envision was his face—rugged and yet entirely too appealing.

Suddenly, I was conscious of the way his hard chest pressed against me, the strength of his arms surrounding me as he held the reins, and the essence of power that emanated from him. I had the urge to squirm, to put distance between us. But I had no place to go. All I could think about was that I was with a man, and I had no idea how to act or what to do.

Of course, I'd watched Mother and Father interact, had witnessed their abiding love and the tenderness with which they treated each other. But I'd never had any practice for myself in mingling or speaking with men my age. I didn't know where to start—or even if I wanted to start.

I peeked at the prince only to find my gaze connecting with his once more. His eyes were beautiful, especially in contrast to his warrior-like expression. They pierced through me and made my pulse lurch with unusual speed.

I closed my eyes.

What was going on? Why was I reacting this way to a stranger?

Mother had taught me the finer lessons of life and had tried to explain the process of courtship and marriage. Even as she'd insisted I'd one day be ready for marriage, and perhaps even fall in love, I'd always proclaimed that I didn't care if I ever met a man and got married.

And for the most part, I'd been telling the truth. I hadn't cared. Only once in a while, like when I'd watch my father slip his arm around my mother's waist, draw her near, and nuzzle her neck, had I wondered what such love would feel like and if I'd ever experience it for myself.

This isn't the time for love or even attraction, I silently rebuked myself. Especially not with the enemy. I had to stay strong, remain vigilant, and continue working toward escape. That's what my father would have wanted me to do—refrain from being mesmerized by beautiful eyes.

I shut my own eyes tighter, forcing myself not to look at the prince and to ignore the curiosity that was growing in spite of my silent lecture to stay detached. But even with my eyes closed, I was still too aware of his strong presence enveloping me and threatening to undo me. Although I worked on keeping my posture rigid, I finally gave way to the weariness that weighed upon me more heavily than it ever had before.

Wakefulness hovered at the edge of my senses, but I fought it away. Instead, I burrowed farther into the warmth and solidness of the arms surrounding me, relishing the feeling of safety. In fact, I'd never felt safer than I did at that moment, knowing with certainty that nothing and no one would be able to hurt me.

Strong but gentle fingers smoothed down flyaway strands of my hair, brushing lightly, almost reverently along one of my cheeks. The other cheek rested against a solid chest, the steady thud of a heartbeat echoing in my ear.

My eyes flew open to the awareness of a horse jostling beneath me, the aching in every joint in my body, and the fact that a man's arm was wrapped around my waist. One glance at the black chain mail brought back the direness of my plight, the realization I'd been captured from my home and was a prisoner.

Panic burst in my chest. But before I could sit forward and claw my way to freedom, the soft fingers glided over my cheek again. The touch was infinitely tender, grazing my skin and combing back my hair in one move.

The prince. I didn't have to see him to recognize the strength of his body against mine, different from Dante, who'd held me much more formally.

I released a breath, allowing the panic to ease from my body. The pressure of the prince's arm around my waist felt somehow secure, not imprisoning. And as his calloused fingertips trailed up my cheekbone, I closed my eyes and rested my head against him, relishing the sweetness of his touch, so delicate and yet so masculine at the same time.

Something in the caress sank into my skin and blazed a path through my blood, pumping it harder so that it spread strange warmth into my chest. I didn't want to move, didn't want to awaken fully, didn't want this moment of tenderness to end.

Yet a voice from my conscience reminded me that while Rex might be a better man than I'd expected, he was still King Ethelwulf's son. I couldn't forget that King Ethelwulf had been the one to murder my birth parents, had hung their bodies from the castle wall after his invasion, and had been hunting my sisters and me for years in order to destroy any threat to the throne.

"I am glad you slept." Rex's low voice rumbled near my ear and made my stomach vault head over heels.

I was tempted to luxuriate in the warmth and strength of his embrace a little longer. I was still weak and tired, I told myself. But with my father's disappointed face rising before me, I sat up straight, moving away from his caress.

"You'll not be so glad if it means I've regained my

strength and energy so that I might more easily get away." As I took in our surroundings, I startled at the realization we were in the open heathland, with hills spreading as far as the eye could see. Majestic rocky crags, purple heather, and crowberry added splashes of color to the pale green. The sky above went on endlessly in all directions, the streaks of lavender and sienna telling me the sun had just made its descent in the west.

For my whole life I'd been surrounded by dense trees. Consequently, I was speechless at this splendor, so unlike anything I'd ever seen.

"The land is a fierce beauty, is she not?" the prince whispered, tugging me close again.

"She is." I had not the will nor desire to resist and found myself reclining against his chest. "My geography books did not do her justice."

"Perhaps I might help in that regard."

While we weren't riding as fast as we had previously, our pace was still steady and hard. Even so, for a short time, I forgot I was a prisoner as the prince answered my questions about the land and the species of plants and brush I didn't recognize, along with the wildlife and fowl that lived in the heathland.

"You are very knowledgeable of the terrain," I said at last, "for one who has not lived in Mercia for long."

"Father Patrick taught me as much about Mercia as he did Warwick." He cocked his head toward the priest who lagged behind with Magnus. "And you. You are knowledgeable as well."

"My parents made sure I was educated," I answered. "And I very nearly memorized every book we owned." My thoughts strayed to the books dumped onto the grass by the prince's men, the pages fluttering in the breeze as though waving good-bye. They'd been my only treasure, and I'd miss them sorely.

For a moment, I prayed Father and Mother had made their escape. If I'd harbored any hope they might be able to catch up to us and help free me, I realized now the futility of such thinking, especially since they had no mounts, and our travels had been too swift, the prince too wise, and the forces too great.

Around us, dusk had settled. The last of daylight was fading, leaving in its place the widest sky I'd ever seen, where the first stars had already made their appearance.

"Do you know the stars?" he asked, tilting his head back to gaze above us as I had.

"A little. Enough to find my way at night."

"Can you name the constellation directly to our east?"

I studied the dark eastern horizon, drawing a mental picture of the few stars I could see. "Is the large constellation Cygnus, the Northern Cross?"

"Yes." His tone registered both surprise and admiration. "And the bright star to the southeast of it?"

As he listed the names of the constellations I didn't know, I soaked in the knowledge, delighted to learn, studying the shapes in the sky and drawing the patterns as he taught them to me.

When he shared everything he knew about the stars, I plied him for information about the galaxies, the sun, and even the moon. Finally, well after dusk, he whistled for his men to stop and make camp. We'd reached a small brook, a perfect place to water the horses and provide refreshment to ourselves.

As my feet touched the ground, the prince steadied me. I was stronger now, having grown more accustomed to the riding, and although still sore, I stood on my own. Through the dark, I eyed the area and mentally sketched my getaway route. I'd go once most of the men were asleep.

"Do not try it, Emmeline," he warned.

I wanted to release an exasperated sigh. How could he read me so well?

"I would not hesitate to chain you to my side whilst we slumber." His fingers circled my arm.

I bristled. "You wouldn't dare."

He leaned in so that I could feel the warmth radiating from his body in the growing coolness of the night. "I would dare it. So do not tempt me."

I didn't need to see his expression to know he was serious. His tone told me enough.

Since it appeared my previous strategy of breaking away and running wouldn't work, I needed a new plan. A campfire was soon blazing, and I joined Father Patrick in front of it. My mind spun with options even as I made small talk with the kindly priest and did my best to avoid Magnus.

We ate and drank and stretched our stiff limbs. It wasn't long before the priest, Magnus, and most of the soldiers spread out their bedrolls around the fire and fell asleep. The prince and several others had taken the first watch, positioning themselves in strategic locations around the perimeter of our camp.

I'd laid my bedroll somewhat away from the others, insisting to Rex that as a woman I needed privacy, but ultimately hoping my location in the shadows and near a boulder would allow me to sneak off undetected.

Once I lay down and covered myself with the woolen blanket, I shivered. I was too far from the campfire to draw its warmth. More than that, my body quivered with the fear of the unknown as I mentally plotted the quickest route to Norland.

Although Father had taught me everything he could, there was one thing he couldn't impart, and that was courage. I didn't know if I had the strength to push forward, especially out here away from all that was familiar.

I hugged my arms around my thin frame and closed my eyes, determined to get some sleep. After all, I didn't dare attempt anything until Rex's turn at watch was over, and he lay down to slumber. At that point, he'd be exhausted and hopefully wouldn't notice me creep away.

Chapter 8

REX

I ROUSED WITH THE FEELING SOMETHING WASN'T RIGHT. A GLANCE at the position of the moon told me I'd been resting for several hours. I hadn't allowed myself to fall into a deep sleep so I could keep my senses alert, especially if Emmeline tried something.

Even so, the moment my eyes opened and landed upon the empty bedroll a handspan away, my chest exploded with the force of a battering ram. The chain I'd shackled to Emmeline's ankle and mine lay undisturbed and unmoved, except that the lock was wide open.

I sat up and unfastened the chain from my own foot, silently cursing myself for sleeping at all. I should have known when she'd offered so little resistance to the chain that she was an expert picklock. Of course, Lance would have taught the princess that skill. And of course, she was also an expert at stealth and had been able to move soundlessly away from me as well as from the guards on duty.

I berated myself again for being so foolish and

underestimating her.

Minutes later, I found her trail and ordered my six fastest men to accompany me. With dawn only an hour away, we didn't take time to saddle our horses but rode them bareback. I guessed she had a two or three-hour lead since she was a fast runner and likely had the endurance to sprint hard for hours.

On our horses, we'd easily span the distance. However, with our delay we risked the rebel search party catching up to us and intercepting Emmeline. They'd apparently discovered their tortured comrade sooner than I'd anticipated, and they'd been on our trail for the past day. While I couldn't be sure how far behind they were, I'd sighted their harpy eagle scouting us, the same eagle they'd used during their days of searching for the princess in Inglewood Forest.

My heartbeat thundered in rhythm to the horse hooves against the heathland. From the trail Emmeline was taking, she hadn't known about the queen's men following us or she would have gone directly to them. As it was, she was heading north, likely planning to travel the Upper Cress River to the Iron Hills and from there hike through the Highlands into Norland.

I pushed my steed harder than I had so far, leaning in low and whispering my encouragement as well as begging forgiveness for the unrelenting pace. I willed the horse to understand my frustration and even my panic. I couldn't lose Emmeline.

Not only would the king be outraged if I let her get away, but I couldn't bear the thought of not having her now that she was mine, and a strange possessiveness rose up within my chest.

For so many weeks, as I'd searched Inglewood Forest,

I'd thought of little else but finding her, so much so that I'd obsessed over it. Once I'd finally had her within my arms and stood before the priest and said my vows, I'd pledged myself to her for eternity. I wouldn't back out on those vows, not for anything. She was my wife now. And I aimed to keep her.

My men knew better than to speak to me as we traveled, but when we started to circle the outer edge of the Cistern Bogs, Dante whistled the signal to stop.

I pulled up abruptly and glared at him.

He nodded to a slight opening in the long grass that surrounded the marshy lowland. "She's gone into the bog, Your Highness."

Certainly, Emmeline had learned about the danger of bogs—the peat formed of spiky grasses and moss that trapped rain and became waterlogged. Golden grass floated like carpet and masked the dangerous water beneath. If that wasn't bad enough, the bog was home to wild boars, adders, and even sundew—carnivorous plants that were hungry for meat.

"She knows better." I dug my heels into my horse's flank. "She went around."

Even if cutting through the bog could save her hours, Emmeline wouldn't try it. Would she?

"I could go in and examine further," Dante said in a rare contradiction of my wishes.

"We cannot waste the time—"

A faint cry echoed from the bog. A cry that was distinctly womanly. A cry that could only belong to one woman.

"The princess," Dante and I said at the same moment.

I had the sudden picture of her sinking beneath the peat, unable to get out, and my heart took up a new rhythm: a drumbeat of fear.

"It's too dangerous for all of us to go in," I shouted as I urged my horse to the bend in the grass. "Dante and Alaric will come with me. The others will stand guard."

I was off my horse and crashing into the bog as soon as my feet landed.

"Your Highness, let Alaric lead," Dante said motioning toward one of the other strong knights who'd come with me from Warwick.

I shook my head curtly, easily locating Emmeline's prints in the muddy grass.

"His family's estate borders Warwick's central bogs," Dante said breathlessly from behind, "and he knows the dangers—"

Before the words were out of his mouth, I slipped, then tripped, and found myself already up to my knees in watery moss, my feet sinking fast in layers of mud and thorny brambles. The ground seemed to suck at my legs like dozens of leeches, a pulling and stinging that tore the breath from my lungs.

I only had to think of Emmeline in the same situation to jolt myself out of my pain-induced stupor.

"Grab on to my belt, Your Highness." Dante had swiftly shed his belt and tossed it out to me.

I caught it but had sunk several more inches to my thighs.

Alaric was already in action as well, tugging at the belt. "The only way to break free from the suction is to twist your body at the same time we heave you upward."

Together Dante and Alaric pulled while I swiveled, attempting to turn like a cork in a bottle top. I gritted my teeth against the pressure, until finally the bog released me, flinging me into Dante and toppling him backward onto Alaric.

We picked ourselves up, and I motioned Alaric ahead of me.

"Your legs, Your Highness?" he called over his shoulder as this time he led the way.

I waved off his concern even though I could feel the trickle of blood beneath my breeches and boots from where sharp thorns had scraped me. For now, all I could think about was Emmeline drowning under a blanket of peat and moss, the pain she would be experiencing, and her desperation to fight her way free.

Alaric picked up his pace, rounding brush and hopping over areas of grass that looked harmless but were death traps.

Another scream resounded in the bog, this one closer and most definitely Emmeline's. The note of agony within it told me she was suffering greatly. My pulse thundered at a frantic tempo that was unfamiliar from my usual calm.

At the edge of a particularly soggy area, Alaric stopped short. I bumped into him and had to grab him to keep him from sprawling into a patch of watery moss.

"There." He pointed to what seemed to be an island in the middle of a lagoon. "She's there."

I followed his finger, and at the sight of her tangled in a mess of vines and hanging upside down by her feet from a tall spruce, my stomach lurched up into my throat. She was slashing at the vines with a dagger, which she must have pilfered from someone on her way out of camp. But with each slash she made against the tangle, the vines wrapped tighter around her.

"It's a sundew," Alaric said in a grave tone.

Sundews were known for catching insects and small

mammals and dissolving them for nutrients. But I'd heard hunters' tales of sundews big enough to trap boars. There were even tales of sundews tangling and killing hunters too. I had to free her now before the vines squeezed the life from her.

But how could I get to her with a lagoon surrounding her?

"Emmeline!" I called.

Her head twisted toward me. "Rex!" Her voice sounded taut, as though she couldn't get enough air. "Help me!"

"How did you get over there?" My gaze landed upon a dozen different routes but discarded each as too risky.

She tilted the tip of her knife upward to the spruce that intertwined with a tree closer to us. She didn't have to say anything more for me to understand that she'd thought to bypass the threat of the lagoon by taking to the trees within the bog. But in doing so, she hadn't been prepared for the whiplike vines of the sundew.

Dante was already leading the way to the base of the spruce closest to us. "You'll need to cut her free, Your Highness, while we prevent sundew tendrils from catching you."

I wasted no time in scaling the trunk, climbing onto a gnarled branch that led above the lagoon. I didn't look down, but for the first time that I could remember, cold fear gripped me. Fear not for myself but for Emmeline. Fear that she could have fallen, fear that she could have disappeared without a trace, fear that she was even now suffocating and that I wouldn't get to her rapidly enough.

The instant I stepped onto the opposite spruce bough, it sank under my weight. In the same moment, a sundew cord whipped out and would have knocked me off, except that my reflexes were sharp, and I slit the vine in two pieces before it could catch me.

I kept moving, scooting slowly along the branch until I finally reached the trunk of the opposite tree and caught sight of Emmeline's boots and skirt twisted among vines. She was still trying valiantly to rend herself free, wielding her blade expertly, but she was already too entangled.

I slipped to a lower limb and prayed it would hold my weight. "Cease thrashing."

She grew motionless.

Above and behind me, came the sounds of Dante and Alaric hacking and chopping, protecting me as best they could from the same fate as Emmeline. Even so, something slithered around my ankle.

From my periphery, I found the source and severed the vine in a backward thrust only to have to fight away another wrapping around my upper arm. How could I free Emmeline if I was struggling to save myself?

I followed the trail of the tendrils until I found what I was looking for. "Dante, up there." I nodded upward. "Slit the sundew at that large knob."

He started in that direction only to have a vine whip out at him and slash him across the back. Even with his chain mail hauberk protecting him, he stiffened momentarily against the pain but didn't let it stop his climb as Alaric severed the vines creeping up from below.

I fought off more vines that came at me swifter than arrows in flight. Bracing myself against the trunk, I parried the climbing plant with my sword while hacking with my dagger at the strands holding Emmeline prisoner. Pieces of the sundew fell away and drifted below into the lagoon, disappearing from sight—a result that gave me pause.

If I continued to cut away the vines, how could I keep

Emmeline from plummeting headfirst into the deadly waters?

As if sensing her plight, Emmeline seemed to gather her last reserves of strength. With an unladylike grunt, she twisted her body and propelled herself into motion like a pendulum on a clock. Nearing the trunk, she thrust out her dagger and attempted to stick it into the tree but only managed to scrape the bark before her momentum took her back the other way. Thankfully, on the second try, her knife stuck.

"Push it in more!" I chopped at Emmeline's bindings and continued to fight the sundew intent upon chaining me.

She shoved harder, but with the plant wrapped so tightly around her arms, I sensed she'd reached the last of her strength and had no more left to give. Even if she could wedge the knife deeper, I doubted it would hold her weight.

Keeping an eye on Dante's slow climb, I tried to inch closer to Emmeline. I needed to come up with a better plan. At the sight of a thick strand swinging toward me, my mind spun into action. I held out my left arm. The moment the slithering plant made contact and began wrapping around my sleeve, I released my grasp on the trunk and let myself fall. The vine acted as a rope as I swung toward Emmeline, grabbed her around the waist, and pulled myself to her, twisting around her as I slammed into the tree.

With her securely in my grasp, I shouted up at Dante. "Now! Cut now!"

Holding Emmeline, I shoved against the tree and pitched us both back out over the open lagoon toward solid ground. With Dante's cut at the source, the pressure of the vines loosened their hold on Emmeline.

Praying the vine around my arm would hold fast a few seconds longer, I leaned forward as we swooped near the land. Then, using the last of the momentum, I leaped. The sundew finally fell away, and I slammed into the hard earth, bringing Emmeline down on top of me to cushion her.

The impact drove the air from my lungs. For an eternal second, I couldn't breathe or move. If Emmeline had wanted to kill me at that moment, I would have been helpless to defend myself. But she only seemed to burrow into me, her entire body quivering.

I wrapped an arm around her to shelter her, alert once more for any other danger that lurked near us. We'd missed falling into the lagoon only by inches. From what I could tell, Dante and Alaric were safe but now battling against a new set of vines attempting to trap them.

"Are you hurt?" I pulled back slightly, only to have her wrap her arms around my neck and cling to me. Though her chest heaved rapidly with the effort of her breathing, she managed to shake her head.

Her hair had come loose during her struggles and now lay in tangled strands down her back, spilling across my body and even onto my face. The dark silk was as long and wavy as I'd imagined it would be.

I rose to my feet with Emmeline in my arms, knowing I needed to set her down and aid my men. However, before I could force myself to release her, Dante jumped the distance while Alaric followed, wielding their weapons expertly to fend away any further entanglements.

Without waiting, Dante took the lead, and we set out at a fast pace. I didn't breathe fully until we broke free of the bog and mounted our horses. Once we were on our way, all I could think about was how close Emmeline had come to death, and I realized my insides were quavering almost as much as she still was.

With the sun now high in the sky, I pushed hard, driving our mounts to a gallop. We'd lost precious time, time that would now put us within easy distance of the rebel search party, who would likely stop at nothing to steal the princess away from me. And while my men were exceptional warriors, I knew I couldn't underestimate the strength of the queen's people.

As we rode, Emmeline's grip around my neck remained tight. But I didn't mind. In fact, I rather liked the sensation that she needed me. When finally we reached the rest of our men at the site of the previous night's camp and I started to dismount, she lifted her head from my shoulder. Although she'd stopped shaking, her eyes were wide and dark and full of fear.

"Thank you for saving me," she whispered.

I nodded, wanting to admonish her never to try something so foolish again, but I suspected once she recovered, she'd continue attempting to escape. All the more reason to win her affection so that she would want to stay with me. But how could I make her like me enough to put aside her plans to leave?

The men I'd left behind were anxious to depart, our supplies packed and their horses at the ready. They informed me that while I'd been gone, Magnus had taken two guards and had set off for Delsworth.

I could only imagine what Magnus would tell the king, likely giving him the worst of the details and leading him to believe I'd lost Emmeline.

"Your Highness," Dante said with a bow. "Shall I hold the princess while your wounds are tended?"

An open slash across his cheek told me he'd suffered injuries of his own, as had Alaric. And how many lashes had Emmeline sustained from the sundew whips? I pulled back and attempted to assess her. Her skirt and bodice were sliced open in several places, exposing red welts. Her wrists and the skin showing at her shirtsleeves revealed bruises. I suspected her ankles and legs were the same.

"We shall tend the princess's wounds and be on our way," I said.

"But, Your Highness—" Dante glanced pointedly at my lower legs.

Only then did the princess squirm and push away from me, giving me no choice but to set her on her feet. Tousled, almost wild, she was more beautiful than ever, making my breath stick in my chest.

I didn't move as she knelt in front of me and examined my legs. My encounter with the waterlogged peat and the thorny brambles underneath had torn patches of my breeches away, along with layers of my skin so that places were open and oozing blood.

She tossed Dante a commanding look. "I need clean water, bandages, and salve—if any can be found among the provisions."

Dante and Alaric scurried to do her bidding even as she turned her attention back to my breeches, fingering the gashes and the blood that had seeped into the linen. "You must sit down and let me doctor your wounds."

"No. We shall take care of yours first."

"Mine are nothing compared to yours."

I waved dismissively and took a step back.

She grabbed my tunic and glared up at me. "Let me at least wash away the dirt."

We'd lose more time. Perhaps that's what she was

counting on.

Her expression softened. "I promise I'll hurry." All traces of hostility were gone from her eyes. Instead, the brown was warm and beckoning and melted my reserve.

I hobbled over to the nearest boulder, lowered myself, and began rolling up my breeches. A moment later, she pushed my hands away and slid the linen up herself, careful not to brush against the gashes.

By the time she'd exposed the bottom half of my legs, Dante, Father Patrick, and another young soldier who was an expert at medical remedies convened with the necessary supplies. When the young soldier knelt next to Emmeline, she took charge, giving him no choice but to watch.

She worked swiftly, keeping her promise. And yet at the same time, her fingers were gentle, the contact of her hands against my legs making me forget about the sting of my injuries. As she finally rose and examined one of the slashes above my knee, I couldn't take my eyes from her.

"Thank you," I said.

"'Tis my fault," she said softly. "I shouldn't have gone into the bog."

She shouldn't have run away at all. But I swallowed my retort and said nothing.

Her fingers moved from my knee to a spot just above it. And as she traced the ragged rip of my breeches there, her touch was like fire and ice, burning my skin and freezing me at the same time. I sucked in a breath.

At my intake, she met my gaze again. From the innocence of her expression, I guessed she wasn't aware of the intimacy of her touch or how it could affect a man.

"I should treat your other wounds too," she said, grazing another spot slightly higher.

I caught her hand and slipped my fingers into hers, preventing her from embarrassing both of us in front of my men. "We need to go." Before she could pull away or protest, I brought her hand to my lips and laid a kiss just above her knuckles.

Thankfully, my men took that as their cue to busy themselves and give me a moment of privacy with Emmeline.

As I let my lips linger, her eyes widened again, as though seeking to understand the meaning behind such a kiss. I refused to look away, holding her gaze and silently communicating the desire she awoke within me.

During my time at court, I'd always had women following me and hanging on to my every word. I'd never learned to be charming or winsome, had never needed such skills. But now I wished I knew more.

When Emmeline's lashes fell and a flush moved into her cheeks, a small measure of satisfaction pooled in my chest. Perhaps there was some hope I could woo her and that she wouldn't resist me forever. I was tempted to kiss her again, this time on the thumping pulse at her wrist.

Even as I chastised myself not to do so, a shadow circled around our camp—the long wingspan and the strong body of a bird of prey. Shielding my eyes from the sun, I peered up to the gliding form of a harpy eagle. My men stopped to watch it too, recognizing it as the harpy eagle that belonged to the queen's search party.

My muscles tensed, and I stood abruptly, putting an end to my attempt at winning Emmeline. How soon before the rebel party was upon us? Were they even now closing in?

Without further ado, I picked Emmeline up. "We must mount and be on our way immediately," I called to the men as I strode to my warhorse.

"I can walk, you know." Emmeline's arms wound around my neck. "I don't need you carrying me every-where."

"You have left me no choice but to keep you with me every second of every minute of every hour."

"Every second?" She gave little resistance to my hold and even seemed to nestle further against me.

"I shall not let you out of my sight again."

"You will tire of watching me eventually."

"I guarantee that will never happen." I was surprised when my voice dipped low and even more surprised when the flush reappeared in her cheeks.

Again, warm satisfaction settled inside and spread.

When she was securely ensconced in the saddle in front of me, I slipped my arm around her waist and drew her back. She held herself stiffly for only a moment before giving way and reclining into me.

I fully realized the battle for her heart was still in the early stages. Even so, I couldn't help feeling as though I'd won a small victory.

Chapter 9

Emmeline

After another day and night of riding hard with only small breaks from the saddle, my body hurt in more places than I'd thought possible—particularly where the sundew vines had wrapped around my limbs, turning my skin shades of purple and blue.

"Are you comfortable?" Rex's voice rumbled close to my ear, making my stomach flip, as it seemed intent on doing whenever I was near him.

I'd just spent the past long hours riding with Dante so that Rex's horse might have a break from the extra burden of my weight.

During our most recent stop when we'd reached the East Sea, Rex had switched me to his mount. I didn't want to admit I'd been anticipating the changeover, but now that I shared the saddle with him, I couldn't deny my attraction.

The feeling had nothing to do with how strong and handsome he was, I told myself. It was because I'd witnessed how good and considerate he was, not only to me but to everyone. Even when he was strict and disciplined and commanding, he never failed to put the needs of others above his own.

As we'd steadily drawn closer to the coast, we'd passed through one small village after another. The couple of times we'd stopped for provisions, I'd been impressed with Rex's fairness and courtesy in his dealings with peasants and tradesmen alike. Perhaps I'd been expecting the brutish behavior my father had always attributed to King Ethelwulf. But Rex, while brusque and businesslike, hadn't shown any cruelty or callousness.

Rex's nose brushed against my temple even as his mouth hovered near my ear, so I could hear his breathing. The graze of his skin and the nearness of his mouth made me suddenly dizzy so that I closed my eyes and reclined my head against his shoulder.

"Is that a yes?" His voice was light, almost teasing.

"Perhaps." I laid my arm across the one he kept around my middle, relishing the hard contours and strength emanating from him. After the hours spent together, I'd realized he was as strong of mind as he was of body. We'd talked of many things, and I'd grown to respect his intelligence in all areas of science, history, and geography.

"You will rest in ease soon," he said, "for God willing, we shall reach Delsworth within the hour."

"Within the hour?" I opened my eyes and strained to see the horizon ahead. "I thought it to be longer since we just stopped."

"We stopped for only one reason." His voice dropped. "I had a need to hold my wife."

At the intimacy in his tone, my insides smoldered

and my thoughts filled with the kiss he'd placed upon my knuckles yesterday, so warm, so tender. I knew I shouldn't think about it, shouldn't let myself react to him the way I was. I had to stay aloof and remember I was his prisoner.

Even so, the longer I was with him, the more I was growing to like him. After the daring rescue he'd made in the Cistern Bogs, how could I not appreciate his valor and kindness? He'd arrived when I'd lost hope, when the danger had been too much to battle on my own. He hadn't hesitated to charge directly into the peril of the bog and the sundew. He'd put his own life at risk for mine. Not only that, but he'd suffered painful wounds that even now needed tending again.

I couldn't keep from admiring him, but the more my admiration grew, the more I betrayed my parents and the sacrifices they'd made. They'd raised me to fight against King Ethelwulf and his son. If they could see me now, they'd be disappointed at how I'd let down my defenses and engaged Rex so easily.

Moreover, Father would have admonished me for another failed escape attempt. I'd had the chance at a complete getaway, but I'd done too many things wrong—like neglecting to cover my tracks, almost as if part of me had wanted Rex to come after me. Which couldn't be true, could it?

Next time, I'd do better and make an escape that would impress even my father, one that also included regaining the ancient key and the labyrinth map. I'd berated myself dozens of times for giving Rex such easy access to the map that Father and I had drawn. While packing to leave for Norland, Father must have placed it inside one of my books for safekeeping, unbeknownst to me. If only he'd been able to warn me. If only I hadn't so foolishly thought to bring my books.

Whatever the case, I resigned myself to remaining Rex's captive for the present. Once I was in Delsworth and away from Rex's constant supervision, perhaps when he trusted me better, I'd have an easier time regaining the key and map and then slipping away.

The coastal road had grown busier, and now that we were so close to the capital, I understood why. A soldier galloped ahead and called out to the people, warning them to move aside for the prince, so that by the time we passed, they were out of the way and bowing in deference.

I noticed again—as I had since we'd arrived in the first small town—that the people weren't excited to see the prince. Most cowered in fear or watched us with blank expressions that I sensed masked discontentment and dislike. A few brave men and women dared to glare at the prince, refusing to bow. If Rex noticed, he paid them no heed.

I, on the other hand, couldn't get enough of the details of the land and people. After living so isolated a life, my senses were alert to everything, from the heavy odors of fish drying on racks along the shore to the dampness in the sea breeze to the shrieking of the gulls.

While I was fascinated, I was also saddened by the conditions. Everywhere I looked, I could see the effects of King Ethelwulf's years of selfish rule, as well as his refusal to provide relief during drought we'd had.

Rather than securing the people's welfare, the king had rewarded his trusted advisors and loyal noblemen by taking land and titles away from others, increasing the wealth and power of his supporters substantially, and allowing his faithful followers to rule their domains as they saw fit so that disorder and lawlessness had become rampant.

The awareness confirmed everything my parents had taught me—that the people of Mercia deserved better. They deserved to have a leader who would make their well-being a priority.

Would my sister, Queen Adelaide Constance, do so? Would she truly love the people and land and be the compassionate sovereign they needed?

The ancient prophecy predicted a young ruler full of wisdom who would use the treasure to help drive the evil from the land and usher in a time of peace. My parents had taught me my older sister was that young ruler.

But, what if they'd been wrong? What if Rex was meant to fulfill the prophecy? He was, after all, the crown prince, having been groomed to reign after King Ethelwulf. He might be ruthless and even harsh at times. But at heart, he wasn't evil.

"What are you thinking about?" Rex had started asking that question whenever we rode together. I'd been rather surprised at the ease with which we could talk and found time passed much quicker during our conversations. "You are thinking of Bede again."

Although I missed my fox, what was worse was knowing he missed me and didn't understand what had become of me. I had no doubt he'd worried, paced, and howled at my absence, causing my parents untold grief.

To ease my ache, I'd shared with Rex how I'd

discovered Bede as a newborn in his fox den. His mother and the rest of the litter had died of starvation during the worst season of the drought. But I'd brought Bede home and fought to save him, laboring over him day and night until he'd gained strength.

Rex had asked about Bede's name and why I'd chosen it, which had then led to a lengthy discussion of history and renowned historians—particularly Saint Bede, who'd written the account of the Great Isle in the early days of its settlement. I'd been reading a copy of Bede's narration at the time I'd found the fox pup, and the name had seemed fitting.

"Bede is never far from my mind," I said. "But as we near Delsworth, I cannot keep from thinking about other matters."

"Such as . . ."

"Why everyone must fight over the throne. Why can we not live in peace?"

Rex was quiet for a long moment. That was another thing I liked about him—he didn't brush away my concerns or questions. Rather, he took his time in giving me serious answers.

At his silence, I glanced at his profile. I tried not to stare at him too often, but my attention seemed to have a will of its own and was drawn more and more to him, to his ruggedness, to the strength in every nuance, to the pride of his bearing.

Whenever he dropped his sights to me, I found myself inwardly flushing under the intensity of his penetrating eyes that seemed to see right inside me and know my thoughts. And this time was no different. As he shifted his attention to my face, I found myself captured and bound to him.

"I want to live at peace," he replied. "More than anything. Which is why I searched so hard to find you."

"You have only stirred up more conflict by taking me." I had the sudden urge to graze my fingers along his jawline and test the scratchiness of his stubble.

His gaze wandered around my face, lingering over my features as though he enjoyed looking upon me the same way I did him. "We may yet have a skirmish, but I pray we have avoided outright war and needless deaths on both sides."

"But your father has waged wars, and you are an elite guard, a warrior—"

"I have no wish for war." His answer was fierce, unexpected, and gave me pause.

I didn't realize I'd hesitated in my response until his gaze dropped to my still-rounded, open lips. Something flared in his eyes, darkening the blue. Without taking his sight from my lips, he leaned closer.

Was he thinking of kissing me? Surely not.

When he angled his head, heat speared my insides, turning my blood hot and sending waves rippling along my skin. My breath caught hard in my throat, and my body tensed in anticipation—dare I say, even readiness?

For several heartbeats, I didn't care we had an audience—his men as well as the people on the sides of the road. I didn't care I'd known the prince for only a few days. And I forgot I was a naïve young woman who could easily be seduced by a smooth-talking man. I could only think about how it would feel to touch my lips to his.

But as he dipped closer, my heartbeat dipped too. The irregular rhythm reminded me of where I was and what I was supposed to be doing. I needed to stay alert and get away from the prince, not allow myself to fall deeper into his embrace.

I quickly lowered my gaze and my chin, turning my head and cutting off the moment of intimacy. Or at least I thought I did. A touch of his lips against my temple told me I'd been wrong. The warmth and the soft pressure were the same as when he'd kissed my knuckles. He was tender and restrained, and yet I could feel his desire for me—a desire that told me our nearness was affecting him as it was me.

At a shout ahead, he stiffened and pulled back. I strained to see the source of the commotion but couldn't see far enough to make any speculations about what was happening.

Moments later, a horse and rider came into view, galloping toward us at full speed. As the soldier neared, I could see his black chain mail and guessed him to be a messenger from the king. Since Magnus had already ridden ahead to Delsworth with the news of our marriage, what if the king had decided I wasn't needed after all? Especially now that Rex had my key and the map to the labyrinth? Would Rex release me?

His vows from after our hasty wedding in the woods whispered in my mind. As I'd gotten to know Rex, I'd learned he was a man of integrity and wouldn't make any vows unless he planned to honor them. But certainly, this was different. Certainly, he wouldn't keep me unless he truly had to.

Did I want him to keep me?

As soon as the question crossed my mind, I

chastised myself for even caring. If he no longer needed me, then I'd be able to make my way to my parents and Bede with all haste. That was what I wanted, wasn't it?

When the soldier brought his horse into stride next to Rex's, the messenger bowed as deeply as he could from atop his mount.

"What news have you?" Rex demanded, wasting no time with formalities.

The younger man was red-faced and sweating, and his horse heaved with the strain of his ride, both testifying to the urgency of his message. "Your Highness, the king tasked me with delivering the news that the usurper and her rebel army, along with Norland's forces, will surround Delsworth's harbor within two days."

Usurper? Did he mean Adelaide?

"How many ships?" Rex asked.

"Over two dozen. Scouts report seeing siege engines on the decks."

"Has word spread among the people that I have married the Princess Emmeline?"

The messenger didn't let his gaze shift to me, although I had no doubt he was curious. "That is why the king has sent me, in order to summon you back with greater haste. He is planning to have the official wedding ceremony today so all the land hears and knows of the marriage."

Rex barked rapid commands to his men then kicked his steed into a gallop.

Could my public union to Rex really bring about peace? At the very least, could it prevent the start of another war?

I wasn't sure the joining of a princess from the House of Mercia to a prince from the House of Warwick would truly satisfy the people and prevent a revolt. The problems ran deep, and the deprivation I'd witnessed today only confirmed it.

However, if there was even a small chance our marriage might prevent bloodshed, how could I not work toward that goal? If that meant I needed to resign myself to a life with Rex in Delsworth, I could do that, couldn't I?

Although deep inside I suspected my father would have argued against my logic and encouraged me to find a way to free myself before the public wedding ceremony, I quietly pushed aside his voice.

Maybe staying wasn't what he would have chosen for me. But if I decided to honor my marriage to the prince, was it possible such a choice would take more courage than running away?

Chapter 10

REX

I STOOD NEAR THE ALTAR OF THE CATHEDRAL, MY SIGHTS FIXED ON the entrance. My muscles were rigid, my body tense, my jaw clenched.

Would Emmeline come? Or had she tried to make another escape?

A mental warning tolled louder with each passing moment of delay, telling me I'd been too trusting and had given her too much freedom during the hour we'd been at Delsworth Castle. Perhaps I should have accompanied her to her chambers and overseen the servants who'd been tasked with making her presentable for the wedding ceremony. She could outsmart them if she set her mind to it, although she would be hard-pressed to slip past the guards I'd posted outside her door.

But another part of me waited expectantly, praying she'd come to the wedding of her own accord, that I wouldn't need to force her to speak her vows, that this time she'd want to be with me.

I knew it was too soon to hope for love. But during our

journey, she seemed to begin to care about me just a little. Hopefully, I hadn't misread her expressive eyes—the shy glances that seemed to relay an interest and even an attraction.

But what if her need to return to her parents still outweighed her attraction? What if she'd been biding her time, making me believe she cared so I'd let my defenses down and allow her the chance to run away again?

"I have heard she is quite beautiful," my mother said from the ornate throne positioned in front of the altar next to the king's equally elaborate throne.

Before I could answer my mother, the king had already reached for her hand, brought it to his lips, and pressed a kiss there. "No one is or ever will be as beautiful as you are, my queen."

Mother smiled tenderly at him. With her long golden hair and her blue eyes, she was as beautiful as always. But I disagreed with the king. Emmeline was more stunning. If Mother was a shining star, then Emmeline was as vibrant as the moon.

For all his brutality, I respected that the king was kind and loving to Mother. He adored her and treated her as a rare jewel. Over the past year, I'd noticed she seemed to be the only person who never angered him, and her presence and beauty had the power to calm him.

While I didn't know my mother well, I'd come to realize she was a simple woman who kept away from the concerns of the kingdom, preferring to spend her days embroidering and tending her rose gardens. If she knew about any of the problems, she chose to ignore them— perhaps had learned to ignore them for her own sanity.

Whatever the case, I inclined my head first to my mother then to the king. With his long black hair styled into three warrior braids and his pointed beard, he exuded strength and dominion. His dark eyes connected with mine and contained a sharpness that set me on edge. Though he might have shielded Mother from the encroaching danger, he'd already spoken at length with me since my return.

And he'd made no effort to hide his frustration that it had taken me so long to find Emmeline. He'd expected me to capture her weeks ago and believed if I'd done so, we would have had fewer men leaving Mercia and joining the rebel army.

I'd wanted to remind him that Captain Theobald hadn't been able to locate any of the princesses in the months he'd searched, and I alone had achieved success. Not only had I found Emmeline, but I'd laid claim to her key and some form of a labyrinth map, which were both now in the king's possession. Nevertheless, as usual, I bore the king's censure without reply.

I glanced again at the doors, past the throngs waiting outside, and hoped to glimpse Emmeline's arrival. The chapel inside was filled beyond capacity, nobles sitting in every pew, lining the side aisles, and standing along the back. Those of high rank not privileged enough to gain an inside view crowded the churchyard. Beyond the yard, masses of common people lined the wrought-iron fences.

Father Patrick sat in a chair near the altar. Although he wore fresh robes, weariness creased his face. I'd had to push him too hard over the past days of travel and needed to reward him for his faithful service.

Magnus stood at my side, also attired in clean garments. He'd complained about having to attend, pleading to have the time to refresh himself after so long away. But of course, he'd accompanied us to the chapel, stifling his frustration.

"Perhaps the princess has run away again," he whispered now, loud enough for our parents to hear.

The king lifted his brow, already aware of my escapades with Emmeline, since Magnus had given him every detail of her capture, including her breaking free and sneaking away from our camp.

"If so, you will need to tame her," the king said in an ominous tone that made my gut clench. If anyone else had spoken of *taming* Emmeline, I would have punished them swiftly.

I lifted my chin and met the king's gaze, conveying my displeasure but knowing I had to appease him nonetheless. "I shall take my direction from your worthy example, Your Majesty. I shall endeavor to love my wife as ardently as you have loved yours. And in so doing, I pray the princess will come to care for me as much as Mother does you."

The king held my gaze, as though testing me. Then he finally relaxed in his chair, a small smile curving his lips. "Well said, son. From what Father Patrick has told me, she is already softening under your influence."

"If you are half as loving as your father," Mother interjected with a smile directed at the king, "you shall have no trouble winning her heart."

"Thank you, Mother."

Before I could say more, cheers erupted outside the chapel, and I knew Emmeline had arrived. Had she come willingly, or were my guards even now dragging her forward?

My heart picked up pace, tapping a strange, almost painful beat. Why did I care so much if she wanted me? Essentially, this was no different from our first wedding ceremony in the forest. She was still my captive, still being held against her will, still being forced to wed a man she hadn't chosen.

The nobility filling the churchyard began to move aside, their cheering growing until at last I caught a glimpse of Emmeline gliding up the stone path flanked by my guards, and my chest seized. She was almost too beautiful to look at. With her dark hair down, it flowed to her waist in gentle waves that had been brushed until they shimmered. A circlet made of gold and pearls adorned her head, making her appear regal. Her creamy gown molded to her body, showing off her womanliness along with her well-toned muscles.

If I'd been attracted before, I was more so now, especially after getting to know her and realizing she was not only beautiful but smart and kindhearted and easy to talk with.

Was she coming to me of her own will?

My pulse thudded harder, and when she stepped through the doors and into the chapel, I couldn't breathe, couldn't move, couldn't do anything but watch her.

With her chin angled up, she held herself with the bearing of a princess and of a future queen—my queen. She continued at a measured pace, her pretty lips set with determination, her shoulders braced in clear resolve.

I riveted my attention to her face, willing her to look into my eyes and see my encouragement and my appreciation. Her gaze moved first to the king, then to my mother, and finally to me. From the rounding of her eyes, I could tell she was surprised to see me in something other than my black chain mail.

Though I'd been left with scant time, I'd taken a quick bath, had my menservants wash my hair, and also managed a shave before donning my courtly garments. My appearance was vastly improved, and I hoped I was as attractive to her as she was to me—although I didn't think that possible.

Her gaze held mine fast for the duration of her walk down the aisle, filling my chest with inexplicable warmth. Something in her expression told me she'd come to the church willingly, although perhaps not necessarily because of her feelings for me. But she hadn't been coerced, and that was progress.

As she reached the altar and ascended the few steps, I held out my hand to her. When she placed her fingers in mine, I felt her trembling and wished I could draw her against my chest and reassure her all was well. While traveling, I'd grown to like having her close, so that having her near but not within my arms was a form of torture.

As she took her place next to me, the king rose. In a show of respect and subservience, the nobility lowered themselves to one knee before the king. I, too, lowered myself and tugged Emmeline down beside me.

The king offered an introductory prayer and then returned to his royal spot next to Mother. When he was finally sitting again, attention shifted back to Emmeline and me. She shot me a sideways glance, and I nodded at her, hoping she could see my sincerity.

Father Patrick led us through the same wedding ceremony he had previously officiated. But this time, he spoke every word and prayer, without leaving out anything, ending with the Holy Eucharist and then the pronunciation that we were man and wife.

At his final signing of the cross, the chapel bells began to peal. The crowds that had swelled the churchyard and nearby streets shouted, clapped, and whistled. Father Patrick closed his prayer book. "There's only one thing left to do," he said. "And that is to seal your union with a kiss."

I was still holding Emmeline's hand, and at the mention of a kiss, she started to pull her hand from mine. Before she could get away, I intertwined our fingers and then lifted my other hand to her cheek. I settled my attention upon her lips—those pretty, oft sassy, and yet innocent lips. I wasn't about to let an opportunity to kiss her pass by.

I'd wanted to kiss her earlier today and had almost succeeded. I wouldn't fail now.

Caressing her high cheekbone with my thumb, I leaned in and let my mouth hover above hers. She drew in a quick breath, caught her lower lip between her teeth, then dropped her eyes to my lips. Curiosity and interest mingled there, igniting my own desire even more.

Before anything could stop me, I closed the distance and covered her mouth with mine. For a heartbeat, uncertainty hung between us. Then I moved my lips, relishing the sweet fullness and the taste of her. A moment later, her lips responded tentatively, testing, trying. I opened more fully to her, giving her room for exploring. But she was timid and began to pull away altogether.

I let my lips cling to hers an instant longer, willing her to feel my devotion, desire, and determination to be a good husband. When I released her, I became aware of more clapping and cheering from within the chapel, the nods of approval, the smiles of relief.

At the joyous atmosphere both from within the church and outside, Emmeline finally smiled—the first real smile I'd seen from her. It lit her eyes and made the curves of her mouth all the more appealing, so that I could think of nothing else but kissing her again.

As a man accustomed to getting what I wanted and doing whatever I pleased, I bent in and touched my lips to hers again. Her eyes widened with surprise. She, in turn, surprised me by lifting on her toes and pressing back, almost as if she'd wanted another kiss as much as I had. This time her mouth meshed with mine, her lips fitting perfectly, eagerly.

The cheering and whistling increased until it was deafening.

Emmeline pulled back, again nibbling on her lip, her cheeks pink, her eyes bright. She avoided my gaze, suddenly shy in a way that made my pulse quicken. I could only pray her willingness to kiss me meant she was beginning to like me as much as I liked her.

Chapter 11

Emmeline

I was overwhelmed by the lavishness of the wedding banquet awaiting us at Delsworth Castle. The kitchen servants brought out a continual procession of delicacies. In addition to capons, pigeons, rabbits, veal, venison, and lamb there were sugar plums, strawberry tarts, pears in red wine, sweetmeats, and more I couldn't name.

Between the courses, pages and squires helped to serve the ale and wine while minstrels played music on their lutes. The king and queen sat side by side at the center of the high table. I was positioned between the queen and one of her important ladies-in-waiting. Rex was seated on the opposite side of his father with his brother, Magnus, next to him.

In some ways, I was relieved I wasn't beside Rex. Something had most definitely changed between us as a result of his kisses, something new and exciting and yet frightening. During the meal, whenever I dared to peek at him and allow our gazes to collide, the desire and possessiveness in his eyes only tilted my world, making me dizzy and breathless with emotions I couldn't begin to name.

I was still uncertain what to make of the pale cream gown I wore, with its rows upon rows of seed pearls embroidered in intricate patterns with golden threads that shimmered in the light. When I'd been ushered to my chambers earlier, a dozen maidservants had crowded around to beautify me for the wedding, some working on my hair while others cleaned and styled my fingernails. Still others lathered my body, particularly my sundew bruises, in creams.

Although Mother had done her best to prepare me for such a moment, drilling me on the proper court etiquette, I'd never imagined so much attention and pampering all at once. Even now, as I ate, several servants waited only a few feet away, ready to jump at my every need. After fending for myself all my life, I wasn't sure I'd be able to get used to depending on others.

What would I have been like if I'd grown up in the royal residence, if King Francis and Queen Dierdal had reigned instead of King Ethelwulf? As I'd walked the halls of the castle, I tried to picture them, tried to picture my sisters. But my thoughts had turned to Lance and Felicia. They were the only family I'd ever known, and I couldn't—didn't want to—imagine my life without them.

"You have captured his heart," the queen said, looking first at Rex and then at me.

"He's an admirable man." I picked off a piece of the tart crust and took a small bite.

"I did not love the king right away, either," the

queen admitted softly. "But he was persistent and loved me until I could not help but love him in return."

I nodded. For all of King Ethelwulf's mistakes, I certainly couldn't fault him for the love and tenderness he bestowed upon his wife. It was obvious with his every interaction with her that he cherished and revered her.

Perhaps he was a good husband, but I wasn't convinced he was a good king. My parents had told me of his cruelty during those early days of his reign, the stories of how he'd sent whole families to the gallows for the slightest infractions. He'd tortured and killed so many that the streets of Delsworth had run red with blood.

From what I'd witnessed of the people and conditions during my ride through Mercia, I suspected he could still be just as cruel and harsh. And the times I'd caught him looking at me, I'd sensed a cool detachment and sharp calculation, as though he were trying to figure out how he could use me to his advantage.

"Rex will love you as well as the king has loved me," the queen continued. "And he will give you little choice but to love him back, even if you are reluctant to do so."

"He has many good qualities." Even so, had I done the right thing in making our marriage public and attempting to win the support of the people? During the short ride back from the chapel, I'd waved and smiled at all who gathered along the roads and hung out open windows. I prayed they'd see me with Rex and opt for peace rather than revolt. If my marriage to Rex could help prevent a war, then that's what we needed, wasn't it?

Self-doubts crowded in again as they had since I'd made up my mind to go through with the ceremony. Deep inside, I knew Father wouldn't have wanted me to give in to the enemy and undermine Adelaide's rebellion. Instead, he would have instructed me to think about my duty to the country, the people who needed freedom, and the true peace that could happen only after it was earned through hard-fought toil and tribulation.

Though I wanted to let my attention drift to Rex again, to reassure myself of his goodness and kindness, I broke off another piece of my tart. Had I allowed him to charm me too easily?

After all, I'd never had the solicitude of a handsome man—or any man—before. Had he wooed me into doing exactly as he'd planned? To use our wedding to distract the people from their discontentment with the king? That had to be it. With our countries on the brink of war, it was too far-fetched to believe he'd be interested in me as anything more than a means to an end.

What have I done?

My insides quivered, and I searched the perimeter of the room, mentally calculating my best route of escape, before focusing on the table in front of me. I couldn't leave. The damage was already done. Would any of the people of Mercia fight with Adelaide against King Ethelwulf now?

At a short blast of a trumpet, the guests grew silent and turned their attention to our table. Only then did I notice that Rex had risen and moved to the front of the raised dais.

When all eyes were on him, he spoke in his usual clipped and commanding tone. "Upon this, my wedding day, I should like the chance to bestow upon my bride three wedding gifts."

I sat up straighter and exchanged a glance with the queen. Her eyes reaffirmed what she'd said moments ago about her son loving his wife well. At her nod, I stood and skirted the table to stand next to Rex.

I had to squelch my misgivings. Whatever might happen, I was here now. Even though my fears urged me to run away, somehow I had to gather the courage to stay and seek peace here, right where I was, in any way I could.

"The first is . . ." He motioned toward a squire, who hurried forward carrying a tasseled cushion. The squire bowed and held out the elegant pillow. Rex gingerly retrieved something and then turned to me. "A ring made of the finest ruby."

Before I realized what he was doing, he'd kneeled in front of me and reached for my left hand. Gently, he slid on the ring, a ruby surrounded by dainty pearls. It glinted in the candlelight and reminded me of the much larger ruby my parents had saved for me as proof of my royal lineage.

He looked up at me, his eyes apologetic, as though to say he wished he could give me back my other ruby, but that for now, this would have to take its place.

I nodded. Maybe I wouldn't have the ruby and the life my parents had envisioned for me. But I could make something of this new life and do some good here, couldn't I?

When the ring was finally in place, Rex pressed a kiss against my knuckles, reminding me of our kisses from the church. As his eyes lifted to mine, their smoldering blue told me he was thinking of the same. "It shall signify my heart, that you shall have it forever."

Delighted murmurs rippled through the guests, followed by clapping. They approved of his gift. His gaze stayed upon me, beseeching me for the same. With such an offer, how could I accuse him of using me or doubt his sincerity?

I wasn't quite sure how to show I accepted his gift, so I did the first thing that came to mind. I tugged him upward until he stood once more, then I reached for his hand and pressed a kiss to his knuckles in return.

At the touch of my lips on his work-roughened skin, the blue in his eyes turned a shade darker, making my stomach dive with pleasure. As I released his hand, I couldn't release his gaze.

"The second gift is..." Without breaking our connection, he motioned another squire to the dais. This one brought a cushion, too, and Rex retrieved the item at the center. "A key."

My first thought was that he was returning the key he'd taken from me—the one to the ancient treasure. But at the sight of the object, I realized it was smaller and plainer.

He held it out to me. "This will allow you to enter the scriptorium, and there you will be able to read any book you wish."

I sucked in a breath and couldn't keep my fingers from trembling as I took the key—from both anticipation and the thrill of such a present. He wasn't just giving me a few books to replace the ones I'd had to leave behind. He was supplying an entire room filled with them. The gesture was not only sweet, but it spoke of his respect for my thirst for knowledge.

If I'd harbored any lingering qualms about his intentions, this offering easily banished them. My heart swelled with admiration so that I couldn't contain a smile. "Thank you, Your Highness. You are as generous as you are kind."

Again, the guests clapped, clearly enjoying the display of Rex's affection as much as I was.

"The third gift is . . ." Rex turned and beckoned to a final squire waiting in the shadows of the great hall. The young man strode forward quickly, but rather than a cushion, he carried a medium-sized wooden box. As he stopped in front of Rex, he bowed but didn't hand over the box. Instead, he held it out and allowed Rex to remove the lid.

"A new friend." Rex glanced inside before beckoning me to step closer and take a look for myself.

A new friend? I rose on my toes and peered in. At the fluffy bundle of fur curled up in a bed of hay, I gasped my delight. At my slight noise, a pair of dark eyes opened and a little nose poked up to sniff the air.

"She may not be a fox," Rex said hesitantly, "but I've been assured this breed of dog is close."

I reached inside and lifted out the puppy. The sight of the adorable creature earned the applause and endearments of the guests. Her fur was a rich, thick red mixed with patches of white—almost like the ruby on my new wedding ring. As I studied her pointed ears and snout, she examined me in return.

She seemed to waste no time in accepting me, raising her head and greeting me with several sloppy licks. At the exuberant kiss, I laughed and buried my face in the puppy's neck. Above the creature, my gaze locked with Rex's, which was filled with pleasure and something infinitely warmer.

Sudden tears stung at the backs of my eyes. Rex's consideration was beyond anything I'd ever known. He didn't have to do any of this for me. He wasn't obligated. Most men wouldn't have gone to the trouble to bestow any gifts, much less three that were so meaningful.

My fears from moments ago had been unfounded. I had no need to escape, for this was where I wanted to be. With him. I wanted to thank him, but I suspected any effort I made would fall short. "I wish there was something I could give you."

"I expect nothing in return," he said. "I only pray one day you might be able to freely offer me your love. That is all."

My heart had yielded a little more with each gift, and now, at his bold declaration, my entire body turned as soft and warm as the puppy in my arms. I wanted—no, needed—to show him how much I already did care and how grateful I was for his thoughtfulness.

I stepped toward him. With one arm around the puppy, I lifted my other to his neck, hooking him and bringing him down so that my mouth met his. Although I was inexperienced in kissing, I pressed to him nevertheless, hoping he could sense everything I was feeling. As his lips responded gently, I melted even more, so that I was afraid I might not be able to stand if I let go of him.

As he fitted his hands at my waist and started to deepen the kiss, the puppy squirmed, released a yip, and then reached up to lick my chin. With a laugh, I broke away from Rex to find that he was grinning and his eyes radiated contentment and happiness. The guests were laughing and smiling, too, clearly enamored by our interactions.

From the corner of my eye, I caught sight of the king bestowing a smile on his wife before he lifted her hand and kissed it. For the first time since I'd met him, his dark eyes lost their edge and filled with tenderness.

With how well everything was going, how could I have made a wrong choice in staying instead of joining the rebellion with my sisters? If the rebels could see the prince the way I had, they'd work toward a more peaceful resolution to the conflict too. Perhaps Providence had even placed me here for that very reason.

Chapter 12

REX

I STOOD IN THE PASSAGEWAY OUTSIDE EMMELINE'S CHAMBER DOOR and blew out a taut breath. Father Patrick, several of the king's closest advisors, other clergy, and a physician waited nearby with eyes downcast, as embarrassed as I was by our mission.

With my hand poised to knock, I hesitated.

The wedding at the church and the feasting in the great hall had both gone well. Emmeline was finally beginning to trust and like me. If I went into her chamber now, I was sure to lose all the ground I'd already won. And I didn't want that to happen. I had only to remember her laughter and her kiss to know I wanted more of that, not less.

I dropped my hand and then spun on the men behind me, giving them my fiercest glare. "I do not care what tradition requires. I shall not subject my wife to your scrutiny."

None dared to meet my gaze . . . except for Father Patrick. He nodded, his eyes brimming with understanding.

"Your Royal Highness, if I might make a suggestion?"

I crossed my arms and continued to scowl.

Father Patrick cleared his throat. "Allow me to enter the princess's chambers and pray over you both, then we shall all be on our way."

Several of the advisors began to object, but the priest spoke louder, cutting them off. "As I have been traveling with the prince and the princess these many days and have seen their growing affection, I am quite confident they shall have a true marriage. You have witnessed the affection this day, too, have you not?"

I wanted to protest Father Patrick coming into Emmeline's chamber. She'd find his presence odd and embarrassing as well. But the priest's suggestion was reasonable and would hopefully satisfy the other men.

By now, Emmeline had likely heard our commotion and was wondering what was going on. I held up my hand for silence. "Father Patrick may accompany me, and he will report back to you."

Under my harsh censure, the men again lowered their gazes. No one dared to contradict me. I suspected a few of them would inform the king of my break from tradition, but after witnessing Emmeline initiating a kiss with me after I'd given her my gifts, how could the king disapprove overly much?

Whatever the case, Emmeline was my wife, and I would place her needs above tradition. I could only hope the king would understand since he felt the same about Mother.

Without another moment of hesitation, I knocked. I didn't wait for Emmeline's invitation to come in. Instead, I swung the door open and stepped into the chamber.

She was kneeling in the middle of the floor and in the

process of tossing a rag ball across the room, sending the puppy scampering after it. She laughed as the puppy fumbled, tripped, and then slid into the rushes that covered the floor. At the sight of me, however, her smile turned suddenly shy.

She stood and reached for the coverlet on the end of the bed, pulling it free and winding it around her frame, but not before I realized she was already wearing a nightgown. One of her maidservants rushed to her side and aided in draping the blanket over her, providing a measure of decency.

When her eyes landed upon Father Patrick behind me, her smile faded away completely, and she backed up a step, wariness tightening her features.

"Everyone leave us," I growled, glaring once again, not only at Father Patrick but at the servants.

The maidservants scurried to obey. Father Patrick raised a brow before retreating into the passageway.

Emmeline had returned her attention to the puppy, who'd retrieved the ball in his mouth and was carrying it to her. She kneeled, picked it up, and quietly praised the pup, before lavishing her with scratches behind her neck and ears. The puppy's tongue lolled, and her mouth curved up as though she were smiling.

Emmeline held the ball out, spoke a short command, then tossed the object. The pup took after it again.

Although the scene was adorable, I had eyes only for Emmeline. Her maidservants had plaited her hair into one long, thick braid down her back. Even by the low light of the wall sconces, I could see that her cheeks were flushed and her eyes were filled with tenderness for the pup.

"Have you decided upon a name for her?" I knelt next to her.

Emmeline watched the pup hop onto the ball and this time roll end over end. "I have taken to calling her Ruby."

"Her coloring lends itself to such a name."

Emmeline's gaze shifted to her ring, and she caressed the shining jewel at its center. "I chose the name to remind me of the one who gave her to me."

At her shy admission, my breath snagged. And when she sent me a sideways look full of admiration, my pulse tripped before racing forward at double the speed.

This time when Ruby trotted to us with the ball, Emmeline directed the pup to drop it in front of me. "First you must praise her and earn her trust, then you can command her."

I did as Emmeline instructed, and soon the pup was obeying me as readily as Emmeline. After several minutes more of play, I finally sat back on my heels. "Emmeline, I regret that I must impose upon you tonight."

Her shoulders stiffened. Apparently, she guessed what I was insinuating.

"As we have only just met, I would like to give you more time." I glanced at the open door and grew agitated once more that everyone was waiting outside. "If our situation were different, I would have commanded your privacy."

She kept her gaze squarely focused upon Ruby, rolling the pup over to her back and scratching her belly.

I leaned in and lowered my voice. "The men have come to usher me to my marriage bed, but I shall only allow Father Patrick inside the room."

Her fingers began to tremble, and she quickly pulled them from Ruby and tucked them within the folds of the coverlet still draped around her.

Before she could hide her hands away completely, I

reached for one and held it tightly. "Emmeline, I promise after he departs, I shall sleep on the floor. I would leave you to yourself entirely if I could. But such an arrangement is the best I can offer under the circumstances."

Even in the low light, I could sense her mortification and wished to alleviate it. But I'd already conceded enough.

After a moment, her hand relaxed within mine. "So we shall playact for everyone but shall privately remain chaste?"

"Rest assured, I shall not be playacting." I stroked my thumb along her wrist and relished the smoothness of her skin.

"And what if I am?"

"Then 'twill not be playacting for long, Princess."

She ducked her head, but I could see a smile tug at her lips.

I lifted my fingers to her cheek and drew a path from her ear to her chin. "And I shall certainly not sleep on the floor for many nights."

When she didn't protest, I took courage and stood, drawing her up with me. "Father Patrick, you may come inside now."

My faithful priest entered the room again, his robes billowing and his brows high as though questioning whether everything was in order.

I nodded and drew Emmeline to my side. "We are ready."

From my pallet on the floor, I held myself stiffly. In the

bed, Emmeline's shifting and turning and soft sighs only made me all the more aware that we were alone in her bedchamber on our wedding night.

Had I been too rash in my decision not to share the bed? Though I'd sent away all the servants, there was still the chance someone could open the door and catch me on the floor. If word leaked that we had not shared the marriage bed, I had no doubt the rebels would use the knowledge to cast suspicion upon the authenticity of our marriage and work against all we'd accomplished through the union.

My thoughts strayed to the crowds during the afternoon when we'd exited the chapel. I'd scooped Emmeline up and carried her to my steed to the roaring approval of onlookers. Throughout the ride back to the castle, people had strained to get a glimpse of the princess. All it had taken was one look at her smile and her beauty for them to be smitten. I'd seen it on face after face. Everyone loved her and loved us together.

After today, I could only pray the citizens of Mercia would stand strong against Adelaide's encroaching army and refuse to welcome her.

"Rex?" Emmeline's whisper was near the edge of the bed.

I glanced up through the dark to see the outline of her face peering down. "Yes?"

"Are you asleep?" she asked.

"Very much so."

She paused. "No, you're not."

I was tempted to tell her I probably wouldn't get any sleep this night or in the nights to come so long as I lay this near to her, but I bit the comment back.

"Will you show me the scriptorium soon?"

"I shall if it would please you."

"I'd like to know what you've read and recommend."

"I have not read nearly enough," I admitted. "But I may be able to suggest a few manuscripts."

She released what could only be described as a happy sigh.

For a reason I couldn't begin to explain, her happiness filled me with a deep sense of satisfaction. During all those months of searching for the princess, I hadn't known what to expect from her, hadn't known whether I'd even like her, had resigned myself to the marriage no matter what. I'd never dreamed my feelings for this woman could develop so strongly and quickly.

"Do you remember what your life was like here in the castle when you were a little boy? Before you were sent away to Warwick?"

Was that a note of wistfulness in her question? Was she wondering what her own life might have been like if she'd lived here with her family—the family my father had destroyed?

Something pricked at the back of my conscience, something akin to guilt.

I'd been but a young lad when the king had started his military campaign to reunite Mercia and Warwick into one country as it had been under Alfred the Peacemaker long ago. With the king's own army along with hired mercenaries, the battle for Mercia had been fierce but quick.

Only after he'd assured his place on the throne of the unified kingdom of Bryttania had he sent for his family. I'd arrived in Delsworth with my mother and the newly-birthed Magnus. Even though I didn't remember much about those early years, I had the vague recollection of the king's anger when he'd learned of plots to bring about my demise. He'd then sent me back to Warwick, away from the trouble, and there I'd remained in seclusion for most of my life.

While growing up, I'd always assumed the king had every right to take the throne of Mercia away from King Francis and his descendants. My father claimed King Alfred never should have split the country between his twin daughters, that he should have given the kingdom to the older twin, Margery.

But everything I'd read and learned about Queen Margery had proven her to be a cruel and selfish woman. Perhaps King Alfred had seen those traits within his older twin daughter and had decided she wouldn't make a good leader. Perhaps he'd thought she only deserved half the kingdom.

There was no denying that Queen Margery's inheritance—Warwick to the south of Mercia—had suffered and fallen into decline. Margery had demanded much of her subjects and had given very little to them in return.

Her son, King Ethelbard, had lived lavishly, too, continuing to drain the country known for its rich jewels, until nothing had remained. Trade and commerce had all but ceased, the people had suffered extreme poverty, and the land had become barren and depleted.

When my father came to the throne, he inherited a kingdom in shambles and disarray. Since he belonged to a lineage of fierce warriors on his father's side, he did what he knew best—he fought.

Within several years, he'd amassed a strong force and had begun attacking Mercia's southern borders. Facing the vast Inglewood Forest serving as Mercia's natural defense, my father had finally changed tactics. He'd sold off the royal family's remaining jewels and hired the seafaring Danes as well as the lethal Saracens, and then he'd sailed to Delsworth, the stately capital of the old kingdom and the main residence of King Francis.

During the Battle of Delsworth, King Francis had been fatally wounded. His wife, Queen Dierdal, had died giving birth to Emmeline and her twin sister. It had been rumored that servants had escaped with the princesses. But for years afterward, no one had known what had really become of the princesses—whether they'd lived or died.

What would my father have done to the three princesses if he'd captured them? No doubt he would have executed them as he'd done with many others in an effort to solidify his reign.

I'd never concerned myself with the fate of the lost princesses before, never cared, never believed they mattered. My mentor, Lord Kennard, had fully supported the king's rule over the united kingdom and had done everything within his power to ensure I was ready to assume leadership one day. He'd certainly never given credence to the rights of the displaced princesses, had always taught me that I'd become the next ruler, and had assured me I'd make a great king.

But now that one of the princesses was my bride, this battle between the two houses over Mercia's throne had grown much more personal. And I realized I hated the idea that the king might have killed Emmeline or her sisters. Even now, he still considered Emmeline his enemy, though she was my wife, and that thought filled me with unease.

"Tell me what you were like as a little boy," Emmeline said softly, bringing me out of my reverie to focus on her again. "I should like to hear about your naughtiest escapades."

"All? They are so numerous my tales would keep you awake the whole night long."

"I don't mind." Again her voice was happy.

"Very well. But I shall only tell one of my naughty deeds at the telling of one of your own."

"I was never naughty."

I chuckled.

"Not purposefully," she added with a breathless laugh.

Pushing aside my concerns, I settled back, crossed my arms behind my head, and let the satisfaction of the moment surround me. I had a feeling the night would go much too fast, but then reminded myself that tonight was only the beginning. We had forever together.

Chapter 13

REX

I SAT BACK IN MY CHAIR AND RUBBED MY EYES WEARILY. FROM THE fading daylight outside the open windows of the antechamber, I guessed the hour to be drawing nigh to supper. With the lengthening shadows across the stuffy room, servants had already lit the wall sconces and candelabrum.

A dozen other men were seated with me and the king around the long oaken table. Their lined foreheads and heavy eyelids attested to their weariness as well. If I called an end to the meeting, they'd surely agree to it.

But they'd also see it as a sign of weakness on my part and rightly conclude I was more interested in seeing my wife than I was in supping.

Unavoidably, the days following our wedding had proven to be busy. With the impending siege from Queen Adelaide Constance, townspeople and castle staff were frantically stocking up on supplies while I oversaw the defense of both the town and castle.

I'd spent hours in urgent meetings with advisors and

military leaders devising a strategy on the best way to protect Delsworth. I'd confirmed we had the necessary weapons and manpower. And I'd toured the walls and ramparts, making sure everything was in order.

By the time I was able to retire at night, the hour was well past midnight, and I was too exhausted to visit with Emmeline. Although I'd promised her I'd show her the scriptorium, I'd quickly realized our time together would have to wait.

Just that morning, I managed one brief break to stroll in the garden with her and the new puppy. With the queen's rebel forces having made landfall at dawn, I could spare no more than a few minutes, enough to answer her worried questions about the siege and to assure her I was doing what I could to work toward a peaceful resolution.

"We must dispatch word to the Danes," the king was saying again from his position at the head of the table. "If we can get a messenger through to them of our need for aid, they will be here within a week."

I toyed with the goblet in front of me. Already we'd discussed the various options. I wanted to send a delegation to the queen and attempt to persuade her to accept Emmeline's place in the new royal lineage for the House of Mercia. Perhaps then we could avoid a war.

Yet, I was afraid the queen wouldn't be swayed. She must have received word of our marriage by now. But even with the news, her army, along with Norland's, were coming ashore and making camp southwest of the city along the banks of the Cress River.

Most of the advisors, including the king, concluded that war was inevitable and favored seeking the assistance of the Danes. If we couldn't negotiate peace, then having the help of the sea-faring warriors was our next best alternative. We needed to instruct them to surround and attack the foreign ships, drawing the queen's forces away from the town. Then, once the rebels were distracted, we would be able to launch our own onslaught.

While the plan was sound, there was one major problem: the kingdom's coffers were empty, and we had no way to pay mercenaries to come to our aid.

Since I wasn't involved in the financial decisions the king made, I didn't have full knowledge of how our steward managed affairs. But I hadn't been surprised when the king had ordered another increase in taxes earlier in the year.

Of course, the king had called upon his elite guards to keep the peace by locking away the most violent and vocal of the protestors. We'd had to make examples of some who refused to pay. After all, citizens had to understand their taxes helped secure the defense and well-being of their nation. The taxes were for the common good of all.

However, even with the increase in taxes, the coffers were still empty. And now, when we were faced with the rebel army, we had no financial reserves to add to our fortification. I wanted to question why we were in such dire financial straits, especially after making the people suffer through higher taxes. But this wasn't the time to bring up such a query.

"Your Majesty," said one of the king's oldest and most loyal advisors. "We all agree that getting word to the Danes is the best solution. But will they come if they have no guarantee of payment?"

The king rubbed the pointed tip of his beard, his lips pressed thinly and his brows furrowed dangerously. The king was normally intuitive, quick-thinking, and decisive. But in this case, after hours of meetings, I suspected he was reaching his limit of patience, and he wasn't an easy man to be around when he was angry.

He narrowed his eyes upon his advisor. "I charge you to find the payment for the Danes, Dobson, since you are apparently the wise one tonight."

The room grew silent, enough so that we could hear distant shouts. Were they from the queen's army even now advancing upon Delsworth?

All eyes fell to the table now littered with mugs, bowls, crumbs, and maps. No one dared to look up and meet the king's gaze. And no one dared to speak, least of all Dobson.

I straightened and sat forward. Tonight wasn't the time for the king to unleash his wrath upon his advisors. Tonight we needed to stay unified and find a solution to our monetary woes. And if I could find the treasure, I would have the solution.

"Your Majesty," I said, breaking the tense silence. Though the king might lash out at me in anger, he wouldn't punish me the same way he would the others. The knowledge gave me the liberty to speak more forthrightly, although I'd learned to do so carefully. "Now that we have a map of the Labyrinth of Death, I will take a detachment of my men and go after the ancient treasure."

"We still have not confirmed the map's accuracy," he replied tersely.

"I shall have the princess inform me of everything she knows regarding the map." I'd yet to ask Emmeline how it came to be in her possession, as well as the validity of it. Perhaps I'd feared that bringing it up would disturb the peace between us. But if I planned to use it to navigate the labyrinth, then I needed her to tell me whatever she knew.

I guessed we could make the trip there and back in under two weeks, especially since we could move swiftly by boat up the Central Cress River to the Iron Hills. From there we'd have a two or three days' ride into the Highlands to the labyrinth entrance.

Delsworth could withstand a siege for a fortnight, especially if I put Dante in charge of the army in my absence.

"Yes," the king said, some of his anger fading away. "But even if we learn the map is trustworthy, you forget something important: we lack the third key."

"Lack of keys has never stopped me from gaining entrance to wherever I want to go."

"The lack of the key will stop you this time. You can be sure of it."

"Then we shall get the third key."

The king met my gaze, his dark eyes sharp. "How?"

"We shall find out where Queen Adelaide Constance keeps it and steal it from her." I could sense the advisors watching our interaction, their weariness now dissipating.

"She likely has it locked away somewhere in Norland for safekeeping."

"My guess is that she brought it and hopes to gain the treasure for herself." If she planned to attack us, she'd certainly try to reclaim the keys and go after the treasure.

"Then you think she keeps it with her?"

"We could easily kidnap one of her guards and glean the information from him."

The king shook his head. "Even if we discover where she holds it, she will likely have it under heavy guard."

"I shall fight them for it."

The king was quiet for a long moment. At his new surge of interest, the others around the table had started breathing again.

"We need a better way," the king said. "Someone with the ability to go inside and take the key."

"A traitor?" I suggested. "One of their own who can be bribed?"

A commotion outside the antechamber door drew my attention. Already on high alert, my mind cleared and my muscles tensed. Was one of my men bringing an update?

"No!" came the guard's voice. "You cannot disturb the king and his men."

"I insist on seeing the prince," came another voice, this one belonging to a woman.

Emmeline?

Shoving away from the table, I stood. In three rapid strides, I was at the door and threw it open. The burly soldier that oft served as the king's bodyguard filled the door frame with feet spread and arms wide, a formidable and impenetrable force. Emmeline stood in front of him, her arms crossed, her shoulders rigid, her eyes heated with fury.

She was a blazing force, too, and breathtakingly beautiful with her dark hair styled in circular plaits atop her head and a gown of richest green.

At the sight of me, she lifted her chin. "Why didn't you tell me?"

Behind me, I could feel the stares of the men, including the penetrating one from the king. I had no doubt he was silently rebuking me for my wife's behavior. Mother would never have dreamed of interrupting a meeting and demanding to see him.

Did I need to reprimand Emmeline? Ought I to chastise her to be more docile? Part of me knew Emmeline would never be quiet and calm and agreeable like my mother, and I didn't want her to be. I liked her spark and fire and the way she made me feel alive.

Nevertheless, my backbone stiffened with the need to show the king and his advisors that I was in control of my wife, that I was still a strong man and warrior, and that I wouldn't be manipulated by the whim of a woman. As the future king, I must demand respect, even from Emmeline.

"You cannot interrupt my meetings," I said brusquely, lifting my chin and glaring down at her. "Whatever your concern, it must wait."

"This cannot wait."

"It must." I nodded to the guard and began to close the door.

She pushed forward. "Why didn't you tell me you captured my parents?"

I froze. In an instant, a dozen thoughts raced through my mind. The first was denial. I hadn't captured her parents. Yes, I'd threatened to go back for them. But out of my desire to show Emmeline mercy, I'd spared Lance and Felicia's lives.

The second was realization, and it hit me like icy water against the face. The king had done this behind my back. But why?

Had he sent out a separate contingent after learning the details from Magnus? Had he considered my decision to free them too lenient? Or had he secured them in order to hold leverage over Emmeline?

A glance at his face gave me my answer. He'd done it for all those reasons and perhaps more I didn't yet understand.

Of course, I'd expected an elite warrior like Lance to chase after Emmline once he'd freed himself. He wouldn't have had any trouble tracking us. But he most certainly wouldn't have been able to travel rapidly, not with his crippled leg, not with his wife slowing him down, and not without swift horses. If he'd been captured, then he'd obviously drawn near over the past days, but not far enough to find sanctuary with the queen's rebels.

A sliver of frustration pricked me. Lance should have gone directly to the rebel party. He'd surely picked up on their trail too. Why hadn't he sought their aid? Was he afraid in light of the coming battle, they'd prevent him from attempting to rescue Emmeline?

At the king's probing intensity, I kept my expression passive and willed my eyes not to show any irritation.

"Magnus just told me," Emmeline said from where the guard was holding her back. "He said they've been taken to the dungeons."

Of course, Magnus would relish stirring up discord by sharing the news with Emmeline. But why was he privy to the capture when I wasn't? I should have been the first to hear of something of such importance since it had to do with my wife.

Perhaps that's why the king had kept it from me. Perhaps he suspected I'd be weak in areas concerning Emmeline, that my attraction to her would cloud my judgment. Maybe it already had.

"I have put Magnus in charge of their discipline," the king said matter-of-factly.

"Discipline?" Emmeline's tone rose.

"They have committed high treason," he continued. "And as a result, they deserve to die a traitor's death."

"No!" Emmeline cried out. She obviously understood

what a traitor's death entailed—slow torture over days. With Magnus in charge, the torture could last weeks. "No, you cannot put them to death. Please. They are good people."

At the anguish in Emmeline's tone, my gut clenched. And yet I didn't move or take my gaze from the king's face. He was still testing me. I could sense it.

"If not for them," the king said, his voice taking on an edge, "I would have become the keeper of the keys and would have found the treasure years ago."

From what I'd learned, kings of old had always been tasked with guarding the keys and keeping the three together. When Lance and Felicia had divided the princesses up for safekeeping all those years ago, they'd gone against tradition and separated the keys.

"If not for them," the king continued, "I would not have a usurper's army sitting on my doorstep. And if not for them, I would have peace and prosperity in my land."

"They only did what your faithful servants would have done," Emmeline replied, "if the situation had been reversed and your sons' lives were at stake."

The king pushed away from the table, clearly done with the conversation. "They deserve death, and I shall not be satisfied with anything less."

I suspected the king's words were for me as much as they were for Emmeline. It was his way of saying he'd been disappointed I hadn't brought Lance and Felicia back to him so he might have the opportunity for vengeance.

"Rex, please." Emmeline's tone turned soft and plaintive behind me. "Do something."

Slowly I pivoted, aware again that all eyes were upon me, especially the king's, gauging my interaction and whether I'd remain strong and loyal to him or whether I'd give in to my wife's pleading.

On the one hand, I understood the king's need to punish Lance and Felicia. He must send a message to the people that he wouldn't tolerate anyone aiding the enemy. And yet, the crime had happened long ago. Surely, the king could show some leniency.

As I met Emmeline's expectant, even hopeful gaze, I wanted nothing more than to cross to her, sweep her into my embrace, and reassure her everything would be all right and I'd do what I could to save her parents. How could I deny her this?

But if I gave in, where would her demands stop? And what example would I set as a leader, as the future king? That I'd be swayed so easily?

I hardened my resolve and shook my head. "If the king wishes to punish them, then so be it."

The glow in Emmeline's eyes flickered and sputtered out. Any warmth in her expression fled, and a chill took its place, making her features rigid, almost haughty. Then she responded, "I thought you were different." She jutted her chin. "I was wrong."

With a final glare that dripped with disdain, she strode away. My heart lurched with the need to chase after her, to talk further and explain my decision. But I only watched her go, telling myself I'd come up with a better plan later, one that could aid her parents without undermining the king—if that was even possible.

As the king finally adjourned the meeting and the men filed out of the room, I started to leave with them, unsure whether to pursue Emmeline or let her go for now.

"Stay a moment, Rex." The king came alongside me and clamped a hand on my shoulder. The move was meant to reassure me I'd done the right thing. Why, then, did I feel worse as I pictured the hope flickering out in Emmeline's eyes?

I acknowledged the king's command with a slight bow and again made sure to keep the emotion from my face. The king considered confusion and indecision a weakness. I couldn't let him see I was experiencing both.

"Princess Emmeline is the one to gain access to the usurper's camp," the king said quietly, "and find the third key."

Protest sprang to the tip of my tongue, but although I bit it back, I couldn't keep it from my eyes. Upon seeing it, the king's lips twisted into a slight smile. "As their lost sister, they will welcome her into their midst with open arms."

"That does not mean they will give her the key."

"She is clever and needs to find a way to get it."

The king was right about Emmeline's cleverness. Even so, I didn't want her going into the enemy camp. Such a move was too risky and dangerous.

"Send your best men," the king continued as though reading my mind, "and ensure her safety."

"Once she is among them, I suspect she will not return to me." Especially now that she was furious with me.

The king stroked his beard, his eyes narrowing in thought. "Then you must give her reason to come back."

"What do you suggest, Your Majesty?"

"Tell her if she gets the key and returns, you will spare the life of one of her guardians—the one of her choosing."

How could I go to Emmeline with such an ultimatum? It wouldn't endear me to her any further. "She might do it for both lives."

"She will do it for one." With that, he moved away from me, signaling for his bodyguard to follow him.

As the king departed, I bowed, outwardly giving him my allegiance and respect as I'd always done. But inside, I couldn't muster the same. Instead, uncertainty roiled around, tumbling and bumping. I wished nothing more than to shield Emmeline from the king's plans, but how could I do so when she was right at the center of them?

Chapter 14

Emmeline

From my spot in the middle of my canopied bed, I rubbed Ruby's stomach absently, unable to gather any enthusiasm for training her as I'd been doing the past few days.

My servants hovered on the fringes of the room, hopping at my every command, clearly sensing the change in my mood. I closed my eyes and fought back a wave of betrayal and hurt. Rex didn't really care about me the way I thought he did. If he'd cared, he would have made some effort to listen to my pleas, to understand how important my parents were to me.

From his reaction, I'd surmised he hadn't known about their capture until I'd told him. Even so, he could have attempted to free them instead of callously turning away from my request and supporting his father's decision.

Tears stung, and I fought them back as I had each time I'd been tempted to cry over Rex's choice. His loyalty to his father went deeper than his concerns for me. I supposed that was to be expected from a man who'd married me because his father had ordered it.

What if his displays of affection and gifts on our wedding day had simply been a show? What if I'd read more into his gestures than he'd meant?

I shook my head. Of course, it wasn't all a show. The night he'd slept on my floor, he'd said he wasn't playacting. I hadn't misjudged him so entirely, had I?

Though I'd witnessed my parents' love for each other and read about the emotion in books, what did I really know of love? My feelings for Rex had certainly been changing. I couldn't deny I found him attractive and that my body responded to him in strange ways. I also couldn't deny I admired many things about him. But how did I know if what I felt was love?

With a silent groan, I buried my face in my hands. Even if my feelings were growing, he didn't regard me highly enough to help my parents.

My pulse sped again, just as it had when Magnus had given me the news. I ached to go to my parents, throw my arms around them, hear their voices, and see their precious faces. Through the long days of traveling to Delsworth, I'd missed them. And now that they were here, within reach, my heart felt like it would break with the need to be with them and make sure they were kept safe.

Except they were far from safe. The glint in Magnus's eyes had told me as much. He planned to make them suffer so that I would suffer, which would, in turn, affect my relationship negatively with Rex—as it already had.

During our travels, I'd quickly learned Magnus had one goal in life: to undermine Rex. He did so subtly, passively, with slight put-downs, misplaced comments, and snide criticism. I guessed Magnus's attitude stemmed from jealousy. Perhaps Magnus had believed himself to be the favored son for so many years, since he'd been allowed to remain in Delsworth. Maybe once Rex had arrived and taken a role as a powerful leader, Magnus had felt pushed aside.

Whatever the case, I feared what Magnus planned to do to my parents. I wrapped my arms around my middle and bent over, fighting back my tears. *Oh God*, I silently called out. *Keep them safe. And show me what to do and then give me the courage to do it.*

I sat up and forced myself to think again, to mentally retrace the various routes for arriving at the passageway that led to the dungeons. I'd explored the castle enough that I was reasonably familiar with the layout.

Even so, getting down into the dungeons without any guards seeing me would be difficult. I had no doubt Magnus would be expecting me to attempt to free my parents and had taken extra precautions.

My chamber door opened and Rex stepped inside, glancing around until his sights landed upon me. Against my will, my heartbeat pattered faster. I didn't want to see him or speak to him, and so I chastised myself and focused on Ruby, who'd fallen asleep in a half sprawl.

"Everyone, leave us," Rex commanded.

The servants responded immediately, their footsteps shuffling hastily in the rushes. A moment later, the door closed with a thud. The quiet of the room made me suddenly fidgety so that I began to pet Ruby faster and with both hands.

I chanced a look at Rex to find that he was watching me, no longer stiff and unapproachable as he'd been a short while ago. Instead, his face was masked with regret, maybe even sadness.

Had he come to apologize and make things right? As the future king, he must have some influence and could figure out a way to set my parents free.

"Emmeline." He stood in the middle of the room. "I am sorry about your parents' capture. I had no knowledge the king was even searching for them."

The gentleness in his voice beckoned me, and I crawled off the bed, leaving Ruby behind. I wanted to go to him, fall to my knees, and plead with him to help me.

"I allowed your parents to go free for your sake," he continued. "I hope you know I had no desire to bring them harm."

I took several steps toward him, then stopped. "I believe you."

He nodded, but his eyes were still troubled.

Gaining hope, I crossed to him and reached for his hand. He was attired in his chain mail as he had been the past days. But he'd discarded his gloves, and my fingers made contact with his. The hard contours, the strength, the roughness of his skin, all reminded me of his power and yet his indescribable gentleness.

As though sensing my reaction, his attention shifted to my hand against his. He stared, his brows furrowing.

"I love them, Rex," I said before he could dash my hope again. "They're the only parents I ever knew. They sacrificed everything for me. And they loved me with body, soul, and strength."

"I know," he said softly.

"Then you understand why I must save them? Why I'll do anything to free them?"

"Anything?" He finally lifted his gaze.

Something in his eyes and tone warned me that he hadn't come to apologize or offer to help. He'd come to manipulate me. I let go of his hand and took a step back. He reached for me as though to regain our connection, but I slipped farther away, widening the distance between us.

"What must I do?" I didn't care that my voice came out hard.

He expelled a sigh, paused, then straightened his shoulders. "You must go meet your sisters and retrieve the last ancient key to the hidden treasure."

"Then you know for sure that they have both come?" When I'd previously questioned Rex about the impending attack, he'd been uncertain if both my sisters were aboard the ships bringing the rebel army. He'd supposed one might stay behind in Norland for safekeeping.

"Our scouts have spotted them both. And now you must go to them and get the final key."

I stared at him, trying to make sense of his command. "I'm to sneak into the rebel camp and steal it?"

"You can go under the guise of meeting them and negotiating peace. But then, yes, you must secretly retrieve the key."

My mind spun in a hundred directions. "Where will I find it?"

"I have already sent out my men to capture one of Adelaide's close advisors or guards. I shall have that information before long."

My stomach lurched. I only had to picture the bare back of the man who'd given away my location in Inglewood Forest to know what method Rex planned to use to gain his information.

I stalked back to my bed, frustration pulsing with every step. I'd thought I was beginning to know who Rex really was. Underneath his fierce exterior, I'd seen a man who longed for peace, a man who wanted to avoid bloodshed.

However, apparently, a beast lurked within him. Why had I expected anything less from the son of a monster like King Ethelwulf? Though I'd longed to believe the best about him, ultimately he used people to his benefit and didn't care whom he hurt in the process of gaining what he wanted.

I stopped at the footboard and wished I could pull the bed curtains around me and hide within. I wanted to get away from Rex, from this battle between our families, from everything. As I closed my eyes, the desire for my forest home rose up so swiftly that for a moment I could almost smell the rich scent of pine and moss and charcoal smoke. I could almost feel the cool air rustling the leaves.

If only things had never changed. If only we could return—Father, Mother, me, and Bede—to our cottage and live in peace. We'd been content, and life had been good.

Now my parents were in the dungeons and would soon face Magnus's torture—if they hadn't already. They were suffering on account of me. And where was Bede? What would become of my little friend now?

My shoulders sagged and my head drooped. I had

no choice but to do whatever Rex asked. Stealing a key wasn't the worst thing he could have required. After all, what could Adelaide do with the one remaining ancient key?

Though I didn't relish the idea of befriending my sisters only to betray them, I prayed they would come to understand I'd had no choice, not if I hoped to save my parents.

Finally, I turned to face Rex, resigning myself to my fate. "Do you vow to release my parents if I get the key?"

The sadness was back in his eyes. "The king will allow you to save one of them."

"One?" Surely I'd misunderstood him.

Rex didn't answer except to lift his chin.

Cold fury rushed through my veins. "You're despicable."

"I may not like every decision the king makes." His voice turned low and steely. "But I must obey him the same as everyone else, perhaps more so, if I hope to prove myself worthy of being his heir and have any chance of someday being a better ruler."

"You will never be a better ruler unless you learn that winning loyalty is best achieved through mercy rather than fear."

"How can a girl as sheltered and naïve as you presume to give me advice?" His tone sliced as sharply as the glint in his eyes. "You know nothing about being a leader."

Before I could formulate an answer, he pivoted, strode to the door, exited, and slammed it with a force that rattled the furniture.

I stared at the door, and a wave of anguish

pummeled me. A sob expanded in my chest. It burst out, but not before I caught it within the confines of my hand.

I wasn't sure which hurt more: knowing no matter what I did, my parents were still in grave danger. Or knowing I'd lost Rex and that whatever love we'd developed was now gone.

The following dawn, my servants awoke me at Rex's command and passed along his message that I was to be ready to ride to Adelaide's camp at full light. He'd clearly gotten all the information he'd needed regarding the location of the third key. I could only pray the poor person he'd seized and tortured hadn't suffered for long.

After a restless night of thinking about Rex, about his sweet gifts, about the tender moments we'd shared, the pain had swelled and at times had been difficult to bear. So had the pain over my parents. I alternated between panic regarding their fate and fury that they'd been captured in the first place. In addition, I couldn't stop thinking about meeting my sisters for the first time and the fact that I would have to betray them.

When I'd finally fallen asleep, my nightmares of being chased and captured by men in black chain mail came back in vivid detail so that upon waking, I was listless and tired, my anger mingling with sorrow.

My maidservants did their best to transform me into a regal woman worthy of being the next queen. But now that I knew how Rex really viewed me—as a sheltered and naïve girl—all their fussing only made me feel more inadequate.

When Rex's guards came for me, I offered no resistance. They led me to the inner bailey where the prince had assembled a group of armed soldiers attired in their finest armor and wearing the standard of Bryttania. Thankfully, I had a horse of my own, for I wasn't sure I could have borne sitting with Rex on his steed, so close and yet so far apart.

As one of his men aided my mount, I glimpsed Rex watching me, but like his men, he'd donned his great helm, shielding his face. Though his eyes were visible behind narrow slits, I turned away from him so I wouldn't be tempted to look into them and search for any hint of the warmth and affection he'd shown me previously.

I needed to focus on the mission at hand, retrieve the key, and then get my mother out of the dungeons. While I loathed the prospect of leaving Father there, he was stronger and would be able to endure the torture for longer, until I could figure out a way to free him. Once I came up with a plan, hopefully, he wouldn't be too weak and injured to make the escape with me.

As we rode into the outer bailey and through the gatehouse, I studied every wall, tower, window, and crenellation with renewed awareness. The fortifications were strong and crawled with soldiers. How would Father and I sneak past all of them? I'd just have to pray Father remembered every nuance and crack in the castle from his days as an elite guard, and that he'd have a plan for making our escape.

A long wooden bridge spanned the moat—a moat

that had once been full of poisonous snakes and maybe still was. Father and Mother had loved to tell me the story of their running through a tunnel that ran under the moat while the snakes hung down from the ceiling like vines. From what I'd been able to glean from castle servants, the king had filled in that passageway long ago.

The fortress stood on a slight northern rise with the town spreading out below like a footstool. Beyond the town walls, at an even lower elevation, the churning waters of the East Sea crashed against the rocky shore. In the distance, dozens of ships blockaded Delsworth's harbor, trapping King Ethelwulf's ships as well as merchant vessels.

Even if the king's fleet was cut off, the sea and its high crags provided a measure of fortification, particularly on the southern and eastern sides. To the north of the castle, a heavily wooded area acted as another defense.

The only direction an advancing army could easily attack was from the southwest. However, the invading army would first need to conquer the town before being able to take the castle. Apparently, that was Adelaide's strategy because her camp spread to the southwest as far as I could see. The plains were covered with hundreds of tents, horses, and campfires, the smoke curling up into the early morning, and crews assembling siege engines along the perimeter of the camp closest to Delsworth.

The early-morning sunshine turned the bright-red royal standards into flaming flags. With the golden lions rearing up, I recognized the insignia. The emblem belonged to the House of Mercia, my family.

My family. I sat up straighter and examined the tents more closely, searching for the larger ones that would signify royalty. I'd finally meet Adelaide today and possibly Maribel. What would they think of me? After I'd already sabotaged their rebellion with my marriage to Rex, would they despise me? Consider me weak?

As I looked out over the plains, the magnitude of Adelaide's resistance efforts impressed me, even if I didn't agree with her methods. She'd gone from a young, unknown woman in hiding to a respected and revered queen in a little over a year.

What was the secret of her success? Would she be a merciful ruler? Better than Rex? A part of me wanted to cling to the hope that Rex could yet be different, that he might let himself be controlled by goodness instead of by evil. However, as he rode ahead of me with his shoulders and back stiff and proud, I feared I'd misplaced my trust.

Our ride through town was solemn. The cheering crowds from just days ago were long gone. Most were hidden away behind closed shutters. Only a few shopkeepers dared to show themselves.

The king and Rex had to be taking some satisfaction in their successful scheming, since the people of Delsworth hadn't thrown open the city gates to welcome Adelaide. They'd effectively used the public wedding and display of affection to manipulate the emotions of the people the same way they'd manipulated mine.

The very remembrance served to stir the anger in me once more so that by the time we reached the southern city gates, my determination to fight had started to return.

When Rex drew his steed alongside mine and lifted his visor, I was ready to hold myself together. I could sense him waiting for me to turn my attention upon him. Instead, I looked straight ahead at the imposing iron grill of the closed gate.

"We shall ride out together," he said, "with the white flag signifying our peaceful intentions."

"Very well," I replied with equal formality.

"If your sister agrees to give you an audience, I and several others will accompany you to the meeting and will request the privacy of a tent. Though the key belonged to Maribel, the queen now keeps it in a pouch at her waist. That means you will need to figure out a way to cut it loose when she is not aware." He held out my knife.

I took it without looking at him. "I pray I succeed, not for your sake, but for the soul of the poor innocent man you tortured, so his suffering will not be in vain."

Rex didn't respond. He hesitated as though wanting to say more. But after a moment of tense silence, he urged his horse forward and signaled to the gatehouse guard to begin raising the portcullis.

As we rode out of the city, several knights moved to the front and unfurled white flags. Across the grassy plains, shouts rose from Adelaide's camp and within seconds a small party of armed knights gathered and began to ride toward us, their swords drawn, their shields positioned.

Though I was surrounded by Rex's men, a knot twisted in my stomach. This wasn't what my parents had risked their lives for—so that I'd betray my family and undermine the fight to regain the throne. They hadn't raised me to cower in fear and bow to the demands of my enemy.

But here I was, married to the enemy and plotting with him to steal from my sisters. A braver woman wouldn't have placed herself into this situation. A woman of valor and integrity would have stayed strong amidst the pressures and done what was right no matter the consequences.

"I'm sorry, Father," I whispered. This wasn't his fault. He'd done all he could to shape me into a worthy princess. But somehow, I'd failed. Instead of being courageous and daring the way he'd wanted, I'd only brought trouble on everyone.

Ahead, Adelaide's soldiers drew to a halt and shouted something to Rex. He responded by motioning his knights with the white flags to cross the remaining distance to deliver his message.

As the soldiers handed over Rex's sealed note, I held my breath, praying that perhaps Adelaide would refuse. Maybe she'd realize the king was plotting something, that he wouldn't send me to negotiate peace without having ulterior motives.

Long minutes later, the knights carrying the white flags trotted back. "Your Highness," one of them called. "They have agreed to a meeting with the princess. They will set up a tent here outside of camp."

As the rebels made short work of erecting a tent, I wished for Inglewood Forest where I might disappear. But with nothing around except open sandy grassland with opposing armies on either side, I had to move forward, plunging further into the deceitful plans.

Finally, Rex nudged his horse ahead of the rest, and the soldiers accompanying us gave me little choice but to move with them. With Adelaide's small army of men watching our approach, I made myself sit higher, knowing they must despise me for marrying Rex. The closer we drew, the more my stomach churned with the need to be sick.

When we halted several lengths away, a broad-shouldered man at the front and center of the group lifted his visor. He bowed respectfully toward Rex. "Your Highness, I am the Earl of Langley, the husband of Queen Adelaide."

Adelaide's husband? I focused on him more intently, studying the little bit of his face I could see through the opening of his great helm. He seemed a young and handsome man with strong features and even an aura of dashing. His eyes—a light brown— shifted to me.

"This is my wife, the Princess Emmeline," Rex said in a hard, almost superior tone. "The future queen of Bryttania."

One of my guards nudged my horse forward, giving me no choice but to pull alongside Rex. Was I imagining things or did the earl's eyes seem to soften upon me, perhaps even grow tender? "It is good to see you, Princess Emmeline." He spoke with warmth. "Your sisters have been awaiting this day for a very long time."

"Both are available?" I asked.

"Yes. And they will be thrilled to meet you."

Thrilled at meeting me? The notion was new and disconcerting. Nonetheless, my racing pulse slowed just a little.

"She is here to negotiate peace," Rex said brusquely. "Not engage in a reunion."

"Can we not accomplish both?" the earl asked.

"With so much at stake," Rex said, "peace talks must take precedence."

Why was he opposing it? He must know the extra time would allow me more opportunity to steal the key.

His eyes met mine in a warning glance, bidding me to remain quiet. Was he offering a mild protest so they wouldn't suspect we were scheming?

"The queen will want to spend time with her sister first." The earl's voice took on an edge that showed him also to be a man of power and strength.

Under different circumstances, I might have appreciated Rex's ingenuity. He'd gotten the earl to give me the perfect opportunity to steal the key. But at the moment, the sickness in my stomach returned. I was an awful sister, and if Adelaide and Maribel only knew it, they wouldn't want to meet me.

As it was, I'd have to go forward, engage in the introductions, and pretend to be friendly, all the while plotting how I might further undermine and destroy them.

Chapter 15

Emmeline

My lungs constricted at the prospect of finally meeting my sisters. Although my parents had always talked fondly of my family, I'd never developed an interest in finding them. I suppose in some ways I'd known the introduction would thrust me into danger and bring an end to my idyllic life.

In the distance, the rebel camp was already busy with men assembling siege engines, along with squires and their knights engaged in various morning rituals—breaking their fasts, sharpening weapons, polishing armor, and drilling for battle. Others stood at the edge watching our proceedings, vying for a glimpse of the crown prince and his wife.

Next to me, Rex sidled close enough that his leg brushed against mine. The tightness of his grip on his reins and the stiffness of his demeanor told me he was on high alert, aware of every movement and every possible threat.

Even with the retinue of his men fanning out

behind him, he was in very real danger here so near to the enemy camp. They could capture him, hold him as a prisoner, and perhaps use him as a bargaining tool to make King Ethelwulf capitulate to their demands. I had no doubt if the roles had been reversed, Rex and King Ethelwulf wouldn't have hesitated to use the situation to their advantage.

In spite of my anger, I had no wish for any ill to befall Rex. He was after all, still my husband, and a small part of me longed for him and the special bond we'd shared, however briefly.

I chanced a glance at Rex. Through the slits in his helm, his eyes met mine. They issued an assurance that he intended to keep me safe and would fight to the death for me if need be.

Even with the rift that had opened between us, I knew I hadn't misjudged him entirely, that underneath the complicated layers, goodness and kindness existed.

"Your Majesty," the Earl of Langley spoke to the group of his knights mounted and waiting on the opposite side of the tent. "I present to you Prince Ethelrex and Princess Emmeline."

I looked around for the queen, but no one moved except one knight. He dismounted, strode forward, and stopped near the tent next to the guards who had set up the meeting place.

Perhaps the queen was already waiting for me inside?

The knight glanced first at Rex and the men behind us. Then he slipped off his helmet.

I stifled a gasp as I found myself looking not upon a man, but upon a woman with long, blond hair that flowed over her shoulders now that it was free from confinement.

Was this Adelaide?

Her gaze shot to me, filled with such hope I had no doubt this was my older sister. She studied my face, taking in every detail.

"Emmeline, welcome," she said, warmth and excitement reaching out to embrace me. "This is a joyous day to finally meet you."

"Thank you, Your Majesty." I bowed my head. "I'm grateful for this opportunity to meet you as well."

Adelaide shifted her attention to Rex again, who lifted his chin. He'd never bow to Adelaide. He likely expected her to show obeisance to him instead.

For a long moment neither Adelaide nor Rex spoke. Adelaide's weapon hung casually at her side, but her grip was tight. Likewise, Rex's fingers flexed around the hilt of his sword. His body radiated tension, and his horse whinnied as if warning against impending doom.

"Prince Ethelrex," Adelaide finally said, narrowing her eyes upon him. "I admit I did not expect the king to send his son to negotiate peace."

Rex removed his helm, revealing his rugged countenance, piercing eyes, and warrior-like intensity. "The king did not send me. I came of my own accord so I might ensure my wife's safety."

"You are afraid we shall not let her return with you?"

"She is mine, and I shall fight to the death anyone who touches her or tries to take her from me."

Adelaide wouldn't seize me, would she? What purpose would a separation from Rex achieve? Even if she wanted me to stay, I wouldn't—not with Mother and Father languishing in the castle dungeons.

The queen studied the prince's face. "You married the princess for political gain. Now that you have influenced the people in your favor, you have no more need of Emmeline."

Of course, the king and prince still had need of me. Today's mission proved that. Likely, they'd continue to make use of me as long as they could. But I couldn't say any of that, not now. Not with my parents' lives at stake.

"Royal marriages may start as political arrangements," Rex replied. "But they can become more."

"Then your intentions toward my sister are noble?"

"I have pledged her my life and love before both God and man. I shall never be swayed to break my vow."

With so public a declaration, I didn't dare look at Rex lest he see that he was softening me much more than I wanted. Even if he genuinely wished to honor our marriage vows, I couldn't forget he was putting his aspirations and his father's whims above my needs.

When Adelaide shifted to scrutinize me, I refused to give way to the need to squirm. Instead, I forced myself to remain calm and unexpressive as my father had trained me.

"I should like very much the chance to visit with Emmeline," my sister said, waving to an adjacent tent. "Perchance Emmeline would join me for refreshments?"

"I would be honored," I said.

Rex was off his horse and beside mine before I could begin my descent. With his hands fitted securely around my waist, he lifted me down and steadied me.

Even then, his fingers lingered, drawing my eyes up to his.

Crinkles at his temples reflected his worry. "Be careful."

I wanted to retort that if he was worried about me, then why was he making me steal? Why wasn't he more concerned about helping me find a way to free my parents instead? I lifted my chin in defiance.

Too late, I realized my mistake. Before I knew what he was doing, he swept down and captured my mouth in a kiss like none we'd yet shared. His lips were demanding and possessive and desperate all at once, so that I lost my bearing and grasped his arms to keep from buckling. His hands upon my hips drew me closer. Even though his armor separated our bodies, I was still very much aware of our proximity, his strength, and his passion. How was it possible one touch could make me as wobbly as a newborn fawn?

He broke our kiss as sharply as he'd begun it, pulling back a fraction so that his breathing bathed my now swollen lips. "If you need me," he whispered, "call my name. I shall remain close at hand."

His lips were so near I could almost feel them and was surprised by how much I wanted them against mine once more. Thankfully, he released me and took a step away before I could make a fool of myself and rise up to kiss him again. Instead, I dropped my focus to the grass and didn't dare look at him. I was supposed to be angry with him, not fall into his arms.

What must Adelaide and her husband think of our display?

With heat rising into my cheeks, I followed Adelaide to her tent, bending past a flap and entering a spacious interior. With the canvas pulled back at a hole in the ceiling, sunlight flooded the grassy floor and showed a table surrounded by several rudimentary benches.

"Please, sit." She motioned me to one of the seats while she retrieved a jug and two cups from the center of the table.

Tentatively, I lowered myself and folded my hands in my lap. With her back to me, I took stock of her armor and wondered how I would be able to get to her leather pouch beneath the iron layer.

"When did you discover your identity as a princess?" She poured amber liquid into one of the cups.

"I've always known."

Her gaze swung to me, and I dropped mine to the tabletop, hoping she hadn't read my thoughts. "Then Sister Katherine didn't find you and tell you?"

"No. Was she supposed to?"

"She sought me at my home in Langley and next found Maribel at her convent in the Highlands. In both cases, she led King Ethelwulf right to us."

"Yes, my father kept me apprised of the happenings. He always brought back news after one of his trips to the market."

"Father?" Adelaide poured liquid into the other cup.

"Lance was like a father to me and Felicia a mother."

Adelaide set the jug back on the table, corked it, and then handed me a cup. Accepting it from her, I noticed again how beautiful she was even in her armor with lines of sweat and dust upon her face.

I sipped the liquid to discover a sweet but spicy ale. Adelaide, too, took a drink, all the while assessing me.

"They raised me to know everything about my family and history." I offered the explanation I expected she was looking for.

She lowered her mug to the table and wiped the rim with her forefinger. "I was surprised to receive the news that Prince Ethelrex spared their lives."

Although I sensed Adelaide had many questions about what had led me to marry the prince, she watched me without condemnation. At least none yet.

"He vowed to let them go unharmed if I handed myself over to him."

She nodded.

"I had no choice but to marry him or watch them suffer."

"Then you married him against your will?"

How honest could I be with this young woman who was still a stranger even though she was my sister? "I attempted to get away from him, but as you can see, he's a strong man..." I twisted my mug. "And persuasive."

"He has persuaded you to love him?" Her question was quiet but hit me as if she'd shouted it.

My gaze shot to hers. "No, I loathe him."

"Not according to the reports I received regarding your public wedding and the feast."

"Reports cannot always tell the whole story."

"Your kiss just now confirmed your affection."

"Because he is persuasive."

"Because he cares about you in return."

"Not enough."

"Why?" The glint in Adelaide's eyes told me my

answer was significant.

I picked up my cup and took a quick sip. How had she gotten to the real reason for my visit in so short a time and with so little effort?

She traced the rim of her mug again. "You are not here to negotiate peace, are you, Emmeline?"

I stiffened, expecting her guards to come in, grab me on either side, and drag me away. No matter how hard Rex fought, we were too close to the enemy camp and would quickly be outnumbered.

When the canvas door flapped open, I jumped from my bench, and it toppled backward into the grass. Rex's name was on the tip of my tongue. But at the sight of the newcomer—a woman—I froze.

One look was all I needed to know she was Maribel, my twin. Although she had the same golden hair and blue eyes as Adelaide, the heart shape of her face, high cheekbones, rounded chin, and long neck were like mine.

As her gaze alighted upon me, she squealed with excitement, then closed the distance and threw her arms around me.

"Emmeline, oh, Emmeline," she said with such joy, squeezing me until I couldn't keep from hugging her in return. "I have lived for this day." She sniffled as she held me tight.

A small ache formed in my chest. I'd never thought I'd needed my sisters, had always believed I fared well enough without them. But what if I'd missed out on something special I hadn't known I'd needed?

Maribel pulled back but didn't let go. Instead, she studied me and smiled again, even though tears now streamed down her cheeks. "You are just as beautiful as they say. Even more so."

"Thank you." I tried to make my voice work past the lump in my throat. "You're both so lovely, I can't compare."

Maribel released a soft laugh full of delight. "Rumors say you are the ravishing, dark beauty who stole the prince's heart."

Ravishing? I smiled at the exaggeration.

Maribel laughed again and drew me into another hug. This time I went willingly and somehow felt as though a part of me had finally come home.

I lost track of time as we ate from the simple fare servants brought us. Maribel kept the conversation lighthearted and pleasant. And thankfully, Adelaide didn't attempt to probe me further regarding the true nature of my visit.

Adelaide told about her childhood growing up with the Langleys, her husband's family, and how she'd always secretly loved Christopher. She also spoke of her time evading King Ethelwulf's men who'd come after her.

Maribel described her life at Highland Convent and how she'd considered becoming a nun until Sister Katherine's visit had changed everything. Maribel relayed her and Edmund's adventures as she'd fled from King Ethelwulf's guards. And she told fondly of how she'd fallen in love with Edmund through it all.

Of course, they wanted to know about my life in Inglewood Forest. Maribel was particularly fascinated and asked all about living with my parents and Bede and what it was like knowing I was a princess all those years and having to keep the secret.

My mind flashed to the few occasions we'd had guests. One time Mother had covered me in blankets in the dormer room, where I'd huddled in fear for hours. During another incident, she'd made me hide in the forest in the dugout tree, a tight, dark spot. I'd been filled with such terror I'd lain paralyzed until she'd finally come after me.

After such experiences, my nightmares about the king's soldiers in black chain mail had always been worse.

"Sometimes I wonder if I may have been better off not knowing," I replied quietly, the morning sunshine streaming in through the opening at the top and warming the tent. "Maybe I'd be stronger and braver like the two of you."

Maribel reached for my hand and squeezed it. "From the moment I learned you had been captured, I have thought you must be so brave to face the prince and King Ethelwulf with such dignity."

"I have only done what I must to keep those I love safe."

"Then God has gifted you with the highest form of courage," Adelaide said, sliding her bench back into the shade, likely growing warm in the layers of her armor. Did I dare hope she'd shed it and provide me an opportunity to get what I'd come for?

"'Highest form of courage'?" I released a shaky laugh. "I am much too afraid most of the time to lay claim to any courage."

"Courage is not the absence of fear but the

determination to persevere when circumstances are at their worst."

I liked her definition, but I certainly didn't feel gifted with courage.

"I also believe true courage puts the needs of others above one's own."

"I agree," Maribel added. "I could not have made such a sacrifice to marry a stranger, especially one who looks as though he could tear apart a dozen wolves with his bare hands."

"He has proven himself kind and even generous," I said, defending him before I could catch myself.

"And yet he has asked you to do something you do not wish to do?" Adelaide's question was gentle and yet direct.

From everything I'd witnessed about her in the short hour we'd conversed, I realized the rumors regarding her gift of wisdom were true. She was insightful beyond her years. And though I hadn't seen Maribel in her role as a physician, her gift of healing was obvious as well. She'd healed the rifts of time and distance, bonding us quickly together.

If my sisters both had such powerful gifts, had God given me one too? Was it the courage of which Adelaide spoke?

I'd never believed I had courage since I'd grown up anxious and fearful. But what if my courage ran deeper than my circumstances? What if I had always been stronger than I'd believed?

"What has the prince asked you to do?" Maribel queried innocently, clearly not realizing my ulterior motives for the visit the same way Adelaide had.

"While he may be kind and generous, he is still his

father's son." I kept my voice low. Rex was somewhere outside the tent, and I didn't know what—if anything—he could hear of our conversation. "His loyalty to the king takes precedence over me."

Adelaide glanced to the tent door and lowered her voice too. "The prince has shown his devotion to you by risking his life to come so near our camp with you. Alas, he would have been wiser to send his trusted men rather than expose himself to capture."

"He's a skilled warrior—"

"He loves you and has no wish to lose you."

Except for an infusion of warmth into my chest, I could find no ready response to Adelaide's declaration.

"He might remain loyal to his father," she continued, "but I see in him worthy qualities that may yet redeem him."

"He does have many worthy qualities," I concurred.

Maribel squeezed my hand again, this time admiring my ruby wedding ring. "He must, if he has gained your affection."

Adelaide shifted on her bench, her body tense. "Tell us why you are really here, Emmeline."

"She's here to meet us," Maribel started, but a sharp look from Adelaide silenced her.

If I told them the truth, maybe they'd be able to help me find a solution to my problems. What other choice did I have? Especially since I had no way of getting the ancient key from beneath Adelaide's armor.

"King Ethelwulf sent you to retrieve the final key," Adelaide stated without taking her gaze from my face.

I knew I should keep my expression impassive, but I was too impressed with her keenness to mask my surprise.

Apparently, my reaction was answer enough, for she shifted back on her bench, letting her body relax.

"I understand if you hate me now." I pulled my hand away from Maribel's and tucked it into my lap. "I deserve it. But I vow it was not my will or desire to deceive you or steal the key."

Adelaide watched me, her eyes clear as though she'd yet to condemn me.

"Although Rex allowed my parents to go free," I said, "King Ethelwulf sent his men out to seek and capture them."

"If only our scout had roused sooner," Maribel said compassionately, "perhaps Edmund and his men could have intercepted your parents first."

My mind returned to the first night of my capture and the battered man tied to the tree. My betrayer. Though I wanted to be angry at him, I couldn't fault him for capitulating under torture.

"The scout was unconscious and barely alive when Edmund's men discovered him," Maribel continued. "They had to leave him behind in the care of a woodcutter. Edmund said they didn't know for sure if the prince had you, but with his hasty departure, they suspected as much and began their chase after him with little thought to what had become of your parents, believing them dead."

I nodded in understanding. My parents weren't their concern, not when so much else had been at stake—and still was.

"I am sorry, Emmeline," Maribel whispered, her eyes filling with tears. "I wish now Edmund and his men had tried to find your home and your parents before leaving the forest."

"They did what they thought was best," I replied, feeling no ill will toward the rebels or my sisters. How could I, when I'd plotted deception against them?

"I am not surprised the king would aspire to have Lance and Felicia," Adelaide added.

"Now they languish in the dungeons where the king has ordered them to be tortured and killed. If I bring him the key, he will spare one of them."

"Oh, Emmeline," Maribel murmured with such depth of emotion I couldn't hold back my tears. They spilled over and began to run down my cheeks, even though I swiped at them.

"My parents were good to me and made so many sacrifices. I cannot bear to think of their suffering."

"We cannot bear it, either!" Maribel said, tears wetting her cheeks too.

Adelaide pressed a finger against her lips as her attention shifted to the tent walls and door.

Maribel dropped to a whisper. "They saved us all those years ago. We must do something now to save them, Adelaide."

For several long moments, Adelaide sat in contemplation, so that the outside sounds penetrated the thin canvas and brought the distant grinding of iron against whetstones, the clanking of swords from soldiers still at drill, and the deep voices of men in conversation.

"His desperation for the key and the treasure means only one thing," Adelaide finally spoke. "He is looking for a way to pay mercenaries to come to his aid."

"I wish I knew," I said. "But I admit I haven't pried for information the way I could have."

Adelaide stared at the tent wall as if staring into the future. "If the king finds the treasure, he will have riches to hire half the continent to fight on his behalf."

"But no one knows for certain if the treasure still remains," Maribel said.

"It does," I remarked.

At my quick affirmation, they both turned wide eyes upon me.

"I've read enough of the ancient history texts to know that King Solomon's ancient treasure has most certainly been preserved. In fact, from the various records I've come across, different powerful kings have added wealth so that the treasure far exceeds what it was in King Solomon's day."

While I'd always known the books hidden in our cottage had been rare, it hadn't been until I'd ventured into the Delsworth scriptorium that I truly grasped their worth. From browsing the titles filling the scriptorium, I'd realized there were no other books anywhere about the labyrinth, that perhaps someone long ago had made a point of pulling all traces of the labyrinth and its clues from the shelves. That meant I'd accumulated a wealth of information regarding the labyrinth that no one else had. Did that also mean I bore an even greater responsibility to my family and to Mercia than I'd realized?

"During the reign of King William, the great-great-grandfather of Alfred the Peacemaker," I continued with what I'd learned, "the kingdom was threatened by invasion. King William secretly finished carving out the ruins of a labyrinth left from ancient times. He moved the treasure into the labyrinth and made sure it was full of deadly traps as well as beasts to act as guardians."

Maribel nodded. "Edmund and I faced a few traps and a terrible beast while we were in the Labyrinth of Death. It was horrific and deadly during the long hours we were within its confines."

As she shared her experience down in the depths of the labyrinth, I listened with fascination and plied her with questions. I was particularly interested in her encounter with the dragon-like creature and in knowing she'd helped to heal it. I was also impressed she and Edmund had managed to navigate the outer rim and find another entrance with only their third of the map.

"Although I wanted to explore further in," Maribel finished, "Edmund said we must not attempt it without a complete map."

"Even with a complete map," I replied, "the treasure was—and still is—nearly impossible to claim."

Adelaide pushed her bench away from the table. "Then you do not believe the king will be able to retrieve it even with the third and final key?"

"Without the right knowledge and guidance, any attempt would be foolhardy."

"If he is desperate, he will surely try."

"Then he will send his men to certain death."

Adelaide was quiet again, perhaps deep in thought or prayer—or both. "When Sister Katherine came to visit Maribel and me, she told us both about an old prophecy that foretells a young ruler filled with wisdom who will use the ancient treasure to help drive evil from the land and usher in a time of peace like never before seen or ever seen again."

"Yes," I answered. "I've read the prophecy in the Book of Dierum. But how can you know for certain if you are that young ruler?"

Adelaide shrugged. "Sister Katherine believed I was and insisted the three of us be reunited so we can use the keys to unlock a treasure that will help restore the land."

"I would like nothing more than a time of peace and restoration rather than continued war and discord. In fact, I'd hoped in part that my marriage to Prince Ethelrex would bring about peace."

"Perhaps it still shall," Adelaide said but her tone was too vague to assure me.

"Then you are of the same mind as Sister Katherine, that unlocking the treasure is necessary for peace?"

"I do not have all the answers to the riddle yet. But I am coming to believe perhaps real treasure lies not in the wealth deep in the labyrinth, but in the gifts God has bestowed upon us—gifts we can use for the greater good of the kingdom and the people."

Everything Adelaide said resonated within me. Even so, I was caught in the middle of the battle over the throne. While I admired Adelaide and wished I could join her, I couldn't abandon my parents and their plight. And I wasn't sure I could yet abandon Rex either.

Adelaide stood and stretched. "Both of you must help me shed my armor."

Maribel hastened to obey, but I held back.

"Come now, Emmeline." Adelaide beckoned. "Do not be shy now. I am giving you the chance to take what you came for."

My mouth dropped open, and I could only stare at my sister.

Maribel smiled at me even as she worked to unlace the pauldron upon Adelaide's shoulder.

I still couldn't move.

"You will tell the prince you did what you came to do," Adelaide said. "In so doing, you will save one of your parents. It is the least we can do for them."

Relief and gratitude swelled within my chest. I tried to stand to thank Adelaide, but instead I fell to my knees, buried my face in my hands, and wept.

Chapter
16

REX

THE EARL OF LANGLEY WAS A CUNNING MAN AND KEPT ME occupied with conversation and food during the entire visit so that I had no choice but to sit with him at the table his men brought into the clearing.

The spot was far enough from the queen's tent to allow the women privacy. But it was also close enough I could hear Emmeline shout if she was in any distress. Even so, I didn't let down my guard. I knew that in coming with Emmeline rather than allowing my guards to escort her, I was in imminent danger. What would the king say when he learned I'd put myself in such a position? Would he care?

Of course, he'd care, I told myself. If the enemy decided to hold me for ransom, he'd do everything he could to save me. Wouldn't he?

When the tent flap opened and Emmeline finally ducked through, I expelled my first full breath since she'd disappeared inside.

The earl's eyes were upon me. "I did not expect to like you."

"There is no reason you should." I assessed Emmeline, making sure she was unharmed. Other than the flush of her cheeks and the redness around her eyes, not a detail had changed.

She scanned the open area until she found me. Although she didn't meet my eyes, the slight release of tension from her shoulders told me she'd been worried about me. It also reaffirmed what her kiss had shown—that perhaps she would be quicker to forgive than I deserved.

I stood. "I am your enemy, Lord Langley. If we meet on the battlefield, I shall kill you."

"And I, you."

I had no doubt he'd be a formidable foe. His reputation in Norland fighting for King Draybane preceded him. Nevertheless, I was more skilled than he and would vanquish him eventually.

"Even so," the earl said, "I like you. I did not believe such a thing possible considering my fierce hatred of your father."

I finally spared the earl a glance to find his eyes somber and his expression sincere. I had the feeling if we hadn't been on opposing sides of this war I might have liked him too. However, he was the husband of the greatest threat to my future ascension as king. As such, I ought to plunge my dagger through his heart and be done with him.

But as he and his men had shown honor toward me and the white flag we'd raised, I could do no less than honor him at this moment. "I thank you for your kind treatment of my wife."

"I can see that you are kind to her as well."

I wasn't sure I'd treated her kindly of late. But his

affirmation was a dose of encouragement I needed after my recent failure to make her happy.

If the king didn't find the treasure to hire the Danes, I feared we'd have a difficult siege, and the battle with the queen's army would drag on. If things didn't go our way, Langley was the type of warrior who would act swiftly and decisively to bring about a victory.

"I pray that whatever the future holds," I said, "you will continue to show Emmeline kindness regardless of my fate."

"Of course. I shall endeavor to keep her safe."

I nodded my thanks. Then I motioned to my men that it was time to go.

We rode in silence back into Delsworth. Once the city gates clanged shut behind us, I slowed my horse to a trot next to Emmeline.

She'd been quiet since leaving Adelaide's tent, giving me no indication whether she'd found the key or not. From the slight redness rimming her eyes, I guessed she'd cried during her meeting with her sisters. I could only imagine what the reunion had been like—meeting family for the first time.

From the night I'd spent on her floor, she'd shared enough for me to know she'd had a happy childhood, that Lance and Felicia had been good to her, and that she hadn't been lonely. Even so, I'd learned that fears overtook her at times—fears likely borne of always hiding and waiting to be discovered.

If only she'd had the chance for a carefree childhood.

One without any worries. One with the sisters who obviously loved her. Perhaps, in spite of forcing her to get the key, some good had come out of the occasion because she'd finally been able to meet her sisters.

"I pray your visit with your sisters went well," I offered, my voice stiffer and more formal than I wanted it to be.

"You needn't worry any longer." She tossed her pouch to me.

I caught it easily. Through the leather, I could feel the design of the key, its weight, even the engraving on the bit, so similar and yet so different from the other two.

"I accomplished what you desired."

What the *king* desired. But instead of correcting her I pressed on and gentled my tone. "I do hope the reunion was satisfying."

She bit her bottom lip, which served only to remind me of the kiss I'd taken from her before her meeting with the queen. That kiss had been intended to show everyone Emmeline was mine. Why, then, had the kiss weakened me and made me feel as though Emmeline had ownership of me instead?

"Did you like them?" I tore my mind from thoughts of kissing her again.

"I loved them." Sudden bright tears shone in her eyes.

I reached for her hand and twined my fingers through hers. I was thankful when she didn't pull away.

"I regret I resisted meeting them for so long," she said. "Maybe if I'd left for Norland earlier when my father first suggested it . . ."

If she'd gone, would I have been able to find her? Would I have missed the chance to have her for my wife? Now that I had her, I couldn't imagine ever wanting anyone else. But clearly, she didn't feel as deeply about me if she wished she could have left the country before I'd found her.

I needed to work harder to win her, especially since she blamed me for the king's decision regarding her parents. Could I convince him to spare them, perhaps hold them as prisoners in the tower rather than execute them? I doubted there was anything I could say to change his mind. In fact, I suspected contradicting him would make matters only worse for her parents. And yet, I had to do something, didn't I?

When we finally entered the castle grounds, I didn't want to release my hold of her hand and break the tenuous connection we'd formed again. So after helping her from her horse, I swept her into my arms and carried her inside. She didn't resist and leaned her head against my shoulder as I made my way to her room.

Once there, I reluctantly lowered her. The king would be waiting for my report on every detail regarding our time with the enemy. He'd want to know about their size, the strength of their siege engines, and any plans I'd overheard.

Most of all he'd want the key.

Regardless, I couldn't make myself turn and walk away yet.

Ruby bounded over to Emmeline, and she bent to scratch the pup's head. The servants had discreetly disappeared, which only made me want to linger and take advantage of the moment of privacy.

As though sensing my need, Emmeline straightened and faced me, her expression turning serious. Even then, she was more beautiful than both her sisters. I reached out and brushed her long hair off her shoulder and in the process let my fingers graze her neck.

At the contact, she drew in a breath.

My attention fell to the rise of her chest, the elegance of her neck, and the pounding pulse at the hollow of her throat. I brushed the hair off her other shoulder, once more letting my fingers skim her neck.

Her breath hitched again, and she closed her eyes as though the merest of my touches could vanquish her resistance. Could it? The kiss earlier had certainly helped. Dare I try it again?

"Rex." She spoke my name in a breathy whisper.

With her neck so close and beckoning, I angled in and brushed a kiss there.

She arched back, giving me more access. It was an invitation I couldn't refuse—didn't want to refuse. I pressed a kiss higher beneath her chin, relishing the softness and sweetness of her skin.

"Rex," she whispered. "Please, will you not ask your father to spare both my parents?"

At that moment, I wanted to give her the world and everything in it. If I'd wondered whether I was in love with her, I had no doubt any longer. I loved her and needed her and wanted her happiness more than anything.

Though I yearned to continue my path up her neck to her lips, I gathered her into my arms, wanting to prove to myself and her that my intentions were honorable, that in response to her request I'd ask for nothing in return.

"Yes," I whispered. "I shall ask him."

She nestled against me. "Thank you."

I rested my chin on her head. "My plea may do no good."

"I know. But I'm grateful you will consider it."

She knew enough about the king to realize he was not

easily swayed, not even by his sons.

I wanted to believe that if the matter was truly imperative to me, the king would listen and try to understand my perspective. But a dark, hidden part of me feared I wasn't important enough to him. It was the same part that a short while ago, during the meeting with the rebels, had wondered what the king would do if the enemy decided to make me their prisoner. What would he have sacrificed to get me back? The keys? The treasure? Even his kingdom?

Although I didn't want to admit the answer, the truth sometimes had a way of creeping out and haunting me—the truth that the keys and treasure and his kingdom were more valuable than his sons, perhaps even more than his beloved wife.

"I see I am interrupting you newlyweds." The king's voice came from the doorway.

Emmeline tugged away from me, her lashes dropping against flushed cheeks, making her all the more appealing. As the king crossed into the room, I looped my arm around her and drew her to my side. In the hallway behind him stood several other men, half peeking, probably curious to know what the king had interrupted.

"The key?" He got straight to the point, clearly anxious enough to seek me out rather than waiting for me to petition for an audience with him.

I loosened the pouch and tugged out the third ancient key. I studied it only momentarily before releasing Emmeline, striding to the king, and kneeling. I bowed my head and then held out the key as my gift to him. "Your Majesty."

He snatched it from my outstretched hands and began to examine it. I stayed on my knees a moment longer, waiting for his words of approval, even a brief offer of thanks. But he was too busy scrutinizing the artifact.

Steeling myself, I stood and returned to Emmeline's side. "Since Emmeline did so well with what we requested, I suggest we give her the release of both parents."

The king looked up. "Since she did so well, I suggest we keep them both right where they are, as we may have use of them again."

"No!" Emmeline cried.

I quickly cupped my hand over her mouth before she could say something that would only anger the king and make matters worse. She struggled against me, but at my warning glare, she ceased thrashing.

The king watched our interaction with raised brows before returning his attention to the key.

"Your Majesty," I continued, "we promised we would release one of her parents—"

"If you are to be a great king, you must learn to take advantage of people's weaknesses whenever possible."

My frustration quickly reached the surface, but I had to mask it lest the king conceive it as a weakness. "If you will not do it for Emmeline, I ask that you consider freeing them for me."

I'd never asked anything of the king before, and I prayed he would realize how rare my request was.

His eyes swung back to me.

"You would do anything for Mother, to make her happy, would you not?"

"Of course."

"It is the same for me. I only follow your worthy example and wish to make my wife as happy as you have made yours."

"If you wish to follow my example, then you will not allow your wife to control you." His gaze was sharp, even piercing, the kind of look he bestowed upon those who displeased him.

I stiffened, wanting to blurt out that Emmeline didn't control me, that rather my love for her did. But I couldn't say it, not now, not under these circumstances.

"Ready yourself and your men to leave for the labyrinth within the hour," the king commanded. "The sooner you can get there and back, the better."

Before I could manage a bow, Emmeline pulled away from me, her eyes wide with horror. "You're going to the labyrinth?" I started to nod, but she cut me off. "You can't possibly go. It's much too dangerous."

"I am not afraid of danger, Emmeline. You should know that by now."

"You don't understand. The labyrinth is a death trap. You and your men will never make it to the treasure alive."

"How can you be so sure?" The king watched Emmeline with a calculated look that set off a warning inside me.

"Because the designer was none other than the great historian himself, Saint Bede, who was the personal scribe to King William."

"And why should that matter?"

"Bede's historical accounts are full of clues to the deadly snares he placed in the labyrinth."

"And you know these clues?" the king asked.

The warning clamored louder. Emmeline needed to be silent and say no more, but I was helpless to stop the king's questioning.

"Yes," Emmeline replied, pulling herself up proudly. "I

have read nearly every one of Bede's books multiple times, and my father and I plotted the location of his traps within the labyrinth as well as the methods for bypassing them."

"How can you know so much when the greatest scholars in the kingdom remain ignorant?"

I tugged at Emmeline's arm, warning her to silence, but she only jerked herself free. "Most, if not all, of Bede's manuscripts were hidden in the cottage where I grew up. I spent much time analyzing the riddles and clues inside the books."

"Then your map?" the king persisted "It is accurate?"

"I believe mostly so—"

"Then you will travel with the prince to the labyrinth, guide him through it, and protect him from the traps."

My heart ceased thudding at the same moment Emmeline recoiled. The king wasn't serious, was he?

"I cannot go—" Emmeline started.

"I will not take her," I cut her off with the first words of defiance I'd ever uttered to the king.

"You must." The king's penetrating eyes narrowed upon me, then Emmeline.

"You would never ask Mother to do anything so dangerous." I could not halt my objection even though I was moving onto dangerous ground. "How, then, can you expect me to take my bride into so deadly a place?"

"She is needed to gain the treasure."

Apparently, not only was the king calloused to my feelings in the matter, but he placed little value on Emmeline's life if he could so easily send her into danger. How could he be so cruel to me after all I'd done for him to prove my loyalty?

"Please, Father. She is my wife. And I—I love her." The

words came out a desperate plea. I was once again counting on the king's love of my mother and praying he'd understand and empathize with my feelings for Emmeline. I didn't dare look at Emmeline for fear of her reaction. Perhaps it was too soon for her to know the truth about how I felt, but it was out now, and I wouldn't take it back.

"Do not speak to me of love." Instead of understanding, the king's eyes filled with contempt. "You hardly know the princess."

"I know her well enough."

"If we gain the treasure, you will not need her anymore."

"Not need her?"

"She can easily be put aside for a better alliance."

"I made vows to her I intend to keep—"

"Enough!" The king's voice bellowed through the chamber. In the doorway, I could see the men in the hallway scurry away, clearly afraid of the king's unpredictability when angered.

The king's features were taut, and his eyes blazed with a fury I'd seldom seen. Fury I'd worked hard to avoid but was now directed at me. I'd crossed a line in not only defying him but also in showing and voicing my emotions. Now that it was crossed, I couldn't go back.

Neither could I go forward. I'd pushed the king far enough and would only further endanger Emmeline if I persisted.

As though understanding the same, Emmeline's shaking fingers slid into mine. "Have no fear, Your Majesty. I'll go with the prince and help him find the treasure."

Though I loathed the thought of her joining the

mission, the determined jut of Emmeline's chin told me that even if I could somehow manage the impossible task of getting the king to change his mind, I would never change hers.

Chapter 17

Emmeline

We traveled for five days and nights without stopping—first by boat up the Cress River and next by horse into the Iron Hills. After my previous journey with Rex from Inglewood Forest to Delsworth, I should have been prepared for his unrelenting pace. But by the end of the fifth day, I was weary and sore.

I suspected without me, he would have pushed even harder and made fewer and shorter stops. I had my own mount, which aided our speed and endurance. Nevertheless, I could see the furrows in his forehead grow deeper every time he glanced over his shoulder to the south. He didn't have to say anything for me to guess we were being followed.

I had no doubt the moment Adelaide heard we were on the way to the labyrinth, she'd dispatched her warriors to stop us. I'd reassured her the king wouldn't be able to get the treasure, that it would be nearly impossible to attain. As a result, she'd entrusted me with the third key. What must she think of me now?

I could only hang my head in shame. Maybe she hadn't seen my marriage to Rex as a betrayal of her cause. But, after learning I was with Rex and his group, she'd see me for the coward I truly was and despise me. Rather than standing strong against King Ethelwulf, I'd given in to the enemy just as I had all along.

At least in sneaking away from the castle and Delsworth with Rex and his knights, I'd discovered a new secret passageway I might be able to use in freeing my parents from the castle after our return—if we returned.

The tunnel wasn't the same one my parents had used to escape when Maribel and I had been only hours old. But from Lance's description, I guessed it was similar, running under the moat and opening up into the dense forestland to the west of the castle. Though I'd been terrified each step through the passageway, I'd pushed myself forward, knowing I had to stay strong so I could come back again and lead my parents to freedom.

Ahead, Rex led us in single file up the narrow rocky path. The summer sun had been especially harsh since reaching the Highlands, where even the tallest crags provided little shade. In spite of the cooler air, I was parched and hot and ready to sleep a few hours— somewhere besides the bottom of a boat or on the back of my horse.

The soldiers riding directly in front of me picked up their pace, sending a shower of pebbles down the steep ridge. I nudged my horse onward and prayed Adelaide would forgive me again and understand I'd had no choice but to accompany Rex.

Would Father be able to forgive me for using my knowledge to help the enemy? All the while we'd studied the labyrinth together, he'd believed that someday I'd use the details to help my sisters. Little had he known I'd wield the information against them.

Even if King Ethelwulf hadn't ordered me to go, I wouldn't have let the prince navigate the labyrinth without my help. There was a reason it was called the Labyrinth of Death. So many had lost their lives that eventually the labyrinth had been sealed off and forgotten.

The truth was despite my knowledge of the traps, we'd still face many unknowns, including the creatures who guarded the treasure. I didn't know how many beasts remained or where they'd be, and if we could outsmart or outfight them.

And I didn't know how I'd be able to crawl down into the tight, dark confines of the labyrinth without panicking. Even now, thinking about the damp walls pressing in made my pulse speed erratically and my stomach roil. What if I got down into the labyrinth and froze with fear?

I held my reins tighter, wincing at the pain of the blisters on my palm. I couldn't think about myself. I had to focus on Rex. Keeping him alive in the labyrinth took priority.

Although we'd had little chance to speak to each other privately over the past days of travel, my longing for him had been growing, especially every time I thought about his bold declaration to his father. *She is my wife. And I love her.*

Maybe at first his decision to love me had been prompted by his marriage vow and his determination to be a man of honor. He'd made an effort to love me with his actions, showing me kindness and consideration.

But somewhere along the way, his love had become more than mere actions. His declaration had contained a deep emotion that beckoned my heart to respond with the same. Could I love him back? Or would his loyalty and faithfulness to his father stand in the way?

The king's true feelings about me had come out in our last conversation—he held no affection for me. I hadn't expected affinity. Nor had I expected devotion. But I had hoped after he'd gone to such lengths to secure my future to Rex's, that he'd accept me.

As it turned out, however, he'd never planned to keep me. Perhaps all along he'd intended to get rid of me when he no longer needed me so he could form a more profitable marriage alliance for Rex. He'd likely have me murdered so the people would never suspect his hand in it.

I shivered at the thought, even with the sun beating down relentlessly.

How far would Rex go to defy his father's wishes? That last moment in my chamber, Rex had spoken out on behalf of my parents and had objected to bringing me on this trip. But he'd accomplished nothing except to anger the king. If Rex had pushed harder to keep me home, as I'd been afraid he'd do, I'd feared he'd only jeopardize his own safety with the king.

I'd pondered the dilemma the entire journey, but I'd been unable to see a way out of the predicament in which we found ourselves. Though he might care for me—even love me—he was helpless to protect my parents, or even me, without incurring the king's wrath upon himself.

In some ways, he was at the mercy of the king too.

At the very least, I could take comfort that Rex had commanded the guards to keep my parents safe during our absence and had forbidden Magnus to start any torture. Even though Rex was doing what he could to compensate for his father's decision, how long could he go on without having to choose between loving me and serving his father?

As my horse scrambled up the last incline, the reins dug into my tender flesh until the warmth of blood oozed between my fingers. At the top, I drew in a breath of relief to find the rest of the party dismounting.

Rex strode toward me, his face dark with stubble and the dust of the trail. His hair was lighter as if it had soaked in the sun's rays. As his blue eyes met mine, my pulse hopped with the need to be with him.

"I didn't expect another break so soon." I flexed my sore back.

He reached up and lifted me down. "We have arrived. The entrance is within that cave."

I followed his nod to a gaping black arch in the bedrock where several soldiers were unloading our packs of food. The interior of the cavern was dark and narrow. How could I go in there? I looked away from it and attempted to swallow my fear. "Are we eating before we enter?"

He peered past me over the miles of rocky terrain we'd traversed. "The queen's party has dropped behind."

I searched the crags and boulders for any signs of movement or dust and saw nothing. "What can that mean?"

"It likely means they have finally stopped for a break."

I wasn't so sure and couldn't keep my disappointment at bay. In some ways, I supposed I'd been hoping they'd intercept us and take the key back so we wouldn't have to go into the labyrinth after all. In fact, what if she'd purposefully given me the key so that I'd set into motion this treasure hunt and draw all three keys out of Delsworth where she could more easily recover them?

"Since we have a lead," Rex continued, "I have decided we shall eat and rest momentarily before we begin the next part of our journey."

"I won't protest." I brushed back a strand of hair, then winced.

He captured my hand before I could hide it and frowned at the sight of the blood there. "You are hurt."

I tried to free my hand. "It's nothing to worry about. Only a few blisters."

With a grumble under his breath, he scooped me up and began to carry me.

I couldn't contain a smile. "I'm perfectly capable of walking. My fingers hurt, not my feet."

He didn't smile. "You should have told me you had blisters."

"And have you decide to leave me behind? No, I won't let you get rid of me that easily." I snuggled against him, relishing the closeness after the days of riding apart.

He called out orders for one of his men to bring him the medical supplies. As we neared the cave, I slipped my arm around his neck and stared at the opening. "Do we need to go inside? Can we not stay out here?"

"There is a smaller second cave next to the larger one. And we shall rest there with more privacy."

If it was smaller, I'd like it even less.

Rex ducked into the opening of the side cavern. Though bright sunlight angled in to fill the room, I was reluctant to release my hold from Rex's neck when he lowered me to a pallet that had already been unrolled.

"Emmeline," he chastised softly as he unhooked my arms. "You have nothing to fear here."

I had everything to fear—especially that I'd lose him when I'd just begun to care about him. I nodded and attempted to hide my quaking. If he suspected my aversion to tight, dark spaces, he'd probably insist I stay behind, and I couldn't let that happen.

For a short while, a young soldier tended my bloody hands while Rex conversed outside the cave with his men. Once the soldier left, Rex returned with a pouch of food and his leather water bag. He spread out cheese, figs, and dried meat then sat down next to me on the pallet.

"This cavern probably served as home to a guardian of the labyrinth," I mused as we ate.

"To keep away intruders?" Rex asked, leaning back on one elbow, his legs stretched out in front of him.

"No. More likely to warn people not to go inside."

Rex paused in his chewing.

"Must we go into it?" I asked, unable to stop my desperation from rising. "Your father will never be the wiser."

Rex resumed eating, studying my face, almost as if he was memorizing every detail.

"Please, Rex."

"The king will expect me to return with the

treasure or return not at all."

Aside from my aversion to cramped dark places, the dangers below were innumerable and the mission nearly impossible. Even with my knowledge of the labyrinth, there was the very real chance of never coming out alive. I couldn't bear the thought that we might be throwing away our lives for a man like King Ethelwulf. "Why must you bend to his every whim?"

"He is my king and my father and as such deserves my honor and service."

"But why should you care so much about pleasing him when he cares so little for you in return?"

"He does care. Maybe not in a way you can see."

"I see nothing but a selfish man who only values how the people in his life benefit him and not how he might sacrifice for them."

Rex stiffened and began to stand.

I grabbed his arm, regardless of the pain to my blistered hands. "Rex, wait."

He halted, halfway up, his back towards me.

"I'm sorry." I tugged him, wanting him to stay, needing just a little more time alone with him.

He didn't bend. "You should rest."

I didn't want our private moment to end like this, with him aloof and upset. "Please don't go," I whispered. "Rest with me."

Slowly he pivoted, his eyes questioning.

I pushed aside the remaining food. Then I pulled him down with me, my eyes beckoning him. This time he didn't resist. He came willingly, stretching out next to me and holding me close.

Within the confines of his solid chest and thick arms, I barely had time to release a contented breath before his lips covered mine, moving desperately and deeply as if he too recognized the danger of what we were about to do.

The kiss was consuming and yet contained a sadness that made my insides ache. I didn't realize my tears had escaped until his lips broke from mine and he gently began to kiss them away.

"I meant what I said," he whispered, letting his lips linger against my forehead. "I love you."

More tears squeezed out. "I love you, too." I'd denied my growing feelings long enough. Why deny them any longer when we were leaving for so dangerous a journey?

At my confession, he pressed another kiss hard against my forehead before pulling back and cradling me gently against his chest.

"Rest now," he whispered.

With his steady breath upon my temple, I closed my eyes and allowed myself to fall asleep, praying I'd have many more days to sleep in his arms and resisting the prospect that this might be my last.

Chapter
18

Emmeline

I awoke to silence and thoughts of Rex—of his body next to mine, of his warm breath against my brow, of his strong arms enfolding me. Yet as I stirred, the space around me felt strangely empty.

"Rex." I reached for him but found a deserted pallet, lacking not only his warmth, but him.

My eyes flew open, and I pushed myself up. A sweeping glance around the cave told me he was gone, and the coldness of the pallet confirmed he'd been away for a while.

I listened for his voice outside barking orders to his men and for the general sounds of camp, but only the lonely whistle of wind greeted me.

My heart sped, and I scrambled to my feet. From the waning sunlight, I guessed I'd slept for an hour or more. As I stepped out of the cave, I berated myself for being so careless. At the emptiness of the camp, I stopped abruptly.

The horses were tied and resting in the shadows of

the caves, and only a lone sentinel on watch stood a distance away. There were no campfires, and nothing had been unpacked, almost as if Rex had never had any intention of allowing his men to rest before going down into the labyrinth. He'd only expected *me* to rest . . .

So he could leave me behind.

I released a huff of frustration.

Perhaps he'd been planning all along to keep me out of the labyrinth and had only brought me to appease his father.

With a burst of determination, I started toward the mouth of the larger cave. Even if he had a lead, I could easily find his trail and track him. Maybe if I hurried, I'd yet have time to intercept him before he and his men left the outer rim and headed into the deadly marked tunnels.

Upon entering, I halted at the sight of two knights standing in front of a gravel pit. I should have known he'd leave guards behind to stop me from following him.

They straightened to their fullest attention.

"How long has the prince been gone?" I asked.

One of the soldiers gave a slight bow. "Your Highness, the prince instructed us not to give you any information."

It didn't really matter. Whether he'd left sooner or later, I'd have to hurry to catch up.

The flat ceiling, the chiseled walls, the loose debris—even if I hadn't known this was one of the labyrinth entrances, I could have guessed it in no time. I swallowed my trepidation and crossed to the pit.

At my approach, both men raised their swords to

form a barrier. "The prince instructed us to keep you out of the labyrinth by any means necessary."

While he had my best interest at heart and was noble to the last, he was being foolhardy. Hadn't I warned him he'd need more than his brawn and elite guard skills to make it to the treasure? Even with my carefully drawn map, he wouldn't know how to navigate through all the traps.

I eyed the soldiers and slid my hand to the small of my back, looking for my knife, the one Rex had given to me the day I'd gone to visit my sisters. Since that time, he hadn't demanded its return. I hadn't been able to figure out why, other than that he trusted me not to run away. Or maybe he'd felt I'd need it for protection from the king? Or Magnus?

Feeling the emptiness there now, I silently railed against Rex. He'd likely anticipated my tactics and had divested me of any way to threaten these guards. Without a weapon, I'd be no match for them. They'd easily overpower me.

"Please," I said. "You have to understand the danger the prince and his men are heading into. I'm the only one who can lead them safely to the center. If you don't allow me inside, they'll all surely die."

"I'm sorry, Your Highness." The guard's expression remained unreadable. "But the prince said not to listen to any of the arguments you might offer."

I bit back my frustration at Rex, unwilling to take it out on these two poor souls who were only obeying him, as they should.

Just then distant echoes of shouts rose from the pit, followed by tortured screaming that made my blood run cold.

I wished I could gauge how far away the men were, but the hollowness of the tunnels made the estimation difficult. From the fear flaring to life in the eyes of the two soldiers, I guessed this wasn't the first time since standing guard that they'd had to listen to their comrades dying.

One thing was clear, if I didn't get down there soon, I'd lose Rex . . . if I hadn't already.

An hour later, I was no closer to entering the labyrinth. All my pleading and attacking hadn't moved the guards. Nor had the intermittent screams that rose from the pit.

With darkness descending, my only hope was to wait until sunset, steal a horse, and attempt to find one of the other labyrinth entrances—the eastern entrance that Maribel had spoken of in her tale of the time she'd spent in the labyrinth with Edmund. Though traversing the Highlands and locating another entrance would be difficult and dangerous in the dark, I'd have to rely on my father's training and pray for a cloudless night so I could use the stars to navigate.

I lowered myself down to a rock outside the cave when the whinny of a horse and the clatter of hooves brought me back to my feet. Had Adelaide's men finally caught up to us?

As several knights in black chain mail ascended the trail into the rocky clearing, I rose from my resting spot. The emblem upon their horses and cloaks matched those of Rex's men and not Adelaide's.

Had more of the king's soldiers been sent out? And if so, why?

As the incoming knights climbed the rise, one stood out among the others. With his dark hair, pointed beard, and penetrating eyes, he was none other than the king himself. At the sight of me near the cave, the king urged his horse faster toward me, even though the beast was clearly weary.

At his approach, I bowed my head to hide not only my surprise at his appearance but also my anticipation. Rex might not have wanted me to go inside the labyrinth, but his father would have no such qualms.

"Just as I suspected." The king halted his mare alongside me. "My son is too weak to accomplish the task."

Rex? Weak? If he believed his son was weak, then he didn't know him the way I did. "After the journey, I was exhausted, Your Majesty. And in the prince's haste to do your bidding, he chose not to wait for me to awaken from my slumber."

"Do my bidding?" The king's lips curled into a sneer as he dismounted. "I was quite clear what my bidding was, and he had not the heart nor the will to do it."

"I am to blame, Your Majesty." I wasn't sure why I felt such a deep need to protect Rex, but from the contempt lining the king's face, my defense was making no difference.

He cast a cursory glance around the camp before homing in on the arched entrance of the main cave. Then, without further stalling, he stalked inside. I followed behind, praying he would send me down immediately and put an end to my miserable waiting.

At the sight of the king, the guards Rex had left on

duty bowed. The king eyed them with disgust before motioning to his bodyguard. "Take them out and kill them both. And tell the rest of the men this is what happens to those who obey the prince rather than me."

Revulsion swelled swiftly, and I feared I would be sick. I covered my mouth and turned away, but not before the king saw my reaction.

"I am still the king," he said in a low voice, "and will not have you or anyone else forget it."

I nodded, too nauseous to speak.

More soldiers congregated inside the cave until the king glared at me. "You will lead me down to the treasure."

"You, Your Majesty? The labyrinth is no place for a king."

"Do you really think I shall allow my son to get the glory for finding the ancient treasure?" In the darkness of the cavern, his eyes glowed with excitement. "I have been waiting my whole life for this moment and plan to be the one to discover it."

"Then why send Rex—"

"Besides testing his loyalty, I also gave him a head start so that he and his men could secure the correct way there and eliminate the dangers."

Suddenly I understood. Adelaide hadn't been following closely behind as Rex had supposed. Rather, the king had trailed us, and he'd planned to come all this time. In spite of the enemy camped outside Delsworth, he was more interested in the treasure than anything else, including his son. In fact, he regarded his son's life so little, that he'd sent him into the labyrinth to face all the dangers on his behalf.

Within minutes, I found myself descending a steep

slope with the king and his men behind me. The farther down I went, the more my limbs shook until finally I slid the last dozen feet.

When I landed at the bottom with darkness and the tight confines of rock walls surrounding me, I bent over and retched.

Chapter 19

REX

I CREPT FORWARD, HOLDING OUT MY TORCH AND SCRUTINIZING the smooth gray walls for any indication of danger. I tested the pathway with my toes and ducked low to avoid brushing the ceiling with its sharp outcroppings.

Behind me, one of my men released a pained cry that sent fresh dread up my spine. With four out of my ten men dead, I couldn't lose anyone else—didn't want to lose anyone else.

Crouched low, I glanced over my shoulder. Alaric, one of my faithful soldiers, grimaced. "A knife, Your Highness. It came up from the ground and sliced through my sole."

A look at Alaric's boot confirmed his predicament. The point of a blade protruded out the top of his foot.

Did we dare attempt to pull it loose now? One wrong step and anyone of us might face the same fate.

In a split second, I made my decision. "Hold out your foot."

Alaric obeyed, and the two men near him lent their aid.

I grabbed the pearl handle wedged deeply through the boot and his foot. When I jerked it hard, it gave only a little. Alaric bit back a groan.

"Clasp his leg more securely," I ordered the other two.

As their grasps tightened, I yanked with both hands and felt the weapon give. With a final pull, it slid out. Blood coated it, while more now dribbled from the slice in Alaric's foot. I tossed the weapon to the floor. At the impact, another knife sprang up and protruded into the empty air.

I had to be more careful, had to focus every bit of my attention so I could find the traps before they found us.

After traversing the outer rim of the labyrinth the first hour and avoiding the obvious obstacles, I'd grown too confident and comfortable. I realized now that the designer had intended to lure intruders into a false security so they'd become unguarded and lazy, therefore more susceptible to the deadly traps in the tunnels marked with letters.

Emmeline's warning was never far from my mind: *The labyrinth is a death trap. You and your men will never make it to the treasure alive.*

Maybe I should have had her school me in everything she knew about the labyrinth before coming down. In doing so, she would have suspected I was going without her and would have found a way to stay with me—although I could have tied her up and forced her to remain, regardless of how angry she might have been.

It didn't matter anymore. What was done, was done. As I skimmed my fingers along the cold stone, I attempted to calm my racing pulse. My nervousness would only make me more jittery and more unaware.

At several points, I thought I heard distant voices.

Another time, I paused at the far-off roar of a beast to the north. I suspected for now we were safe from any of the creatures roaming the labyrinth, that they avoided the middle area because of the poisons that came from out of nowhere, the pits that swallowed men up whole and then disappeared, and the pikes that slid out from the walls in random places, impaling whoever was in the path.

By now, Emmeline would have awoken and realized I'd left without her. I could only pray she hadn't managed to outsmart my guards and enter the labyrinth. Hopefully, they were following my instructions and holding her at bay. I'd told them that if I didn't return within twenty-four hours, they were to take Emmeline to the queen and ask her for sanctuary.

In all likelihood, the queen's small army would arrive while we were down in the labyrinth. I had no doubt she had spies all around Delsworth, all the way to the Cress River. They'd likely seen us rowing upriver and gone back to her with news of our leaving. Perhaps she planned to let us do the deadly work of locating the treasure only to fight us for it once we exited the labyrinth.

I was counting on the men I'd left behind to defend our position until we returned to the surface. However, even if we survived the labyrinth and won the skirmish against the queen's forces, I couldn't keep from wondering if Emmeline should go to her sisters anyway. She'd be safer with them, out of the reaches of the king, who'd made it all too clear he didn't care if Emmeline was dead or alive.

During the long journey into the Highlands, I'd had too much time to think about all the king had said and what he was asking me to do. And with each passing day, my bitterness had eaten away until acid churned in my gut.

How could he expect me to give up Emmeline?

He'd been the one to set the example of how to love a wife. He'd treated Mother with such devotion that I'd vowed I would do the same with my wife. Now that I was married and attempting to cherish my wife in a similar fashion, how could he undermine me? How could he value Emmeline's life so little and ask me to do things he'd never consider?

I didn't understand his double standard. Mostly, I didn't understand why he was unwilling to show compassion toward me after my complete devotion to him.

Emmeline's words from earlier came back unbidden: *Why should you care so much about pleasing him when he cares so little for you in return?*

I didn't want to believe her. But what if she was right?

"Rex?" Her voice cut faintly through the chilled air, causing me to hold up a hand and motion everyone not to make a sound.

I didn't move and fervently prayed her voice was only a figment of my imagination.

"You're on the wrong path." This time her voice echoed through the hollow tunnels much more clearly.

Anger, close to rage, burst through my insides and ravaged what was left. I would kill my guards for falling prey to her whims. I'd warned them severely to resist her every effort to come down, and they'd disobeyed.

"Emmeline, leave the labyrinth at once!"

"I can't." Her words wobbled with fear.

My gut clenched with the knowledge that something was wrong. But I wasn't in a position to discover what it was.

"If you've reached section double R," she continued

urgently, "then you must retreat, keeping to the right side of the path and using only your right hand to guide you."

Already my men had moved to do as she'd instructed, retreating slowly and staying to the right side.

"When you leave double R, you must enter section C and immediately begin crawling as low to the ground as you can go until you intersect with W. Once there, you have to move always to the west."

I motioned for my rear guard to show me the map and quickly found the spot, assessing where she was leading us. So far, her directions seemed sound enough.

For long minutes, she guided us through several sections safely, her voice growing louder until we rounded a bend and she waited at the other end of a passageway that was narrower than any we'd yet traversed. In the small alcove behind her stood a dozen more soldiers.

And the king.

As my eyes connected with hers across the distance, I finally understood why she was here. It had nothing to do with my guards. The king had come after the treasure for himself. I should have known that with his obsession, he wouldn't be able to stay away, not when it was within his grasp. Had he been on my trail the whole ride, rather than the rebel's contingent?

The king stepped next to Emmeline. "Son, I am disappointed you disregarded my instructions." Although his tone was pleasant enough, the hardness of his features spoke louder. I'd offended him and would pay for it.

I knew I ought to bend my knee and beg his forgiveness. But I couldn't make myself bow. Another look at Emmeline's pale face and the fear radiating from her eyes only made my fury blaze hotter.

Even if Emmeline was an expert on the traps within

the tunnels, the king had no right forcing her down here.

"You have always had a propensity to be too soft," he said. "And a soft king is a weak king."

Maybe I was softer at heart than he was. And maybe that made me weaker. But at this moment, I didn't care.

"Perhaps I was wrong in thinking you should inherit my throne," he said, as though reading my defiant thoughts. "Maybe Magnus is the one I should have been grooming. He can do the hard things without failing me."

Magnus? I stiffened in protest. The king wouldn't truly consider raising my brother above me? Not after how diligently I'd worked all these years to train my body and mind in readiness for leading a nation. Not after the past year of fortifying his army and city in preparation for war. Not after the difficult things I'd forced myself to do to prove my loyalty—like carrying out his arrests, torturing people for information, and even capturing and marrying Emmeline.

How could the king so easily disregard all I'd done for him—all that I was even now doing by seeking the treasure he wanted, a treasure I'd never desired the same way he had. I'd jeopardized my own life and the lives of my men on this mission in order to prove again that I was worthy of the kingship. And now he would so easily hand the throne over to Magnus, who'd never done anything worthwhile?

An angry retort pushed for release, but I bit it back.

"I should have left you and your men to die down here," the king continued, "as a fitting punishment for your disobedience. But I shall allow you to atone for your mistake by leading us to the treasure and showing your allegiance."

"Showing my allegiance?" My voice came out harder

than I intended. "Have I not already demonstrated it in my willingness to sacrifice my life?"

"You must prove it by your willingness to give up what was never truly yours to begin with."

Emmeline. He wanted me to sacrifice Emmeline as the ultimate proof of my loyalty to him. Something akin to hatred burned in my veins, but I was helpless to act on it.

His tight smile only taunted me. "Shall we move on, Princess? I have a feeling you will be extra careful where you guide us, now that your husband has joined us."

Not only was he manipulating me, but he was manipulating Emmeline to do his bidding by making me the bait.

For a long second, I could only stare at the king and see myself reflected in all his tactics. What made me any different? After all, I'd manipulated Emmeline into doing my will too. I'd coerced, forced, threatened, and even demanded she do whatever I asked without thought to what she would have to give up or suffer as a result.

"Let us be on our way." The king waved Emmeline ahead of him. "I have no doubt the usurper will learn of our treasure hunt and will attempt to stop us before long."

I agreed with him on that account. The queen's forces would try to stop us. But maybe that would be for the best.

As Emmeline began to call out directions once more, the king took the spot closest to her—likely to ensure her cooperation as well as his own safety. He commanded me and my men to lead, putting me ahead of Emmeline, which only stirred my anger since I wanted to be as near to her as possible to protect her from danger.

We crept cautiously onward. I consulted the map at

every turn in order to keep my bearing. And Emmeline continued to call out instructions and warnings.

When the corners grew more frequent, the tunnels shorter, and the cobwebs thicker, I guessed we were getting closer to the center. The roar of a beast, this time much louder, confirmed my suspicion.

I had a feeling the creature had smelled the blood of the men who'd perished, and that the scent had stirred and awakened it to our presence. Even now, Alaric's bloody foot injury was probably drawing the creature. While I prayed we could locate the treasure and leave before encountering the beast, I doubted we'd be so lucky.

"Section double D," Emmeline called out. "Wait just a moment."

We halted at a bend in the passageway as we had on several occasions while she muttered under her breath and tried to piece together the clue with the section letter.

"'Dash, dash, as fast as a deer.'" Her whisper echoed against the stone walls. "We need to run through tunnel D," she finally said. "Run as fast as we can."

I lifted my torch to light the passageway, surprised at the length of it—one of the longest yet.

"Can you run?" I asked Alaric. So far, he'd hobbled along, our pace slow enough that he hadn't held us back.

"I'll try, Your Highness." His breathing was labored, his face pale, and his brow dotted with perspiration. Worst of all, black streaks ran up the veins in his neck.

Poison. The knife had been coated with poison. Even if the blade had been in his flesh only for a minute, the contact was long enough to expose him to the deadly toxin.

The resignation in his eyes told me he knew it too.

"Can you remember the way and the clues so that you can make your way out of the maze on your own?"

"Yes, Your Highness."

"Then retreat, and when you get to the surface start the blood-letting."

He bowed and began to sidle past the others, backtracking carefully. I could only pray in his weakened condition he'd have the strength to make the return journey as well as the keenness of mind to navigate the traps.

Whatever happened, he'd have a greater chance of survival if he went back rather than remaining with us.

Once Alaric was gone, we took turns sprinting across the long tunnel. Even though I knew Emmeline was fast, my pulse thundered when she had to run. Only when she was safely out of the passage did I start to breathe easy again. But only for a moment . . .

As we rounded the last corner and entered a circular room at the center of the labyrinth, a vicious roar filled the air, causing us to recoil. There, straight ahead, stood a large reptile-like creature that was taller than any of the elite guards present.

It crawled on four stout legs, each foot containing claws as long and sharp as knives. Its body was coated in red and black scales like shields stacked in perfect symmetry. And its tail was thick, tapering into a thin whip covered in sharp spikes.

With a hiss that revealed a forked tongue, the creature swung its tail directly at us.

Chapter 20

Emmeline

The creature was beyond terrifying, a beast found only in nightmares. Though I'd read about such animals in a few historical accounts and fables, none of the stories or Maribel's description had prepared me for the reality.

Or its deadliness.

Before I could voice my protest, Rex had positioned himself at the forefront, weapons in both hands, a mace already rotating in a lethal arc. His knights moved just as quickly next to him, their weapons at the ready.

The tail rent the air with a sharp whir. Rex and his men sliced at it, but it was too fast and struck several unprepared soldiers with lightning speed, carving into one man's neck, another's stomach, and a third soldier's legs. In the same moment, another of King Ethelwulf's guards backed into the tunnel to avoid the attack only to be riddled with jagged spikes dropping from the tunnel ceiling.

The agonized screams of the injured men rose up along with Rex's sharp orders.

I stared in frozen horror. Just as I'd feared, I'd brought Rex and the others this far only to lead them to the worst yet.

"My men and I shall distract the beast!" Rex shouted at his father. "Take Emmeline and find safety!"

King Ethelwulf grabbed my arm and tugged me away from the carnage to another one of a dozen entrances spaced evenly around the circular room. I was too terrified to resist and could only stare at Rex as he charged closer to the beast, yelling at it and swinging his mace.

Why had I ever thought I could be brave down here? Maybe I'd been able to mask my fears for a short while, but I couldn't keep my panic at bay any longer.

The walls seemed to close in and the ceiling drop, pressing hard, tightening my chest, forcing the air from my lungs. What had I gotten myself into?

As more cries of agony rose around us and echoed off the walls, I closed my eyes and stumbled blindly behind the king. I was proving to be the weakling I'd believed of myself.

What had Adelaide said? *Courage is not the absence of fear but the determination to persevere when circumstances are at their worst.*

In the midst of all my fears and insecurities, could I still display courage?

"Oh, God," I whispered, swallowing my rising bile. "I need your gift of the highest form of courage for today. I want to persevere and not give in to my circumstances."

A glance at Rex over my shoulder showed him and

several other elite guards wielding their weapons fiercely while attempting to dodge the creature's tail.

I didn't know what my purpose was yet in this battle between the king and Adelaide. I didn't even know which side I was on—my husband's or my sister's. But there was one thing I wanted: peace within the kingdom. Running from the battle might bring temporary relief. But I had to resist the urge and instead push forward and do whatever it took to bring about lasting peace.

Though I cared nothing for the hidden treasure, what if the ancient prophecy was true and the treasure could open the way for the peace I sought? Now that I was at the heart of the labyrinth, didn't I owe it to myself, to my sisters, even to Rex and the king, to see if I could usher it in? If I retreated with the king, I might never get another chance.

"Which tunnel is safe?" King Ethelwulf stopped in a part of the room farthest from the creature at another of the arches that framed long, dark passages—all as deadly as the one we'd just left. "I command you to lead the way to safety."

I scanned the room, taking in the details for the first time. I'd expected some kind of vault in the middle or another locked door that led to a treasure chamber. But the spacious room was empty apart from a scattering of what appeared to be bones. The walls were just as plain and gray as the rest of the labyrinth. The ceiling mirrored the floor—flat and smooth. Except for one thing . . .

My focus locked on a circular engraving on the floor directly at the center of the room near the beast. I didn't see any keyholes and couldn't make out what was on the engraving, but I couldn't leave without getting a closer look.

"There," I said above the cries of the wounded and the shouts of battle. "At the center of the room. An engraving. It could be what we're looking for."

King Ethelwulf studied the spot. Then he motioned to several of his knights. "Escort the princess and stand guard around her as she examines the engraving."

My legs shook at the prospect of going so near the beast, but I pressed my knees together beneath my gown. Before doubts could assail me, I forced myself to walk directly toward the creature, keeping my unwavering gaze upon it. I let one thought drum through my head: *Be courageous. Be courageous. Be courageous.*

"Emmeline!" Rex shouted, catching sight of me as he ducked out of the tail's path. "What are you doing?"

I didn't slow my stride or the litany in my head but stayed focused on the creature. I couldn't worry about Rex. I couldn't worry about the outcome of this moment. I couldn't worry about what the creature might do to me.

The only thing that mattered was remaining strong and showing this beast it couldn't scare me.

Finally, as though sensing my approach, the reptile swiveled its head, lifted its snout, and sniffed the air. Its glassy eyes searched for me, and it released a low, menacing growl.

"Emmeline, no!" Rex's voice rose with desperation.

Even as he rushed toward me, likely intending to toss me over his shoulder and carry me away, I held out my hand to stop him. In the same moment, the creature ceased its thrashing and dropped its tail.

Rex reached for me, but I sidestepped his grasp.

The soldiers who were still alive and uninjured rushed upon the now quiet beast, causing it to thrash again.

"Cease your attack upon the creature!" I shouted at the men.

Rex hesitated only a moment before issuing a command for his men to halt. As the soldiers obeyed, the beast stilled, returned its attention to me, and sniffed the air again.

I continued until I stood directly over the engraving at the very center of the labyrinth, only a foot from the beast. A strange peace had settled over me, sweeping away my trembling fears. My blood pulsed with new energy and confidence and determination.

As the creature hissed and sent its forked tongue toward me, I watched in fascination.

Next to me with weapons still drawn, Rex tensed, his fierceness palpable.

I laid my hand on his arm in both caution and reassurance and at the same time held my head high as the tongue flicked my cheek. The touch stung but then was gone in an instant. The beast hissed again, bared its sharp fangs, then lowered its snout until it almost touched my face.

At the sight of a scar near its eye, I realized this was likely the same creature Maribel had saved while she and Edmund had been in the labyrinth. Did the beast recognize me as Maribel's twin in some primal way?

Rex's muscles flexed, and I sensed his desire to plunge his weapon into the unprotected spot on the creature's neck. I squeezed his arm, hoping he understood he'd do more harm than good if he attacked now.

With a final sniff, the beast jerked away and roared so that its breath hit me full in the face. Not only was it hot and damp, but the stench was unbearable. I guessed it was making one last attempt to intimidate me, but I refused to back down. Instead, I stiffened my shoulders and lifted my chin, glaring at it and daring it to hurt me.

After releasing its terrifying roar, it watched me for another moment before turning and lumbering away toward the arch to the far north. I wasn't sure it would be able to squeeze through the opening, but it shook itself so that its scales overlapped, diminishing its size until it resembled an enormous lizard—one that could easily traverse the tunnels and withstand its dangers.

As its spiked tail disappeared into the black corridor, I wasted no time and dropped to the floor to examine the engraving. I doubted the beast would stay away for long, and we'd need every second of reprieve to find the treasure.

Rex knelt next to me. His expression contained an awe mirrored in the faces of the soldiers surrounding us.

"We need to hurry," I said. "The creature will be back."

Rex rapidly focused on the spot on the floor, his muscles radiating with urgency.

I smoothed my fingers over the engravings. One was a replica of the wild boar from my key. Another was the tree of life, and the final was a pomegranate with seeds spilling out. The symbols on the keys. I traced them—courage, healing, and wisdom.

Adelaide's words pushed to the front of my mind: *Perhaps real treasure lies not in the wealth deep in the labyrinth, but in the gifts God has bestowed upon us— gifts we can use for the greater good of the kingdom and the people.*

Long ago, King Solomon had understood the same thing—that his purpose and strength as a ruler wasn't found in earthly treasures. He'd believed true wealth resided inside us by using the gifts God bestows.

I'd always struggled with fear and never believed I was courageous, but perhaps courage had been building inside me through the tiny steps I'd been taking all this time by doing things even when I was terrified. Now, in the face of the biggest challenges yet, God was helping to unleash the gift.

While I might never know if the keys my sisters and I had each guarded for so many years had played a role in which gift we'd received, I did know courage had surged through me when I'd most needed it.

I fingered the circular outline of the engraving, noting that tiny pieces of the chinking had come loose and had broken away in some places. I reached for my knife wedged in Rex's belt. He relinquished it, and I wasted no time prying it into the thin rim and chipping away the rest of the remaining mortar. Rex followed my lead, and within seconds we'd separated the center engraving from the stone floor surrounding it.

Rex jabbed his sword into the space, straining and lifting in the same motion. Another of his men aided him in pressing up from the bottom while a third hoisted from the top. After hefting for long moments, the round stone with the engraving scraped upward and came free.

By now, everyone had gathered near us, and one of the men held a torch over the hole. At the sight of three key ports, I blinked back stinging tears of relief. "We did it," I said, catching Rex's gaze.

He nodded solemnly, studying my face as though trying to make sense of who I was.

I wanted to smile and reassure him everything would be fine. But untold dangers still lay ahead. Though I may have earned us a window of safety, we wouldn't truly be out of harm's way until we left the labyrinth far behind.

King Ethelwulf had come forward and was now kneeling next to Rex, peering into the hole. Rex dug into the pouch under his chain mail and pulled out the three ancient keys now hanging together on a golden key ring. They clanked together as he placed them into the king's outstretched hand. The king eagerly lowered the keys to the hole.

"Your Majesty," I said. "We should take care which key we insert into which port."

The king halted. "Which do you suggest first?"

I glanced at the engraving, hoping it held a clue, but was unable to decipher what it was. "My guess is that the pomegranate—wisdom's key—comes first since that's what King Solomon asked for first."

"Very well." The king found the key with the pomegranate, inserted it, and turned.

I held my breath, listened, and waited.

When nothing adverse happened, all eyes focused upon me. I mulled over the account of Solomon from the Holy Scriptures. When the young king had asked for wisdom, God had been so pleased with his request that He'd granted him the things he hadn't asked for—

riches and honor. Finally, God had promised long life if Solomon obeyed his commands.

Honor. Courage brought honor. Was my key second? And healing. It was linked with a long life. Was Maribel's key third?

We had no choice but to try them and see what happened. I couldn't let fear hold me back and forsake my courage now. "Insert the boar key second and the tree of life third."

The king lowered his hand back into the hole and twisted the keys into each of the ports. Then we all stared and waited. I wasn't sure what we were looking for next. If we'd inserted the keys in the wrong order, I suspected we'd find ourselves in greater danger than before.

A moment later, the floor began to rumble, quake, and then give way beneath our feet.

Chapter
21

REX

"Everyone back away!" I shouted. "Move to the wall."

Entranced by the crumbling floor, Emmeline didn't budge. I grabbed her around the waist and hauled her back with me. When I reached the smooth, circular wall, I pressed against it, wrapping my arms around her and securing her against me.

The crashing and cracking continued, so loud that for a moment we could only stand and watch and pray we wouldn't be swept down with the rubble.

Finally, after long minutes, the rumbling stopped, leaving a cloud of dust in the air. But even with the haze, we could see the original hole had crumbled away so that the diameter was now several feet wide.

Did we dare cross the floor and return to the chasm? What if our weight caused another avalanche? What if more dangers arose from the depths?

My embrace around Emmeline tightened as I pictured her face-to-face with the beast, so near to death and yet so calm. The very thought of how close she'd come sent chills up my backbone. And yet, how could I be angry with her for putting herself at such risk when her daring challenge had likely saved all of us?

"Someone needs to return to the center," the king said from where he stood plastered to the wall a few paces away.

"I'll do it." Emmeline jolted free before I could grab her back, and she stalked across the floor.

"Emmeline." I jumped to follow her. "Let me test the safety of the floor first."

She didn't slow, and I knew I wouldn't be able to stop her now, any more than I had in the tunnels or with the beast. As much as I wanted to sweep her up, escape from the labyrinth, and never look back, I sensed this was where she needed to be, that this was more a part of her destiny than it was mine.

When the rest of the ground remained secure under our weight, the others, including the king, returned to the hole, attempting to see past the dust to what was inside. One of our torchbearers held his light above the opening, revealing a winding stone stairway.

"Are there any more traps we should be aware of?" the king asked, his eyes alight with the excitement that came whenever he spoke of the hidden treasure.

"I cannot guarantee we're out of danger," Emmeline said. "But I pray we have suffered the worst."

"You must lead the way." The king waved toward the stone steps.

"Your Majesty." I stepped forward. "Please allow me."

"Your wife will go first and determine our safety."

Was this still part of proving my allegiance after disobeying him? With Emmeline in the labyrinth, I'd swallowed my fear time after time. And I'd swallowed my frustration with the king for disregarding my need to protect and cherish Emmeline.

But how could I let her put herself in danger yet another time? I couldn't. And yet how could I defy the king again? He'd punish me severely, perhaps carry through with his threat to give the throne to Magnus. I couldn't let that happen. The land would suffer with a man like Magnus on the throne.

Just like the land has suffered under my father . . .

The thought came unbidden and unwanted.

Quickly, I shook it away. I couldn't allow myself to analyze his methods of leadership. Not now. It would only stir my growing discontent and dislike.

As Emmeline descended onto the top step, I resisted the urge to jump ahead and lead the way. Maybe with this descent, I'd finally prove my loyalty to the king, and he'd permit me to take Emmeline to the surface. After all, she'd finished guiding us here. She'd done above and beyond what the king had wanted. In fact, if not for her, we wouldn't have survived this far.

I took a torch from one of the guards and followed after Emmeline, holding her arm to keep her from stumbling and from getting too far ahead. As we moved past the dust from the rubble, a damp, musty scent enveloped us.

"Test the step carefully before putting your whole weight on it," I instructed as we navigated the narrow, cracked stone slabs.

Thankfully, Emmeline followed my order and climbed down cautiously. Nonetheless, my heart pounded so hard that my chest ached from the pressure. This search wasn't worth Emmeline's life. In fact, she was more precious than all the treasure in the world. I'd gladly give it up to make sure she was safe.

Did I dare stop now and abandon this cause?

With a gasp, she halted abruptly. I was glad for my quick reflexes that I didn't bump into her and send her toppling.

"Look," she whispered.

I stretched the torch out over the abyss below and drew in a sharp breath. A chamber twice as large as the one above spread out in a circular shape, and it was filled with chests, goblets, relics, and artifacts I couldn't even name. Layers of dust and cobwebs covered everything, turning the room a dusty gray from centuries of lying undlsturbed, but there was no denying the vast riches.

"It's here," I called to the king, unable to keep the wonder and excitement from my tone.

"Is it safe to descend?" he asked.

Anger pricked me again, rapidly deflating any sense of thrill. As Emmeline moved down the stairs, I had to bite back my retort and force myself to continue, though everything within me resisted, my loyalties tearing so that I feared I might never be able to respect the king again.

Behind me, his footsteps tapped against the stone, and more torchlight filled the cavern, driving away the darkness and revealing the immensity of the treasure that spread out in all directions.

After two dozen or more steps, we finally reached the bottom. A single narrow path led through the center of the room lined on either side with mounds of priceless items.

I studied the ceiling and floor, searching for any signs of peril. "What do you know of this room and the dangers that lie within?"

Emmeline was examining the ceiling and floor as well.

"Saint Bede left no further clues beyond the tunnels."

"Then we have nothing to fear here? No knives, pikes, or shards?"

"I cannot say." Emmeline took a tentative step down the path.

I gripped her arm to hold her back. "You have gone far enough. I shall test the path."

She shifted to look at me with her wide brown eyes. "I'm not afraid, Rex."

Her expression reflected the same confidence she'd had when facing the beast. I didn't understand it or even like it, but I could grudgingly admire her determination. "Stay here. You have put yourself in harm's way long enough."

Before she could argue with me, I strode down the path, observing everything and trying not to miss a detail. When I reached the opposite end without any problems, I pivoted to find the king on the bottom step watching me. Several soldiers were also on the stone stairway, holding their torches above the room and illuminating the treasure.

Their eyes, like the king's, reflected the same exhilaration that had filled me only moments ago. But I couldn't muster it again, not even after traversing the length of the chamber without triggering any deadly traps.

"Have the princess open one of the chests," the king ordered.

"I have proven my allegiance," I blurted before I could stop myself. "Now I would leave Emmeline out of any further danger."

The king met my gaze. "I am the king, and you will do as I say."

Would he have me kill my spirit to uphold his desires?

For that is what would happen if I obeyed him rather than my conscience.

"She will open one of the chests," he said again, this time his voice ominously low, daring me to defy his order.

My anger kindled hotter, along with something much more painful. But before I could protest again, Emmeline grasped the lid of the nearest chest and started to lift it.

"Emmeline, wait!" My footsteps slapped against the floor at the same time the creak of rusty hinges echoed within the chamber.

She had to use two hands and heft it hard. By the time I reached her, she'd pushed it all the way up. We stood silently, watching the chest, waiting for disaster to spring out upon us.

After several tense moments, I allowed myself to breathe again. Before Emmeline could do anything else, I pulled her to my side. "You are finished here," I said harshly.

As she sidled against me, I found no relief from my internal war. And I could find no joy as the king descended the last step, walked safely to the open treasure chest, and smiled at the contents—thousands of gold coins, untouched by the elements and age. They were polished and smooth and engraved with an ancient writing. The torchlight refracted their brightness, making them glitter.

The one chest would provide more than enough to pay hundreds of mercenary soldiers to come to our aid in defending Delsworth. Adding in the dozens of chests and mounds of other items, the king would easily become the richest ruler in the world.

And the most powerful.

As the next in line, I'd stand to inherit it all. The prospect sent a tremor through me—one I didn't understand, one that filled me with doubts. Could the king or I really be trustworthy stewards of such wealth?

The king picked up a handful of the coins and let them slip through his fingers, the clinking a tempting sound. As if needing to touch the gold to reassure himself it was truly real, he removed his gloves and with bare fingers dug deeper, stirring and reveling in the riches, his royal onyx ring dark against the gold.

"You see." He smiled at me, his eyes alight. "This is why I needed to push you to remain strong and do the task no matter how difficult and no matter the sacrifice."

I bowed my head in acknowledgment of his statement, although I disagreed completely. If I had to do everything over again, knowing I would reach the treasure, I still wouldn't have brought Emmeline down into the labyrinth.

The king stepped to the next chest, opened it, and laughed with delight. The gold was piled even higher, the coins as gleaming and bright as the previous chest. This time, he dug deeper into the treasure before tossing the coins into the air so that the clinking sounded even louder.

I wished I could be happy for him during this long-awaited and long-hoped-for moment. But though he was rich, I felt strangely impoverished.

"Your Majesty," came an anxious voice from one of the soldiers at the hole at the top. "I believe the beast is returning."

Chapter 22

Emmeline

"Go!" Rex propelled me toward the stone steps.

"We cannot leave without the treasure." The king held handfuls of the gold coins, his fingers curled tightly around them.

"The beast will trap us down here if we linger," Rex said.

"Send Emmeline up to deal with the creature."

I paused in my scramble up the steps. I may have helped us avert danger once with the beast. But when it came back, I wouldn't be able to use the same tactic to divert it. It would no longer find my courage fascinating or honor Maribel's scent—if that's what it had smelled.

No, when it returned, it likely wouldn't be dissuaded until it killed every living thing in its periphery. "The creature won't go away this time," I said. "Rex is right. If we remain, it will trap us here in this room, and we'll never get out."

Still the king hesitated, his gaze unswerving from

the gold coins heaped before him.

Rex approached his father. "Please, Your Majesty."

"We've come all this way and endured so much to find it." The king ran his fingers through the coins again. "I cannot leave it behind."

"We know where it is now," Rex said more firmly. "We shall be able to return, and when we do, we shall bring more men and greater weapons so we can defeat the guardian of the treasure."

From above came the faint roar of the beast as well as the shouts of the remaining soldiers. I guessed we had a minute, maybe two at the most.

"Make haste," I said to Rex.

His anxious gaze urged me to keep going, to take myself to safety. But he surely knew I wouldn't leave him behind.

As though sensing my resolve, Rex closed one of the chests and hefted it, his arms and body straining under the weight. Two of his men picked up a second chest of gold and toted it between them. The king's awed gaze swept over the treasure room again, before he finally followed Rex and the soldiers to the steps.

"You must vow you will come back and retrieve the rest of the treasure," he called to Rex.

"I vow it." Rex climbed behind me with surprising speed in spite of having the chest.

I didn't know how we'd possibly outrun the creature with so heavy a load, or how we'd traverse the deadly tunnels that had been difficult enough without anything slowing us down. But without the two chests, I doubted Rex would have been able to persuade his father to leave.

I scrambled out of the gaping hole to the ferocious

roar of the creature as it reappeared from the black depths of the dark tunnel it had gone into a short while ago. Crawling on its stout legs, it moved faster than I expected, slinging its deadly tail back and forth.

The guards who remained were already approaching the beast, raising their swords and maces. In one swipe of its tail, it took out two men, killing them instantly.

"Follow me!" I sprinted toward the tunnel we'd used previously.

Behind me, the clank of the gold in the chest told me Rex wasn't far behind.

A tortured scream was followed by a crash and the jangle of a thousand coins hitting stone. I glanced over my shoulder to the sight of the second treasure chest overturned and the two men who'd been carrying it lying lifeless on the floor, their blood staining the coins crimson.

The beast's tail rose and swept around again, this time aiming directly for Rex. My heart jumped into my throat, but I managed a warning. "Rex! Watch your left!"

He shoved the chest ahead of him, then dove, rolling out of reach. Meanwhile, two other soldiers took hold of the chest and continued with it. As they approached the mouth of the tunnel, I waved them ahead. "Remember, run as fast as you can! You have to sprint and can't slow down for even a second."

The king had stopped only feet from the arched entrance and was staring back at the gold coins scattered in every direction. He bent and scooped up several.

"Run!" Rex shouted, racing toward the tunnel.

Seeing the spiked tail sweeping our way, the king finally bolted forward too, stumbling into the entrance.

"Faster, Emmeline!" Rex called. "We shall follow!"

I began my sprint through the corridor. When I crossed to the other side, Rex was directly behind me with his arm around his father's waist, having risked his own life to aid his father across.

Even now, the king paused and peered back the way we'd come. "We cannot leave the treasure behind. Not when we are so close to having it all."

Heavy breathing filled the bend that separated us from the next deadly passageway. The glow of torches showed only eight men left in addition to Rex and the king. We'd lost so many already, and we couldn't risk anyone else.

"You must go back for more," the king insisted, turning the gold coins over in his hands and rubbing them.

"I shall return," Rex said. "But only after I have additional men and weapons."

"Now," the king demanded. "Go back and get more of the treasure, now!"

"We have enough to aid the war efforts." Rex nodded at the chest the soldiers still carried.

The king's eyes were almost feverish in their intensity. "If we can get one chest out, we can get more."

"It is too risky—"

The sharp edge of a blade pressed against my throat, pricking my skin so that I cried out from the shock and pain. It took me a moment to realize the king had unsheathed his sword and held it against my neck.

"Leave her be," Rex said harshly, his expression turning fierce.

"Go get the treasure." The king's reply was equally harsh.

Rex stared at him, his eyes sparking with fury. "Very well, Your Majesty," he said after a moment, his voice calm.

"Now," the king demanded, the blade wavering, causing more pain and the warmth of blood to trickle down my neck.

Rex's gaze flickered to the blood, which only seemed to add fuel to the fire burning in his eyes. He took a step back toward the tunnel.

No. I couldn't let Rex expose himself to danger yet again. Though the beast hadn't yet followed us into the tunnel and was likely distracted by the dead we'd left behind, the creature wouldn't hesitate to attack once more.

Deftly, my fingers found the hilt of my knife. I'd kill the king before I allowed him to send Rex back to the beast and his death. I'd kill him and be rid of him forever.

But even as I closed my hand around the handle, a terrible ache formed in my chest. Could I really take a life in order to save one?

I squeezed my eyes closed, already knowing the answer. Killing the king would be the easy way to save Rex. I'd need more courage to do the hard thing . . . the right thing.

I had to let Rex go. I had to trust God to keep him safe.

With a silent prayer for courage, I released my knife. In the same instant, the blade fell away from my throat and the king stumbled backward, hitting the wall before sliding down to his knees. His sword clattered to the ground, as did the coins he'd been holding.

I stared, unable to comprehend what had happened. No one had attacked the king that I could see. Why had he fallen?

Two of the king's guards quickly knelt beside him. But without a glance at the king, Rex tore off a piece of his tunic beneath his chain mail and reached for me. As he lifted the linen to my throat his hand trembled for a second before he pressed the cloth against my cut to stave the bleeding.

On the ground, the king cursed and then attempted to rise, his guards each taking one arm and assisting him back to his feet. "What are you waiting for?" His voice rasped. "Go get the treasure."

Rex didn't take his eyes from my neck, continuing to put pressure against my wound.

The king uttered another oath and started to reach for his sword. But his hand was shaking too hard to make his fingers work.

His black fingers . . .

I blinked to make sure I was seeing correctly. The torchlight could often cast strange shadows. But another look revealed the same. His fingers were as black as if he'd dipped them in an inkpot, with stains running up his wrists and disappearing beneath his sleeves. In addition, his face was pale and his forehead wet with perspiration.

"Rex?" My thoughts returned to the young soldier Rex had sent out of the labyrinth. "Do you think the king is poisoned?"

The king jerked his arms free of his guards and slid down so that he was sitting against the wall, his breathing labored.

"Poisoned?" Rex released me and knelt beside the king. "Your Majesty, what ails you?"

"What ails me?" The king's voice rose with a slightly hysterical note. "My worthless son is ailing me. We are here in the heart of the labyrinth. The treasure is ours for the taking. And you have no will to retrieve it."

"I would see the princess safe first—"

"You will go get the treasure or forfeit your right to the throne."

Rex stared into his father's eyes. If the king had ever shown affection or kindness for his son, it was gone. Only loathing remained in its place.

Finally, Rex's shoulders slumped, and he bowed his head. "I am doing what I should have done from the start. And I only regret I did not do it sooner."

The king nodded. "Good—"

"I am protecting my wife."

The king's lips stalled before his expression contorted. "Then you have proven you are not worthy, and I revoke your right to be the next king. I give the throne to Magnus."

The other soldiers watched the interaction between the king and Rex with wide eyes. My surprise matched theirs, leaving me speechless. Part of me wanted to assure Rex I could fend for myself through the labyrinth, that he had no need to defy his father on account of my safety. And yet another part of me couldn't release him to die for the king. The king didn't deserve such a sacrifice.

"Did you hear me?" the king shouted breathlessly. "I give the throne to Magnus."

"So be it." Rex remained with his head bent. The king rained down curses upon Rex, cajoling and belittling him until he choked on his words and began to wheeze. He clutched his throat with black fingers, his eyes widening. "You poisoned me."

"I would never hurt you!" Rex slammed a hand against the floor. "I have remained loyal to you and attempted to gain your affection."

I bent and stared at one of the gold coins that now littered the floor. Had there been a deadly invisible trap within the treasure chamber after all? Had it been within the chests themselves? Perhaps a deadly poison covering every coin?

The king had been the only one to touch the gold, had reveled in it, had been holding the coins.

"The gold," I said. "What if the gold was coated in a layer of poison?"

Rex glanced from the coins on the floor to the king's black fingers. With alarm tightening his features, he then peered up at the guards surrounding us, then at me. "We need to get the king above ground and find the medical bag as quickly as possible."

I nodded. "I'll lead the way."

He started to shake his head, but I cut him off. "We'll need to move fast if we have any hope of saving him."

Rex didn't argue and instead commanded one of the guards to help him carry the king. Two others took hold of the treasure chest, leaving the gold coins where they'd fallen. I led the way back through the maze, consulting the map, but moving rapidly the way we'd already come.

When we finally reached the entrance, the faint light filtering from the opening told me we'd spent the entire night in the labyrinth and that dawn was breaking. As Rex and his men labored to heft the king up the steep slope, I wiped a weary hand across my eyes.

Though the king was still breathing, he'd lapsed into unconsciousness. His hands had turned completely black like charred wood, stiff and brittle. It wouldn't be long before the poison streaked through the rest of his body.

The remnant of soldiers left behind to guard the camp hefted us above ground. Once we were in the cave, Rex laid the king out and began issuing orders for his care.

Although I wasn't skilled in the healing arts, I knew enough to assist the blood-letting in an attempt to drain the poison from the king's body. Another soldier mixed a concoction for the king to drink, something that would purge the poison.

Even so, the king's breathing became shallow.

Rex kneeled next to me on the cave floor, watching his father's face. His expression was grave, especially because the other poisoned soldier lay only a dozen feet away and was barely alive, his neck and face already streaked with black.

As we worked to save the king, a guard rushed into the cave. "Your Highness," he said without waiting for permission to speak. "We've caught sight of the usurper's war party, and our guess is that they'll be upon us within an hour."

Chapter 23

"PREPARE TO LEAVE IMMEDIATELY." I ROSE FROM MY SPOT BESIDE the king.

"But your father." Emmeline tipped the king's arm, allowing his blood to dribble out to the cave floor. "He won't be able to travel."

"I shall ride with him." I strode toward the mouth of the cave. "Bandage him and get him ready for the journey as best you can."

After consulting further with the lookout who'd spotted the incoming war party, I knew we'd have to leave in a circuitous route to avoid any conflict. I couldn't afford to lose any time with a skirmish, not with the king's life at stake. If we rode hard and evaded confrontations, we might reach the Iron City of Middleton in less than two days. There I'd be able to locate a skilled physician who could lend his expertise to saving the king.

"The treasure chest, Your Highness" One of the soldiers who'd helped carry it out of the labyrinth approached me and bowed. "What should we do with it?"

I glanced to the cursed box just inside the cave. We'd been fortunate the chests themselves hadn't been covered in poison. I shuddered to think of Emmeline lying next to the king in the same condition.

If the king were coherent, he'd demand we take the gold along. But I wouldn't risk any other lives by having the men touch the gold to put it into sacks that we could more easily transport. The poison was especially potent, and even though they were wearing their gauntlet gloves, I didn't want to expose anyone else.

"We must leave it," I said.

The soldier bowed again, but not before I caught sight of the relief upon his countenance. I guessed all the other men would feel the same way, and likely now considered the gold cursed for what it had done to the king. Perhaps it was. Perhaps the whole quest to find the treasure was cursed.

As I readied our horses in the dawn light, my mind spun in a dozen different directions. Without the gold to pay for mercenaries, we'd have to endure a prolonged siege. The people would suffer even more than they already had under the king's harsh rule.

Yes, he'd ruled harshly. As much as I wanted to continue to ignore or make excuses for his methods and philosophies, I no longer could. He'd been a selfish man, using the people around him—including me—to advance himself and his plans to find the treasure.

Maybe a part of him had held some affection for me as his son. But ultimately, his love of power and gold had been greater than anything else. He'd been willing to make any sacrifice to get the ancient treasure and retain his throne.

For many years, I'd given him my deepest allegiance

and had worked to earn his approval. I'd even put my loyalty to him above Emmeline's needs. But it had been for nothing. In the end, he'd rejected all I'd offered him, renounced my inheritance of the throne, and, most of all, revoked any love he may have harbored.

I let my focus drift to the arched entrance, to the silhouette of Emmeline kneeling beside the king, rolling a bandage around an arm while one of my men wrapped linen around the cuts in the other arm.

For the briefest of moments, my mind flashed to the memory of her inviting me to lie down with her in the smaller side cavern after our arrival yesterday. Her eyes had been a luscious warm brown filled with such welcoming trust. Although I'd kidnapped, manipulated, and used her since the day I'd met her, she'd opened her heart to me anyway.

I didn't deserve her. Not after the way I'd treated her—with the same selfish tactics the king employed. Although the king believed we were different, I was like him in more ways than I wanted to admit.

I'd rejected her need to free her parents. I'd subjected her to stealing from her sister and betraying her conscience. I'd given in to the king's whim to bring her to the labyrinth. And even when we'd been deep inside the tunnels, I'd gone along with him time after time, putting her in harm's way.

Turning away from the sight of her, I leaned my head against my steed, nausea roiling in my gut. I wasn't worthy to be her husband. Not in the least. Especially now that I wouldn't be king.

I mentally tallied the number of soldiers who'd heard the king's declaration. Several of them were among his most loyal bodyguards and would carry out his wishes to make Magnus king. I could kill them all now and keep only those who swore loyalty to me. But by using murder and cruelty, I'd only continue down the path to becoming more like the king, and that was a path I wanted to change.

If I abdicated to Magnus without a fight, he'd relegate me to a position far away from Delsworth and the court—if he didn't kill me first. And then what would become of Emmeline? I suspected he'd show her no mercy.

What about the people of Bryttania? Could I really stand back and allow Magnus to take over where the king left off? Knowing Magnus's temperament, he'd show even less compassion to the people.

A shudder worked its way up my spine and served only to solidify the resolve that had been growing since we'd climbed out of the dark depths of the labyrinth. The kingdom was in ruins. The city of Delsworth was under siege. The king was dying. And now Magnus would be the next ruler.

For the love of this kingdom and its people, I comprehended with sudden clarity what I needed to do. As Father Patrick had once admonished, I had to do what was right in the sight of God and man.

"The king is bandaged," Emmeline said from behind me. "But I don't think you should attempt to move him."

At the realization of the hurt I would cause Emmeline, pain pierced my heart as deeply as if someone had plunged a dagger into it. In the short term, she might not understand and might hate me. But maybe eventually, she'd see the wisdom of my plan and realize I only wanted her safety, along with the security of her future.

"Perhaps we can offer the hand of peace to Adelaide," she suggested. "And negotiate a truce with the promise of half the treasure?"

Her presence behind me was strong and beckoned me to spin and pull her into my arms. Instead, I took a deep breath and pushed past the pain in my throat. "The queen will have it all."

"She will?"

"I am leaving the chest of gold here."

"I see," she said after a moment, her voice laced with disappointment. "Then you hope to defeat her soldiers by subjecting them unknowingly to the poison."

"No." I turned so I was facing her and forced the words I knew I must say. "You will stay behind and warn them of the poison."

"I cannot—"

"You will be safer this way."

Her luminous eyes searched my face, and she stepped closer as though sensing the chasm growing between us—a chasm of my own making. "I don't need you to worry about my safety. I'm stronger than you know."

"It is precisely because of your strength that I am leaving you behind." Ultimately, she would overcome the hurt I caused her and go on to have a good life, one with her sisters and even her parents—if I could get to them in time.

"I don't understand." She lifted her hands to my face, but I stepped out of her reach. If I let her touch me, even slightly, I'd be lost. I wouldn't be able to think clearly, and my desire for her would overshadow my resolution.

I climbed up into my saddle, putting myself even farther from her. "You will be better off with your sisters."

"That's my decision to make."

"You belong with them."

"I belong with you."

I shook my head, my frustration mounting. "I took what was never mine to begin with." Those were the king's words, but I was beginning to believe them.

"But we're married. It's too late to have regrets." Her voice hardened, and her chin jutted out with her telltale determination.

"It is never too late to make things right."

"You vowed you would love and cherish me."

Yes, I'd vowed I would love and cherish her until death. And in the deepest region of my heart, I would. Even so, I'd broken my vow by siding with the king instead of with her. My integrity, my word, my promises—they were already useless. What was one more offense?

"I have failed you one too many times."

"What about what I want?" Suddenly, her tone was threaded with desperation.

I stared off into the distant craggy landscape, watching as the rising sun turned the rocks to crimson, and I steeled myself for severing our bond. It was the only way to save her, and I had to stay strong though everything within me demanded I dismount and draw her into my arms.

"You will build a new life for yourself," I finally said. "And eventually, you will forget about me."

"You're despicable," she said, the same words she'd uttered once before. Only this time I knew she was right. I was despicable, just like the king, which was all the more reason to let her go.

I shouted orders to my men, attempting to ignore Emmeline's eyes upon me and the hurt within them. After a whispered conversation with my second-in-command, my men hoisted the king into the saddle in front of me.

Only then did I chance a final glance at her.

She stood back, her arms crossed, her beautiful eyes blazing with fury.

I gave her a curt nod good-bye. Before she could react, I twisted away and kicked my horse into a gallop. I needed to put as much distance as possible between us so I wouldn't give way to the longing to throw aside all caution, gather her into my arms, and beg her to stay with me forever.

I couldn't do it. I had to leave. If I didn't, I'd never be able to follow through on the difficult task set out before me.

Chapter 24

Emmeline

I stood staring at the trail where Rex had ridden away, unable to pull my eyes from it, praying I'd see his proud but strong frame as he rode back for me.

But with each passing minute, my chest throbbed more painfully with the realization he'd left me and had no intention of returning.

Inside the cave, one of Rex's knights had remained to tend Alaric in his dying moments. He knelt beside his comrade and was doing his best to make him comfortable.

"You should leave now," I called to the knight, "before the queen's army arrives."

He stood and exited the cave. "The prince has ordered me to stay, Your Highness."

"They will take you as their prisoner."

"Aye, they will."

"And what if they put you to the sword?"

"So be it, Your Highness."

"And if I command you to leave?"

"I will obey the prince and stay."

"You don't owe him such loyalty." I couldn't keep the anger from my tone. The prince didn't deserve my loyalty either. Why, then, was I waiting for him?

"I don't owe him, Your Highness." The knight stared off in the direction Rex had gone, his eyes sad. "But I'd willingly do whatever he asks, even lay down my life for him."

Something in the man's expression sent a shiver of trepidation through me. I wasn't surprised that the knights Rex had brought from Warwick were loyal to him. He was a hard master, but I'd learned he never asked them to do more than he was willing to do himself. He advanced on danger fearlessly, took the lead, protected his men as best he could, and showed them compassion when it most counted.

My eyes clouded with moisture, and I blinked rapidly to keep my tears from spilling.

Rex was a good and decent man. So why had he broken his vow to me? His promise from after the hasty wedding in the forest had stayed with me: *I meant my vow to you. And I will choose to love and cherish you unto death.*

The heat of my anger turned suddenly cold. I spun and looked at the trail with understanding. The only way he'd break his vow was if he suspected he would die in the fight to come.

I started toward one of the remaining horses. I needed to go after Rex and stop him. We could find a way to end the conflict without him having to give up his life.

Rex's faithful knight abandoned his work and raced after me. "Your Highness, the prince asked me to give you something."

He was trying to stall me so that then he could grab me and keep me from going after Rex.

I didn't break my stride and was near my horse when he rounded me, putting himself between me and my means of getaway.

"He wanted you to have this." The soldier held out a key. It was plain, similar to the one for the scriptorium.

I took it hesitantly.

"The prince said you'd know what to do with it."

I turned it over and studied it. I'd seen the key recently, but where? My mind flashed with the image of Rex using it as we'd crawled through the tunnel underneath the moat leading out of Delsworth.

Why had Rex given this to me? Did he expect me to use it to gain entrance into the castle?

"The prince was wrong." I held the key out to the knight. "I don't know what to do with it."

Without taking the key, he crossed his hands behind his back. "Your Highness, if the king dies . . ." The look in the soldier's eyes told me he knew as well as I did that it wasn't a matter of *if* the king would die, but *when*. "The prince may have to battle his brother for the throne."

"You don't think the king was serious about giving the throne to Magnus, do you? You all love Prince Ethelrex and would fight for his right to be the next king."

"Aye, we'd fight for the prince. But the king's loyal men would fight for Prince Magnus, and we'd soon find ourselves warring each other at the same time we're battling an invading army."

Rex, with his small band of knights, would be at a disadvantage against Magnus and the king's much bigger army. Even if Rex had sufficient forces, I doubted he'd want to fight his brother for the throne and cause even more strife in his kingdom.

"Why did he want me to have the key?" I fingered the key again.

"He didn't come right out and say, Your Highness. But my guess is that he doesn't want his people to suffer any more than they already have."

I tested the commander's words and tried to make sense of them. Was Rex giving me a way to bring an end to the conflict not only with his brother but with Adelaide? Was he inviting me to betray him, capture his city, and ultimately doom his life and his claim to kingship?

If so, Adelaide would likely put both of King Ethelwulf's sons to death and eliminate their threat to the throne. And if she spared their lives, they'd find themselves her prisoners, locked away in a tower, secluded from the outside world.

I shook my head. I couldn't set into motion plans that would ultimately result in Rex's downfall and possible death. I loved him too much to even consider it.

Several dozen men wearing the standard of Mercia surrounded our camp within the hour. I came out of the cave with my hands up in surrender. Rex's faithful knight stood close by.

"I am Princess Emmeline," I said loudly, hoping my voice carried. "Except for one soldier who remained behind for my protection, I'm alone. King Ethelwulf and his son are gone."

Adelaide's forces stayed hidden, and no one made a sound.

Did they suppose I was attempting to lure them out so the king's men might attack?

"Emmeline," came a woman's voice. "It is I, Maribel, and my husband, Edmund, Lord Chambers."

I searched the rocks for Maribel but didn't see her.

"I give you my word," I called. "I am alone. The king and his men abandoned me an hour ago."

Several moments later, a knight stepped out from behind a tall crag. He walked cautiously, his weapons drawn as though expecting an attack. Of course, Adelaide's men wouldn't believe me. Why should they?

"I am Lord Chambers," he said, halting and peering beyond me into the cave.

A harpy eagle swirled in lazy circles high above our camp, and I felt certain it was the same one we'd seen when we'd been riding away from Inglewood Forest.

"Your Highness," Edmund said with a slight bow. "May I look around?"

"Certainly." I stood aside and waved to the cave behind me.

He approached slowly, ducked inside, walked to the labyrinth entrance, and peered down before finally coming back out. "The princess is speaking the truth. She is alone except for a guard and a dying man," he called. "The king and his men have indeed abandoned their efforts."

As Edmund spoke, Maribel rushed forward, worry turning her eyes a wintery blue. "You're injured!" She focused in on my neck where the king's blade had left its mark.

"It's nothing." At least compared to everything else we'd experienced down in the labyrinth.

I insisted Maribel tend to Alaric first. Although she gave him a tonic to ease his pain, she shook her head sadly, confirming what we'd already known—that he would die.

Afterward, Maribel led me to a shaded spot outside, made me sit down, and set to work pulling out an assortment of supplies to doctor my wound. As she cleaned the cut and applied salve, I answered Edmund's questions, relaying all that had happened since leaving Adelaide's camp and arriving in the Highlands. By the time I finished, both were staring at me with wide eyes.

Edmund tilted his head toward the chest that sat just inside the mouth of the cave. "Then the treasure is useless? It will kill anyone who touches it?"

"It would appear so," I said.

Maribel gently dabbed my wound. "I should like to concoct a cleanser, a bath of sorts where we could soak the gold to rid it of the poison."

"Is such a thing possible?" I asked.

"We must try. Think of all the good we could do for the people with just this one chest of gold."

"Would Adelaide use it for the people?" I doubted King Ethelwulf would have done so even if he'd had several chests of the gold. His greed had consumed him so that in the end his love of the treasure had superseded his love of his son.

"Adelaide seeks nothing for herself," Maribel said. "You have heard the stories of her generosity, have you not?"

My father had brought back tales of Adelaide, stories of how she'd saved an entire village by drawing from her own purse of gold for them, of how she'd ruled her tenants with the same generosity, and how she'd continued to pay the ironworkers in her father's smelter by selling off her family's possessions.

"Her reputation precedes her," I replied, "not only as a wise queen but a caring one."

"Then you will allow us to take the chest of gold?" Edmund asked. "Even if Adelaide does not win the throne, she will want to aid the people in any way she can."

Adelaide deserved to win the throne. The truth was too strong to deny any longer. Though Rex was a good man and might be able to help restore the land, his father's evil legacy would always haunt him. And of course, if Magnus became king, the evil legacy would continue.

Though I'd been hoping my union with Rex would stave off conflict, I could see now that King Ethelwulf's evil had to be uprooted. Even if I'd grown to care about Rex, I shouldn't have abandoned my family's cause.

If I was honest with myself, I'd abandoned the fight for the throne long ago, even before I'd met Rex. For too many years, I'd let fear control me so that all I'd wanted to do was hide in the woods and stay out of the conflict.

But I could do so no more. My father's words from long ago surfaced to spur me on. *God made you for more.* This was the time for more.

Adelaide and Maribel had each used their gifts to bring about needed change, but they could go only so far. Now it was my turn to rise up and do my part in bringing about restoration and peace.

It was my turn. The words reverberated through me, bringing an ache to my chest that hurt beyond anything I'd known yet.

Maribel started to slather another ointment over my wound, but I stood quickly, the pain in my heart far worse than the cut in my neck.

She sat back on her heels, her brows rising.

I pressed a hand against my chest to ease the ache, though I suspected nothing ever would take it away.

Edmund waited quietly, patiently. The gentleness in his eyes told me he sensed my pain and just how much I was sacrificing for the cause.

My throat constricted, and I had to swallow hard to force the next words out. "I know how to defeat the king and his sons."

To do so, I'd have to turn against the man I loved. And that would require the greatest courage of all.

Chapter 25

REX

With bowed head, I kneeled beside the king's bed. Next to me, Mother sobbed softly, and I laid a gentle hand upon her back, wishing I could comfort her but knowing no one could.

He has passed. The physician's words clanged through my mind. Not unexpected, they still brought a swell of inner turmoil.

The king had survived until we'd reached the city of Middleton. There, skilled healers had administered tonics and tinctures to help prolong his life. While he'd lasted the boat ride back to Delsworth, he'd never regained consciousness and had only continued to degenerate over the past several hours since we'd managed to elude the rebel patrols and sneak into the castle through the secret tunnel under cover of darkness.

An hour ago, at dawn, he'd stopped breathing and hadn't started again. With the head physician's pronouncement of death, I'd finally given the order to ring the bells and spread the news throughout the city and kingdom regarding the king's passing.

Now, in the distance, the church bell tolled slow and sad. It wouldn't be long before everyone knew the king was dead, including the rebels.

How long before Queen Adelaide Constance acted and took advantage of the moment of weakness, this uncertain time where soldiers and townspeople alike would be distracted?

And how long before Magnus made his move?

He'd been with us during the king's last hours. During that time, several of the king's faithful bodyguards had pulled him aside and conferred with him. By now, he'd be well aware of our father's rejection of me as the next king and would likely be planning my demise.

I inhaled a breath of the bitter odor of bloodwort rising from the incense pots around the king's large, luxurious bed. Though the physicians' medicinal supplies remained scattered over the bed, they'd stepped out, as had the servants, to allow us a private time of mourning. Magnus had stayed only for a short while before leaving, and now I feared what he was plotting.

A knock on the chamber door was followed by rapid footsteps. I glanced up to find both Father Patrick and Dante entering. "Long live King Ethelrex," they said in unison, kneeling in the rushes and bowing their heads.

Once word spread regarding the king's rejection of me and decree regarding Magnus, how many would stay with me? I had too few men left after losing so many of my most trusted knights to the labyrinth. While I'd gained the respect and support of others in Delsworth over the past year, I still didn't have the same networks and connections that Magnus did.

Even so, I couldn't let Magnus take the throne without

a fight. I refused to stand back and relegate the people to a ruler like my brother.

"Your Majesty." Dante rose and bowed once again. "I regret the news I must bring you at so sorrowful a time."

My chest pattered an extra beat. Was Emmeline finally doing what she needed to? I'd hated leaving her behind, especially knowing I'd hurt her. But I'd had no choice. I'd had to cause a rift in order to force her to side with her sisters—which was where she should have been all along.

Even though I'd done the right thing, my body burned with my need for her, a need I would always have. Though I'd set her free of any obligation to me, in my heart she'd always be my wife. I'd never want or love another woman ever again.

I thought about her every moment, prayed for her safety, and hoped one day she could forgive me and find happiness.

"Your Majesty," Dante said, this time his tone containing an urgency that forced me up from the bed. I gave him my full attention and nodded at him to continue. "The usurper's army is on the move. They are drawing near with their siege engines."

I stifled my disappointment. I'd been hoping to avoid the frontal attack, and now that it was upon us, I had no will to fight. I wanted to open the city gates and let the rebels in. But the king's army wouldn't allow it. They'd battle until they defeated our foe or a new ruler's flag was raised over Delsworth. Either way, the fighting would be fierce and would take a great toll on the town and the people.

"Any other news?" I asked.

Dante cocked a brow, likely sensing a deeper question—one he had no answers for. At least none that would please me.

"Very well. Gather the bulk of the army and go to the city wall. I shall assemble my guard and meet you there."

Dante bowed again and strode out, leaving me with Father Patrick. The priest drew me to a far corner from my mother before speaking in a whisper. "Your Majesty, your brother is spreading rumors among the castle servants."

"They are not rumors. They are the truth. I refused to obey the king in the labyrinth, and he renounced me as his heir."

The priest studied my face and then offered a gentle smile. "You made a difficult choice, Your Majesty. But I am proud of you for doing what was right no matter the consequences."

"I will not subject the people or the land to Magnus being king."

"And I do not think you should."

"Then you support my claim to the throne?"

"I could not do otherwise."

I tilted my head to acknowledge and thank him for his loyalty as well as to dismiss him.

Instead of going, he pulled his short stature higher. "Your Majesty, you have my fullest support in everything except in the matter regarding your wife." His voice rang out in the chamber, no longer clandestine.

I glared at him, daring him to say more.

He cleared his throat and continued just like he always did. "I do not support you setting aside your vows to her."

"I shall do as I please." I stalked toward the door.

He rushed after me. "You must honor the commitment you made, even in the worst of circumstances."

I paused, one hand on the door handle. "I have no

doubt her sister will nullify our marriage and find her a better husband, someone noble and good, someone like the Earl of Langley or Lord Chambers."

"Princess Emmeline will never find a better husband than you, Your Majesty."

The sincerity in Father Patrick's voice gave me a moment of hope . . . until all of my faults came rushing back. I'd forced Emmeline into a relationship with me, had given her no choice with our marriage. If I survived the battle against Magnus as well as the battle for the kingdom, I wouldn't coerce or manipulate her into coming back to me. No, she was free to choose what she wanted, and I'd have to live with the consequences.

Before I could formulate my thoughts into words, rapid footsteps and loud voices rumbled outside the chamber. Was Dante returning with more news?

I swung open the door only to find the king's closest guards gathered, their weapons drawn, their expressions severe. The two guards I'd left on duty were slumped in the passageway with blood pooling beneath them. Behind them stood Magnus.

He'd waited until Dante departed with the majority of the army before coming after me. I could admit that was a smart move. But he underestimated me if he thought he could conquer me with a handful of soldiers.

In an instant, I had my weapons out. A quick thrust of my dagger into the closest guard sent him staggering back into the hallway. A swipe with my sword at another brought him to his knees. I used my speed, power, and agility to my advantage. If Magnus believed I'd risen to my position as head commander of the elite guard because I was the king's son, then he was wrong. I'd earned my spot because I'd become the best.

I spun away from the men pouring into the bedchamber, fighting them off and taking them down in quick succession. From the corner of my eye, I saw Magnus stalk across the room. A warning rang in my head, but I was too outnumbered and too busy to stop him unless I threw my knife into his back—which I couldn't do.

An instant later, he shouted above the clamor of fighting. "Surrender or I will kill Father Patrick."

Even as I parried a thrust and ducked away from another blow, I caught a glimpse of Magnus's knife pressed against Father Patrick's throat. I'd witnessed Magnus's cruelty often enough to know my brother never issued an idle threat.

I took several rapid steps, trying to decide how I could hurt Magnus and free Father Patrick simultaneously. My gaze landed upon Mother, who'd risen from the king's bedside and was watching the conflict with horror rounding her beautiful eyes.

How could I live with myself if I injured Magnus? I couldn't do it, especially not in front of Mother.

"Do not harm Father Patrick," I said, lowering my weapons.

Magnus didn't loosen his hold on my wise teacher. His blade nicked the priest's fleshy neck. The remaining guards surrounded me and cautiously crept closer.

"Drop your weapons. Now," Magnus ordered. "Or your priest dies."

I released my grip on my sword and dagger. They clanked against the floor. It was over. I knew it, and from the gleam in Magnus's eyes, he knew it too.

He'd known exactly how to control me and make me do whatever he commanded. He'd perfected the use of the different, but no less deadly, weapons of threats, manipulation, and force—just the same as the king. But no longer for me. I could no longer be that kind of man, not even now.

At the sight of Father Patrick's pale face, I was all the more relieved I'd left Emmeline behind. If she'd been here and within Magnus's grasp, I most certainly would have killed my brother. As it was, I could submit, at least for the time being. And later, I'd find a way to regain control.

"Chain him," Magnus called out to his loyal guards. "Then take him out to the inner bailey and flog him."

"Magnus, no!" Mother held out a trembling hand.

"Be silent, Mother," Magnus said. "Or you will join him."

Magnus would never harm our mother, would he? I suspected the threat was aimed more at me than Mother, another attempt by Magnus to exert his authority and make me comply.

"Everyone knows that nothing good comes from Warwick." Magnus stated the familiar slur with disdain.

I didn't resist as the guards finished disarming me and then wrapped a thick chain around my wrists and shackled my ankles. And I didn't resist when they yanked me toward the exit.

Chapter
26

Emmeline

I'd insisted on going first and leading the way. Though my heartbeat rammed against my chest, all my anxiety had fled the moment I'd unlocked the tunnel door and ducked inside.

Rex would have guessed I didn't need a key, that I had the skill to break in without it, just as he had. That he'd left me the key was all the more confirmation of what he'd wanted—for me to lead Adelaide's army into the fortress. It had also likely been his way of telling me he forgave me for betraying him.

I had a role to play in restoring the land, and I couldn't stop until I helped Adelaide bring about the peace the people needed, even if that meant I had to hurt Rex in the process. Regardless of my decision, my heart hadn't ceased aching since the moment I'd made up my mind to fulfill my destiny as one of the lost princesses.

Adelaide crawled behind me. Thankfully, she'd easily forgiven me for taking Rex to the labyrinth after she'd given me the last of the ancient keys. In fact, I'd learned she'd handed over the key with the hope the king and his men would go after the treasure. Without all the pieces of the map, Adelaide wouldn't have been able to navigate the labyrinth anyway.

She'd sent Edmund's band of knights to intercept the king's men if they made it out of the labyrinth alive and with the treasure. What she hadn't expected was that the king would so willingly put his own life at risk by going inside the labyrinth himself. As it was, his greed had led to his downfall.

Although the ancient prophecy proclaimed the treasure would rid the land of evil, none of us had realized the fulfillment would happen so literally. I now knew without a doubt Adelaide was the young ruler who'd set everything into motion. She was strong and wise and good, but she alone hadn't been enough. She'd needed—and perhaps always would—the gifts of others to truly become a great leader.

During the whole process, Adelaide had concluded that a secret passageway existed, one that led in and out of Delsworth castle, allowing the king and his men to go after the treasure. But her scouts hadn't been able to locate the tunnel entrance.

Using all the skills Lance had once taught me, I'd retraced my path through the thick woodland and found the hidden place. Though the way was narrow and at times required us to slither on our stomachs, I'd pushed myself onward with Adelaide following behind me, assuring me I was doing the right thing.

The Earl of Langley—Christopher, as he insisted I call him—was next in line, leading Adelaide's strongest and bravest men. Among them was her captain of the guard, Firmin, a giant of a man who'd previously lived in the castle as one of the king's guards. Once we were inside, Firmin planned to take half the men through the fortress for Magnus while I would lead Adelaide and Christopher to Rex.

Even from my short time living in the castle, I knew the best places to find Rex—if he wasn't already at the city wall readying for the fight there. Additionally, if I encountered any of the king's guards, they'd recognize me and wouldn't question my presence in the castle until too late. At least I hoped so.

Courage, I silently admonished myself. *Be of great courage.*

With the cold, damp earth beneath my fingers and the darkness of the tunnel blocking out everything, I put one hand in front of the other and crawled onward. My mother and father had once bravely carried me out of the castle to safety. And now it was time to return just as bravely and not only free them but free the land from the curse it had been under for far too long.

When I bumped headlong into an iron door, I halted abruptly and whispered instructions to Adelaide. "We've reached the end. I'll unlock the grate, go inside, and make sure the way is clear before I signal for you."

"We must move swiftly and without hesitation," she replied.

I guessed she was warning me not to let my personal feelings for Rex influence what I did. When I'd returned from the Highlands with Maribel and Edmund, we'd gone directly to Adelaide who'd delayed an attack until she learned the status of the treasure. I'd told her everything that had happened including Rex's defiance of his father as well as his instructions to his knight to give me the key to the secret tunnel.

She knew as well as I did that Rex could have stationed guards at the entrance or even flooded it. As it was, he'd all but offered himself up to her. With such an act, I prayed Adelaide would show him some mercy. I'd asked her to spare his life. But she hadn't promised me she would.

Even though I feared for Rex, I had to keep going.

With a click of the key, the grate unlocked, and I carefully slid it aside, peering through the opening to find that the storage room was deserted except for crates and barrels and old furniture. It was the same storage room in the lower level of the castle that my parents had been in when making their escape. The last time I'd been there, I'd searched for any sign of the door they'd used, but it was long gone.

I scrambled out of the rectangular opening that was big enough for only one person at a time to fit through. The others followed just as silently and crept up the winding stairway until we reached a passageway that led to the kitchens and other servant quarters. For the early morning hour, I'd expected the castle to be bustling with activity. But maybe with the king's death, everyone was in mourning.

We'd heard the church bells tolling his death not long after dawn and had been surprised to learn he'd only just died, that he'd lasted as long as he had. Adelaide had suggested we take full advantage of the distraction the king's death would provide. She'd issued orders for a frontal attack to draw attention away from us as we left for the secret tunnel that would take us into Delsworth.

Apparently, the tactic had worked well. No one was around to see us infiltrating the fortress.

We continued up steep, spiraling stairs to the next level where the great hall and king's antechamber were located. As previously arranged, I planned to go ahead of the others and check both areas for Rex.

Before I could slip through the doorway, Christopher touched my arm and pointed to a window on the landing. It was narrow and slanted, made for shooting arrows at an enemy while staying secluded. "I think we may have found Prince Ethelrex," he said.

I stepped into the landing, peeked through the slit, and found myself gazing over the inner bailey and main courtyard. Amidst a gathering of servants and soldiers, a broad-shouldered young man had been chained to a center post, his arms suspended above his head, and his legs spread. He'd been stripped to his waist, revealing a thickly corded muscular back that was already laced with a crisscross of red welts.

His head was bent, but his fair hair and warrior braids were evidence enough.

"Rex," I whispered, nausea swirling as a whip struck his back. At the contact, his arms jerked and he arched up, but he didn't make a sound, which only caused the slap of leather against flesh to echo all the louder.

"Magnus has taken control," Adelaide whispered as she peered out the narrow slit.

Of course, Adelaide was right. And somehow I sensed this was what Rex had feared all along—that his brother would learn of the king's declaration and make himself king.

I wanted to bend over and retch, but I took a deep breath, straightened my spine, and prayed for more courage. "He doesn't deserve to die this way."

Before anyone could say otherwise or stop me, I dashed through the door and into the passageway that led to the great hall. My footsteps pounded hard, matching the thud of my heartbeat. I didn't care if Adelaide would eventually sentence Rex to death. I wouldn't let him die so cruelly, especially not at his brother's hand.

With footsteps slapping the floor behind me, I ran faster. There wasn't a servant or guard in sight, and I guessed Magnus had ordered everyone to be present for the display that would show his authority over Rex.

Was Magnus overseeing the proceedings from somewhere out there?

It didn't matter. Whatever the danger, I had to go to Rex.

When I reached the door leading to the inner bailey, I flung it open. Magnus and two guards stood on the forebuilding. At the slam of the door against the inner panel, they spun, first surprise and then confusion flitting across their faces. I didn't give them time to question or halt me. I flew past them down the stone stairway.

"Stop the beating at once!" I called to the soldier wielding the whip. Already, I had my knife out and aimed at his arm. Though I didn't want to hurt him, I'd impale my blade into his hand if he attempted to thrash Rex again.

Behind me, Magnus issued clipped orders to his guards. At the same moment, the guard with the whip pivoted, his expression one of surprise—and relief. Were some of the king's guards reluctant to side with Magnus? Or perhaps this one was simply hesitant to bring bodily harm to a royal son.

"Throw me your whip!" I sprinted toward him, knowing I needed to keep ahead of Magnus's guards. I couldn't allow Magnus to catch me yet, not until I freed Rex and gave him the ability to fight back.

The soldier with the whip hesitated only a moment before tossing it to me. I caught the handle and then, gathering my strength, swung the multiple strands in an arc over my head before spinning and aiming for the guards pursuing me. The cords swept across their faces, tearing and slashing. One cried out and dropped to his knees, covering his eyes with his hands. The other drew back, his sword now drawn.

"Bring her to me alive," Magnus called from where he still stood on the forebuilding. Not far from him, I glimpsed Adelaide and Christopher in the doorway. I didn't know what they were planning, but I had to give them more time—time for the rest of the invading army to infiltrate further.

As one lunged at me with his sword, I slapped him with the whip and then sent it zinging toward the other, forcing them back.

"Get her, you imbeciles," Magnus roared, his voice laced with derision and frustration.

The men crept more slowly this time, and I once again slashed at them, this time hitting the neck and face of another and bringing him to his knees.

"What are you standing and waiting for?" Magnus waved impatiently at several guards who stood on the fringes of the gathering. "Capture her. Now!"

As additional soldiers advanced, I crouched lower, the whip in one hand, my knife in my other. I wasn't a warrior princess like Adelaide, but with my father's training and now God's courage, I wouldn't back down from the challenge. I'd fight until Rex had the chance to get away.

"Set Prince Ethelrex free," I called to the soldier who'd given me his whip. A second later, at the jangle of iron against iron, I was relieved to see he was obeying. As the shackles fell from Rex, he slid down the post into a heap.

I caught movement from the periphery of the castle, and I prayed more of Adelaide's men were penetrating the inner bailey. However, with Magnus's soldiers advancing, I had to stay focused, twirling the whip up and moving it faster in front of me. It sliced through the air with a sharp snap.

Even as I provided a shield in front of Rex and myself, Magnus's guards spread out and formed a circle around us. As they neared, the soldier who'd freed Rex unsheathed his sword, apparently willing to fight the onslaught. I welcomed his aid, but two against six or seven would make us easy targets. Nevertheless, I steeled myself to do battle.

At a command from one of the men, Magnus's knights converged at the same time.

Once, I would have been frightened. But a strange calm settled over me—the same calm I'd experienced when facing the beast in the labyrinth. Was it possible that when we made up our minds to face our monsters, God gave us the right amount of courage at the exact moment we needed it?

I swung my knife while spinning with the whip,

hoping to rake the sharp cords across as many of the soldiers as possible. A roar rose behind me at the same time that Rex sprang from the ground. In one swift movement, he reached for the sword of the soldier who'd set him free and sliced the three men advancing at my rear. Each man fell, one after another, crying out with pain.

Meanwhile, I unleashed the whip against the frontal attackers. While the momentum stopped two soldiers, several more pressed onward, close enough that I swiped with my knife only to miss.

At my failed momentum, one of the men grabbed my arm while the other yanked the whip from my other hand. Though I thrashed to free myself, they clung tightly. But Rex spun upon them, again roaring his fury. They shrank back but were too late. One swipe of Rex's sword dropped them to the ground where they lay unmoving.

Rex swept up an abandoned sword and then straightened, weapons in both hands, his feet spread apart, the muscles in his bare arms bulging. I retrieved the whip so that I was well armed and ready to continue to fight next to him.

The inner bailey was silent with all eyes upon us.

Magnus stood stiffly on the forebuilding and motioned to several other guards at the gate. "Get him and then kill him."

The soldiers hesitated—out of fear of fighting Rex or loyalty to him, I didn't know. Either way, if they advanced, they'd soon find themselves dead at Rex's feet.

A piercing whistle rent the air. It came from behind Magnus on the forebuilding. He spun only to find himself surrounded by Adelaide's warriors. Throughout the inner bailey, along the wall, in the gatehouse, and even on the outskirts of the gathering, her soldiers stepped from their hiding places, showing themselves and their weapons and easily disarming the rest of Magnus's knights.

Adelaide herself strode out the castle door confidently and regally to the place Magnus had stood only moments before. Still attired in her armor, she shed her chain mail hood, revealing her long, golden hair, making her beautiful and fierce at the same time. As she swept her gaze over the assembly, she ended at Magnus, who was cursing and struggling against the men who now held him.

"I am Adelaide Constance Dierdal Aurora, the true queen and heir of the house of Mercia." Her voice carried forcefully and clearly across the bailey. "If you bow your knee to me and acknowledge me as the rightful ruler of Mercia, I shall restore your land, your prosperity, and your safety. I shall show you the mercy and kindness you long for."

Magnus spat at Adelaide's feet. "You are the usurper and will never be accepted here. I shall never bow my knee."

Adelaide narrowed her eyes upon the young man. "So be it. You have sealed your fate." Her gaze swept over the gathering and came to rest upon Rex.

For the first time since I'd started the fight for his life, my stomach quivered with fear. Even with his back bruised with welts, Rex was easily the strongest man there, possibly the strongest in all the Great Isle. He was a dangerous opponent. And his presence was commanding. If Adelaide eliminated him, she'd secure her reign and never have to worry about him challenging her.

Even as I fought against my urge to plead for his life, Rex began to cross the bailey, swords at his side, his focus locked upon Adelaide.

Christopher stepped next to Adelaide, his bow fitted with an arrow aimed at Rex's heart. The large guard, Firmin, and his retinue broke away from the perimeter and pushed toward Rex.

Adelaide raised her hand. "Let him come."

The men halted but kept their eyes upon the prince.

As Rex reached the foot of the forebuilding, he jabbed first one sword into the ground, then the other, the thud of metal against earth echoing ominously. Then he lowered himself onto one knee, bowed his head, and spoke in a clear voice, "I acknowledge you as the true queen and rightful heir of Mercia."

At the sight of their warrior prince bowing in subservience to Adelaide, the servants began to lower themselves until every person in the bailey knelt with bent head.

When only Adelaide's soldiers remained standing, my throat constricted at the realization of what Rex had just done. He'd not only handed over the authority to Adelaide, but he'd led the way for his people to do so as well avoiding bloodshed and bringing about peace.

Tears stung my eyes—tears of love and sorrow. In laying aside his rights in order to save his people, he'd proven himself to be a worthy prince. Perhaps he would have made a good and kind king and ruled with justice and fairness in a way his father never had.

But now, he'd never get the chance to find out.

Chapter 27

"I'VE COME TO SEE THE PRINCE." EMMELINE'S VOICE SOUNDED outside my tower prison.

I pushed up from my bed and winced at the pain in my back.

"Your Highness," the guard replied. "He's not allowed any visitors."

"I'm not just any visitor. I am his wife."

Wife. My mind flashed to the image of Emmeline earlier today when she'd rescued me from the whipping. As she'd faced the oncoming soldiers, her brown eyes had flashed with both fury and determination. She'd never been more beautiful.

With Magnus looking on, I'd never been more frightened for her life, not even when we'd been down in the bowels of the labyrinth. I'd realized I had no choice but to defeat Magnus's loyal guards so they couldn't capture Emmeline and hand her over to Magnus who would torture her in order to make me his puppet.

In fact, I'd been so angry with her for walking into the

midst of the courtyard and right into Magnus's clutches that I'd nearly gone mad waiting for the guard to set me free. Even then, I'd pretended to be weak until Magnus's men were nearly upon us before I'd risen and taken them by surprise.

When the queen had finally made her appearance, I'd wanted to fall down and weep with relief that Magnus wouldn't be able to get Emmeline, that she was safe. I'd willingly handed the kingdom over to Queen Adelaide Constance, especially since it meant Magnus could no longer have it.

"You must let me in," Emmeline insisted.

"The queen said the prince isn't to have any visitors except those who are tending to his wounds."

I moved to the edge of the bed. Maribel had already bandaged my back shortly after I'd been ushered to the tower. Her husband, Lord Chambers, and several other soldiers had come with her and stood guard as she'd cleaned and dressed my wounds. Some ran deep, but thankfully I hadn't suffered the flogging for long and the soldier hadn't put his full force into the beating.

"Of course the queen would allow me," Emmeline said confidently. "You needn't worry."

"I should check with the earl, Your Highness," the guard said.

"I'll not take long. I promise."

After several moments of silence, keys rattled in the door. At the squeal of the hinges, I reached for the coverlet and draped it around my torso. Maribel had insisted the wounds be left uncovered temporarily, and so I'd rested on my stomach, letting the warm breeze coming through the high arched windows bathe my irritated flesh.

As Emmeline entered, I rose but didn't make a move to approach her. She came in halfway, glanced around at the sparse furnishing—the worn table and chair, the small bed, a chamber pot, and pedestal holding a basin of water.

Although I'd spent the afternoon admonishing myself to keep my resolve to free Emmeline from her obligation to me, now that she was here, I could do nothing but stare at her beauty. She'd worn one of the gowns I'd bestowed upon her after our public wedding. The deep purple contrasted with her pale skin and dark hair that she wore in long, loose waves.

"Thank you for keeping my parents safe," she said, darting a glance at my chest, her cheeks turning rosy before she dropped her attention to the straw on the floor.

Only then did I realize the coverlet hung open, revealing my shirtless body. At another time, I might have used the opportunity to tease her, but I forced myself to draw the coverlet closed. "The moment I arrived in Delsworth, I had them released and taken to safety."

"That's what they said."

"Then you have seen them?"

She nodded, her eyes alight with happiness. "I spent the afternoon with them."

"They are faring well?"

"Now that we're together again, they're well, and so am I."

"Good."

"Bede found me on the ride back from the Highlands. I've brought him here, and Ruby has adopted the fox as a brother."

At the mention of the puppy, my gaze snagged upon

her ruby ring. She was willingly wearing the jewel I'd given her. My pulse sped with a desire for her that wouldn't go away, even though I'd tried so hard to reject it.

Holding out her hand, she gave me a full view of the ring. Then she smiled at me shyly, her head tilted just slightly, her eyes so inviting. "On our wedding day you said this ring signified your heart, and that I'd have it forever."

The guard discreetly backed away from the door but left it open. Emmeline started toward me with slow, timid steps.

I swallowed hard. I should call the guard back. But as she stopped in front of me and lifted her hand so that the ring sparkled a bright red, I couldn't tear my eyes from hers.

"Do I still have your heart?"

I had to resist her. Had to resist. Had to—"Yes." My answer was breathless as I took her hand and lifted it to my lips.

At the touch of my kiss, desire filled her eyes—so deep and consuming that my own need for her flamed to life unbidden. "Rex," she said just as breathlessly. "You have my heart too."

I lifted my other hand to her hair, to the glorious dark waves. As I brushed my fingers into the thick strands, I told myself this was the last time I'd touch her. I wouldn't do it again, for it would make our parting too difficult.

She tilted her face up, whether an invitation to kiss her or not, I did not know. Nor did it matter. I wanted to kiss her again. But the ache inside—the one that had been growing since I'd ridden away from her—pushed up hard and swift.

"Emmeline," I whispered, tearing myself from her and

pacing to the table. "I will always love you."

Her warm brown eyes chased after me, beckoning, pleading me to come back to her.

I shook my head. "But I cannot relegate you to a life with a prisoner like me."

"I don't care—"

"This is no way to live."

"I want to be with you, even here."

"No." I wanted more for Emmeline, more than I could give. "Besides, the queen will never allow us to be together."

"Then we'll run away." She jutted her chin stubbornly.

I could be more stubborn. "There is no place to hide that your sister would not be able to find us."

"The cottage in Inglewood Forest," she whispered with a glance to the open doorway.

"That is likely the first place she would look."

She studied my face, her lips pursed with determination. "So you would give up on us so easily?"

"I would set you free to live as you never have before."

"The only life I want is with you, no matter what it is like."

It was the only life I wanted, too, but I couldn't say it. I'd already revealed too much. If only I'd been cold and aloof instead of melting under her smile.

She waited for a long moment, then stalked across the room to the door. "I won't let you push me out of your life." She paused. "For good or bad, we're bound together until death separates us."

As she exited and the tap of her footsteps on the tower stairway grew faint, I lowered myself to the bed. Father Patrick had said the same thing. Had it only been that morning when the priest had told me I needed to honor the commitment I'd made to Emmeline, even in the worst of circumstances?

But how could I honor our marriage vows now? I'd lost everything—my home, my land, my people, my loyal friends, and my freedom. I had nothing to offer her . . . except for my love.

But was love enough?

Over the next few days, I waited for Emmeline to return. With every set of footsteps ascending the stone stairway, I longed for them to be hers. But she didn't come again.

Maribel visited several times each day to apply salve and ointments to my wounds. The Earl of Langley also came to question me on affairs of the kingdom. I gave him all the information he required, holding nothing back. I wanted Queen Adelaide Constance to be successful, and to do so, she needed to have my fullest cooperation.

He also questioned me extensively on the labyrinth and the treasure. I had no doubt Emmeline had already given him a great deal of information, so I relayed everything I knew and cautioned them against returning.

"If the queen decides to seek more of the treasure," I said, "I beg you to take me instead of Emmeline. Even if she insists, I would ask that you allow me to go in her place and spare her the danger."

The earl had looked at me long and hard. No doubt he knew by now how valuable Emmeline's knowledge of the labyrinth was, that it was only because of her we'd been able to reach the center.

"The queen has decided we have all the treasure we

need," he'd finally said. "She is filling the labyrinth with rubble and then sealing the entrances."

I'd released a relieved breath. "All I want is for Emmeline to be safe and happy."

"Then you truly love her?"

"More than my life."

With each passing day of my confinement, I only loved her more. By the fifth day, at the clatter of boots on the stairway, I bolted up from the chair where I'd been reading the small history book that had been among the contents of the pouch I'd taken from Emmeline when I'd first met her. Though I knew I ought to give the book back, it was the only thing I had that would forever remind me of her.

When the door opened, I wasn't surprised to see half a dozen of the queen's toughest soldiers. "Your Highness." The largest knight bowed. As he lifted his head, I recognized him and tried to place his name. He'd once belonged to the elite guard under Captain Theobald and had been one of the first to rally to the queen's rebellion. In some ways, I hadn't blamed Captain Theobald's men for defecting. In the short time I'd known Theobald, I'd never liked him or his methods.

"Firmin?" I asked.

"Yes, Your Highness."

"I believe you chose your leader wisely."

His eyes rounded. "Thank you, Your Highness."

The other soldiers waited behind him. And suddenly, I knew they'd come to take me away. I glanced around the tower room, seeing nothing there I needed. I wore the clean garments my servants had brought me earlier in the day. They'd assisted me in bathing and grooming and dressing so that at the very least I could leave with dignity.

Leave for where, I didn't know. But I guessed the queen would have me taken to a secure fortress in a remote area where I would remain heavily guarded for the rest of my life. That is, if she allowed me to live.

She could very well be putting me to death today in front of all my people in a display of authority. But while that was something my father might have done, I suspected the queen had different plans. She'd already proven herself to be not only a wise and just queen but also a compassionate one. Her greatest act of compassion had been in burying the king rather than taking revenge for the lack of respect he'd shown her parents so long ago. Though I hadn't been allowed to attend the burial, I'd heard it had been respectful and simple with my mother at the graveside.

Firmin didn't need to say anything else. After stowing away my few belongings, I held out my hands and allowed him to shackle me. Then, with his guards surrounding me, we descended and left the keep by way of a side door. We mounted steeds, and they led me through the gatehouse and into the city.

I'd steeled myself for the sight of the queen's flag of Mercia waving from the turrets all around the town wall. But I wasn't prepared for the people who lined the streets, staring at me silently as I passed by. I couldn't keep from remembering those same people on my public wedding day, their smiles and cheering as I'd ridden through with Emmeline.

My chest ached at the reminder of losing her. If only I'd figured out a way to be with her . . .

Even as the weight on my heart settled heavier, I held my chin and head high. Over the past few days of contemplating everything that had happened, I'd realized that while I had plenty of regrets in how I'd used Emmeline, I had no regrets in handing the kingdom over to the queen.

Like great King Alfred the Peacemaker, who divided the kingdom for peace, I'd opted for peace, as well, even if I had to give up my own rights. Perhaps I was a soft man, as my father had claimed, but I wasn't weak. The very act of bowing my knee in submission to the queen had taken more strength than fighting her. My entire body had protested that bended knee. But I'd forced myself to do it. For the people and for peace.

When we passed through the city gates and Firmin directed me to the waterfront, I realized I was being taken to a ship. Was the queen sending me to an island, perhaps a place where I'd be isolated and alone?

So be it. Wherever she chose would be an act of compassion I didn't deserve, especially in light of the way my father had treated her and her family.

The crowds only increased as we drew nearer the waterfront until Firmin shouted for the people to make way. As they moved back and we finished the final distance to the shore, I caught sight of the harbor. One of the ships wasn't flying the flag of Bryttania or Mercia. Rather, the old flag of Warwick fluttered in the wind— two leaping golden lions against a black background.

How long had it been since I'd seen such a flag?

I didn't have time to contemplate the meaning. My attention shifted to a gathering of people on the wharf. Queen Adelaide Constance stood at the center attired in a regal gown rather than her usual chain mail. She wore the ancient queen's crown, the one that had belonged to her mother. The two original rubies that had been taken out so long ago had been restored to their rightful place within the crown.

The Earl of Langley waited next to the queen with Lord Chambers and Maribel, as well as a host of other nobility.

But I wasn't interested in any of them. Instead, my attention locked in on Emmeline, who was standing slightly away from her sisters at the edge near a longboat that was no doubt there to row me out to my ship. She, too, was dressed as fashionably as the queen, except that with her dark beauty she was more captivating than I could put into words.

She'd come to say good-bye.

As I slid from my mount, I didn't wait for Firmin or anyone else to direct me. I strode to her, fully intending to push aside anyone who tried to stop me. Thankfully, no one did.

She watched me expectantly, but I couldn't read her expression, nor did I care to. Instead, I grabbed her, bent down, and covered her mouth with mine. With my shackled hands, I couldn't wrap my arms around her the way I wanted, but I pulled her tight nonetheless. And I kissed her deeply, letting my love and passion say what I couldn't with words.

She responded by wrapping her arms around me, rising on her toes, and meeting my passion with her own.

I angled in and let my lips fuse with hers more firmly. If this was to be our last kiss, our final good-bye, I didn't care that I was taking my time and making everyone wait.

But Emmeline broke away and put a body's length of distance between us, her cheeks flushed and her smile radiating her pleasure.

She took hold of my wrist manacles, lifted a key, and unlocked first one and then the next. They fell to the wharf with a clank. I started to pull her to me again, but she stepped out of my grasp. "No more now," she whispered with a breathless laugh. "We shall have plenty of time later."

Plenty of time later? I searched her face for an answer. But truthfully, I didn't need one. Though I'd wanted to spare Emmeline the life of isolation and deprivation that I'd endure, Father Patrick's admonishment had circulated through me countless times. *You must honor the commitment you made, even in the worst of circumstances.*

Emmeline had come to me wearing the ring I'd given her and had told me the only life she wanted was with me, regardless of what it was like. If she could commit to me even now, then I couldn't leave without her. I had to honor our marriage vows no matter where we were, no matter what life might bring, no matter the hardships.

She glanced to the queen, who'd stepped toward us. Though Queen Adelaide Constance didn't smile, I could see from the light in her eyes that she approved of my display of affection toward the princess.

My heart gave a strange leap. It was too much to expect the queen to allow Emmeline to be with me, wasn't it? Even so, I would plead for her.

"Your Majesty." I lowered myself to one knee and bowed my head just as I had that day in the bailey. "I do not deserve anything but your wrath and justice for my many misdeeds as well as those of my father. Nevertheless, I beg you for one thing."

She didn't immediately deny me, so I continued with my head still bowed. "I beg you for my wife. Princess Emmeline means more to me than anything else. She is all I need and all I ask for."

Next to me, Emmeline placed a trembling hand upon

my shoulder, one that told me she supported me and still wanted to be with me.

Silence hung over the shoreline, broken by the lap of the waves. Though overcast, the summer morning was warm and the damp air laden with rain. There would be storms ahead, but I could face anything with Emmeline by my side.

My muscles tensed. What else could I say to make my case to have her? I didn't deserve her, but I wanted to spend my life cherishing her and making myself worthy.

"Rise, King Ethelrex," the queen finally said in a loud voice that carried over the gathering.

I stood, confused that she'd addressed me as king. Emmeline took my hand and smiled up at me with an excitement and joy I didn't understand.

"Since you acknowledged me as the true queen and rightful heir of Mercia," the queen continued solemnly, "I am fulfilling my promise to show you mercy and kindness."

"Thank you, Your Majesty."

She held my gaze levelly. "You have proven yourself worthy of being a king. Therefore, I restore unto you the lands of Warwick and all its holdings so long as you promise to treat the people there with as much compassion as you have shown here."

For a moment, I couldn't find the words to respond. I couldn't think, couldn't speak, couldn't move. In my wildest dreams, I'd never imagined the queen would give me Warwick. Why was she showing such great consideration?

"Warwick needs a king who cares enough to rebuild and restore the kingdom," she said, as if sensing my question. "Someone with strength and courage to meet the many challenges there. I believe you are suited to that task."

"You are equally suited."

The queen didn't waver. "I have challenges enough here in Mercia. Moreover, Warwick will fare better under a ruler who resides there, knows the struggles, and is vested in rebuilding."

Everything she said made perfect sense. And I relished the challenge of returning to my native country and helping to invest in the people and land. However . . .

I laced my fingers through Emmeline's and drew her closer. "I am grateful for your trust in me. But you must know, I would give up my kingdom and power if it meant I could be with my wife."

Finally, the queen's lips curved into a semblance of a smile. "Your wife has done nothing for the past several days but plead with me to allow her to go with you. In fact, she has made all the travel arrangements herself."

Emmeline squeezed my hand, her eyes full of life and love. And suddenly, I understood the magnitude of the gift the queen had given me. Not only was she bestowing upon me the chance to rule as a wise and compassionate king, but she'd also given me Emmeline.

"I allowed your followers a choice to leave with you," the queen said. "And they are already waiting for you on your ship."

I followed her gaze to the vessel flying Warwick's flag. On the deck, I glimpsed my mother, Father Patrick, Dante, and the remainder of my loyal men.

"Although I gave Magnus one more chance at peace, he chose the way of strife and is therefore sentenced to spend his days in solitary confinement."

"You offered him more than he deserved, Your Majesty."

"God oft gives us more than we deserve. I can do no less for others."

I nodded my acknowledgment of her wisdom.

She motioned to a nearby squire who came forward holding a tasseled pillow of bright ruby red. On the top lay the onyx signet ring belonging to the royal family of Warwick. It sparkled brilliantly, obviously having been polished and cleaned to perfection.

As the squire bowed before me and held the pillow out, I shook my head. "I regret that I must decline your gift, Your Majesty. But I have no wish to be anything like my father, not even in the ring I wear."

"'Tis only what you do with what you are given that counts."

I sensed this was her admonition to take the freedom and new life she was offering and to be different than my father. I could do nothing less. Without another moment of hesitation, I took the ring and slipped it on, vowing I would live and die only for peace.

"I have also bestowed to Emmeline her dowry," the queen continued. "I am giving her a portion of the treasure you recovered. I pray you will find it useful in the restoration of Warwick."

A lump formed in my throat, and I struggled to speak past it. "You are more than generous, Your Majesty. I fear I cannot find the words to thank you for the kindness you have shown me."

"You can thank me by loving Emmeline and making her happy."

I glanced down at Emmeline's upturned face. "Rest assured, Your Majesty, I would have done so regardless. And now, I shall do so doubly."

At my declaration, the queen smiled her satisfaction.

I pressed my lips to Emmeline's forehead. "You are sure you want to do this?" I asked her quietly.

"No matter what you told me that day in the tower, I wasn't planning to let you leave without me."

"No matter what I said, I wouldn't have been able to leave you behind."

"Then you would have kidnapped me a second time?" Her eyes twinkled with a challenge.

"Most definitely."

"If you'd been able to catch me."

I bent into her ear. "I told you I never lose, that I always win, didn't I?"

She laughed, and I captured her lips and laughter in another kiss. This one sweet and soft with the promise of many more to come.

Chapter 28

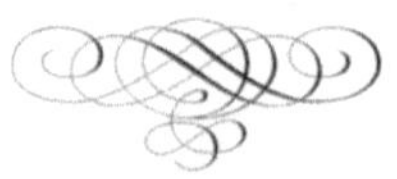

Emmeline

I stood next to Rex on the forecastle of the ship and watched Warwick's shoreline draw near. The wind whipped the sails above us and wrested my hair loose from the elegant knot my maidservant had styled earlier in preparation for our arrival.

We would disembark in the small coastal town of Grayson and then travel upriver to the larger capital city of Kensington. Two of Rex's men would ride ahead and spread the news of his coming as the new king.

Rex was rigid, studying the land with his usual keen gaze. I did likewise, taking in the forested shoreline with its steep cliffs and rocky crags.

We'd spent large portions of the journey meeting with his loyal followers and planning how we could begin to restore prosperity to Warwick. Most of the industries had either failed or were in decline. The land was depleted of resources and infertile. And the people were bitter and suffering. We were arriving at a dark and uncertain place.

Through all of the planning, we'd reminded our-selves changes would take time, energy, and an enor-mous amount of hard work in order to bring about the healing the land and people needed. The task ahead was daunting. But we were their faithful servants, and together we would set out to accomplish the rebuilding with the courage God had given us.

Once again, Adelaide had shown her great wisdom by giving Rex this mission. From Mercia, she would have had a difficult time bringing about the changes Warwick needed. The kingdom likely would have continued to languish. But since Rex had already established goodwill among the people of Warwick, they'd more easily accept him as king along with the changes he needed to institute. And of course, our marriage ensured his alliance with Adelaide.

My good-byes with my sisters had been tearful. We'd only just been reunited and were separating again. I would miss them, yet I knew we were each using our gifts to bring about peace to the land such as it hadn't known in a long time. The people of Mercia had welcomed Adelaide as their new queen, especially as word of her wisdom and her mercy toward Rex had spread.

As the royal physician, Maribel had made her first order of business that of helping all the nuns who'd been hurt and displaced by King Ethelwulf. She'd begun the process of rebuilding the convents in the Highlands and Iron Hills, making sure the nuns and friends she'd had while growing up were restored to their positions.

We'd learned that Sister Katherine, the nun who'd

been so instrumental in saving us as infants, had taken refuge in her final days among a small band of nuns who'd been hiding in ruins in West Moorland. She'd died peacefully in her sleep the same day she'd received news that Adelaide had entered Delsworth and had been crowned queen.

Although Sister Katherine had gone to great lengths in seeking out Adelaide and Maribel and encouraging them to accomplish their duties, she'd apparently never made any attempt to find me. Had she somehow known my destiny was intertwined with Rex's? That he must be the one to find me instead of her?

Whatever the case, my sisters and I had each played our parts to fulfill the ancient prophecy. We'd learned like Solomon and other wise kings that real treasure is found in God's gifts rather than in chests of gold. We prayed future generations would read our account and understand the same truth. But we also realized that over time, greed might raise its ugly head and wreak havoc on the land, bringing about the need for another wise young ruler to rise up and fulfill the ancient prophecy once more.

Adelaide had burned my drawing of the labyrinth and then hidden the original map pieces in three different places throughout the kingdom, putting cryptic clues to their whereabouts within the shanks of the keys as before. She and her descendants would remain keepers of the keys. And we could only pray that once again the legend of the treasure, its keys, and the labyrinth would become more fable than reality.

"Who would have guessed this is where we'd end up," my father said from beside Rex, his arm around my mother. Attired in his black chain mail and all his weapons, he looked nearly as fierce and warlike as Rex.

"I never would have imagined it," my mother replied quietly. Before leaving, I'd done everything I could to discover what had become of both Mother's and Father's families in those early days of King Ethelwulf's purge. We'd learned every member of Mother's family had been brutally murdered, just as she'd suspected.

However, Father's family had received his message in time and had been able to survive by living under false identities. We hadn't needed to search too hard to find his brothers and sisters alive and well with families of their own. Although his mother had since passed away, she'd apparently been proud of Father for how brave he'd been to save the princesses.

"I'm glad you decided to come with us." I bent to rub my free hand over Bede's head and then did the same to Ruby.

Father smiled at me, which made him look more like the charcoal burner I'd grown up with than the warrior he truly was. "Eighteen years ago, I wouldn't have imagined I'd be sailing to Warwick to live. Even a week ago, I wouldn't have imagined it, especially that we'd be going willingly."

I smiled in return. "I guess that means you're no longer angry at Rex for tying you and mother up?"

"Aye. I'll let him live . . . for today."

"That is gallant of you," Rex interjected. "And I shall allow you to live another day, but only because you are the best elite guard trainer I have."

"The only elite guard trainer," my father said wryly.

I loved that the two most important men in my life

had made their peace and liked each other. Rex had asked for forgiveness for stealing me away and coercing me into marriage. He'd also apologized for the crimes King Ethelwulf had committed, especially that my father and mother had been forced to live in hiding for so many years.

To show his gratefulness to Father for his love and care for me all the years I'd been growing up, Rex had offered him the position of his closest advisor and commander of his army. But Father had decided he was more suited to being on the sidelines of the action rather than in the middle of it and had decided to train Rex's army instead.

Rex drew me into the circle of his arm. "Are you ready for this?"

"Yes." I was surprised by how much I meant it. Though I missed my forest home, I'd known I could never go back. But even more than that, I was different. Rex and I were both different. And stronger because of it.

I wrapped my arm around his middle and leaned into him. "As long as we're together, I'm ready for anything."

"Then, welcome home, my queen," he whispered. "I cannot promise you riches or ease in the days to come. But hereafter, I can promise I will choose to love and cherish you unto death."

"That's all that matters," I whispered in return before lifting my lips to his and sealing our love with a kiss.

Jody Hedlund is the best-selling author of over twenty historicals for both adults and teens and is the winner of numerous awards including the Christy, Carol, and Christian Book Award. She lives in central Michigan with her husband, five busy teens, and five spoiled cats. Learn more at JodyHedlund.com

Young Adult Fiction from Jody Hedlund
The Lost Princesses

Always: Prequel Novella

On the verge of dying after giving birth to twins, the queen of Mercia pleads with Lady Felicia to save her infant daughters. With the castle overrun by King Ethelwulf's invading army, Lady Felicia vows to do whatever she can to take the newborn princesses and their three-year old sister to safety, even though it means sacrificing everything she holds dear, possibly her own life.

Evermore

Raised by a noble family, Lady Adelaide has always known she's an orphan. Little does she realize she's one of the lost princesses and the true heir to Mercia's throne . . . until a visitor arrives at her family estate, reveals her birthright as queen, and thrusts her into a quest for the throne whether she's ready or not.

Foremost

Raised in an isolated abbey, Lady Maribel desires nothing more than to become a nun and continue practicing her healing arts. She's carefree and happy with her life...until a visitor comes to the abbey and reveals her true identity as one of the lost princesses.

Hereafter

Forced into marriage, Emmeline has one goal—to escape. But Ethelrex takes his marriage vows seriously, including his promise to love and cherish his wife, and has no intention of letting Emmeline get away. As the battle for the throne rages, will the prince be able to win the battle for Emmeline's heart?

The Noble Knights

The Vow

Young Rosemarie finds herself drawn to Thomas, the son of the nearby baron. But just as her feelings begin to grow, a man carrying the Plague interrupts their hunting party. While in forced isolation, Rosemarie begins to contemplate her future—could it include Thomas? Could he be the perfect man to one day rule beside her and oversee her parents' lands?

An Uncertain Choice

Due to her parents' promise at her birth, Lady Rosemarie has been prepared to become a nun on the day she turns eighteen. Then, shortly before her birthday, a friend of her father's enters the kingdom and proclaims her parents' will left a second choice—if Rosemarie can marry before the eve of her eighteenth year, she will be exempt from the ancient vow.

A Daring Sacrifice

In a reverse twist on the Robin Hood story, a young medieval maiden stands up for the rights of the mistreated, stealing from the rich to give to the poor. All the while, she fights against her cruel uncle who has taken over the land that is rightfully hers.

For Love & Honor

Lady Sabine is harboring a skin blemish, one, that if revealed, could cause her to be branded as a witch, put her life in danger, and damage her chances of making a good marriage. After all, what nobleman would want to marry a woman so flawed?

A Loyal Heart

When Lady Olivia's castle is besieged, she and her sister are taken captive and held for ransom by her father's enemy, Lord Pitt. Loyalty to family means everything to Olivia. She'll save her sister at any cost and do whatever her father asks—even if that means obeying his order to steal a sacred relic from her captor.

A Worthy Rebel

While fleeing an arranged betrothal to a heartless lord, Lady Isabelle becomes injured and lost. Rescued by a young peasant man, she hides her identity as a noblewoman for fear of reprisal from the peasants who are bitter and angry toward the nobility.

A complete list of my novels can be found at jodyhedlund.com.

Would you like to know when my next book is available? You can sign up for my newsletter, become my friend on Goodreads, like me on Facebook, or follow me on Twitter.

Newsletter: jodyhedlund.com
Goodreads:
goodreads.com/author/show/3358829.Jody_Hedlund
Facebook: facebook.com/AuthorJodyHedlund
Twitter: @JodyHedlund

The more reviews a book has, the more likely other readers are to find it. If you have a minute, please leave a rating or review. I appreciate all reviews, whether positive or negative.